What She Craves

What She Craves

LACY DANES

APHRODISIA

KENSINGTON PUBLISHING CORP.
http://www.kensingtonbooks.com

KENSINGTON BOOKS are published by

Kensington Publishing Corp.
850 Third Avenue
New York, NY 10022

All Kensington Titles, Imprints, and Distributed Lines are available at special quantity discounts for bulk purchases for sales promotions, premiums, fund-raising, and educational or institutional use.

Special book excerpts or customized printings can also be created to fit specific needs. For details, write or phone the office of the Kensington special sales manager: Kensington Publishing Corp., 850 Third Avenue, New York, NY 10022, attn: Special Sales Department, Phone: 1-800-221-2647.

ISBN-13: 978-0-7582-1567-3
ISBN-10: 0-7582-1567-3

First Trade Paperback Printing: March 2007

10 9 8 7 6 5 4 3 2 1

Printed in the United States of America

Acknowledgments

Thank you Bri, Debbra, Linda, Ria, Sasha, Shelli, Steph, and Steve! Without you I would never have learned how to write a good story.

Huge hugs to Eva Gale who pushed me to write *Night of the Taking*, the story that sold this book for me and to Sasha White for teaching me to write hot!

Thank you Karen Hopkins and Pattie Steele-Perkins for guiding me to my fabulous agent Roberta Brown.

Thank you Roberta for having faith that I write a good story and it wasn't just a fluke. You truly are the best agent! I am extremely lucky to have you!

Thank you John Scognamiglio for taking a chance on me off a ten thousand word short. Your guidance has been wonderful and my stories are stronger because of it.

Thank you Mom for being understanding about what I write and supporting me when I needed it.

My life changed drastically because of this book. I am truly grateful for the support and education given by my friends and family during this emotional time of change.

Lacy

Contents

Lust's Vow 1

Checkmate 87

Night of the Taking 171

Lust's Vow

1

Longing

Surrey, England, 1815

"Come on, Emma, hit him harder."

WAACK.

"Uhhh."

"Oh . . . God . . . good girl, Emma, good girl. Again."

She shouldn't listen to this. Hannah's brows drew together as she strained to hear the voices coming from Lord Brummelton's secluded summerhouse.

What were they up to?

The tone of their voices intrigued her. She stepped forward to continue on her daily ritual to the mill—*blast*, she couldn't get her feet to move. She needed to know what mischief was about.

Her maid, Gertie, said Mr. Roland arrived back from the war with friends but—

WHACK!

Another pleasure-filled groan floated on the fall breeze.

She stared at the octagon-shaped structure. Floor-to-ceiling windows that faced the river reflected the dappled light of the late-afternoon sun, marring the view within. Nothing. She couldn't see a thing.

"Oh God, Emma, his arse is so red. Reach around and touch his prick."

Hannah's eyes widened. *Oh my.* They were engaged in a sexual act.

"He's not ready, Rupert," Emma said in an exasperated voice. "Even though you could spend, I want this to last." Emma's squeaky voice paused. "Isn't Kenneth supposed to join us?"

"Who cares about Kenneth? Get on with it, woman!"

Biting her lip, Hannah hesitated. Maybe at a different angle she could see . . . something. Her heart pounded in her chest as she stepped forward.

CRUNCH.

She stopped. Blast. Fallen leaves. The sound was so loud to her ears in the silence of the woods. They would surely hear.

The leaves scattered in a thick carpet all around the structure. She frowned. There was no way she could approach silently, but if they were engrossed in the love act, they might not notice.

A groan came from a man with a baritone voice, and shivers cascaded down her arms. Hannah closed her eyes. Good Lord, she longed for that sensation.

She didn't care if they heard. She needed to learn how to pleasure a man. At least two men were in that summerhouse engaged in wicked futter and were thoroughly enjoying it. Enjoying the act as her husband never had with her. Surely she would learn to pleasure a man if she could see them, and if by chance they saw her . . . Well, she didn't give a damn.

Hairs on her arms and neck stood in anticipation as she determinedly crept forward, shuffling her feet so as not to make a sound. She would finally understand what made Simon leave her bed.

The path that followed the river went directly in front of the summerhouse. *Please let there be no reflection on the glass at a different angle.* Her heart sped in her chest as another groan filtered through the trees.

Once in front of the structure, she scooted behind a birch tree. The width was a bit narrow, but she could hide her face if she needed to. She inhaled the crisp fall air and closed her eyes. *Please let me learn.* Then she peeked through the windows of the cottage. Oh my. Her eyes bulged in shock.

A man with pale skin knelt on the floor, his breeches pushed down past his knees. A blond woman, younger than herself, stood behind him, a long thin switch in hand. She held the birch out to the side, and *swoosh*, the twig hit his bottom with a loud crack. Ouch. That's not what she expected.

The kneeling man flinched from the impact and groaned. Another deep groan came from a man who stood farther back in the structure.

He watched them as she did.

While giving orders to Emma, his penis jutted out of his pants. His long fingers stroked the length, settled at the tip, and then rolled. Hannah bit her lip. His well-proportioned hands stroked in a musical rhythm. Beautiful. His hands held an artistic quality.

In her mind, those big graceful hands slid down her body; working their magic on her bare skin. She trembled and her eyelids fluttered. *Oh my!* His fingers caressed her breasts, tapping as if playing a fine instrument. Then circled her nipples and he scraped his nail over the hard peak. Her nipples budded into the confines of her corset and she sucked in a tight breath with longing for his touch.

His hands slid up her inner thighs. The heat of him seeped through her dress as he jerked her legs apart, lifting her skirt so he could access every part of her.

She groaned and remembered the pictures from the books she read. Engravings of a man placing his tongue where his phallus normally fit. How she desired to experience a touch like such.

If this man lifted her skirts just like so, and kneeled between her legs he could give her that experience and more. His hair would tickle her inner thighs. His hands would burn marks into her bottom as he lifted her sex opening to his mouth. Her heart pounded against her ribs. Oh, how she wanted to feel a man's tongue tasting her inner core.

Her insides quivered. What would lying with this man be like? His hand slid over his prick again in a controlled move. Amazing. His expertise in this act shone in every motion. She licked her lips, wanting him to touch her, and create that wonderful tingling sensation in her body with his hands. What a shocking, yet delightful thought.

The man on the floor did not cry out in pain as the switch hit him again, but moaned in pleasure.

How could anyone find pleasure from a spank? Her eyes narrowed, and she tilted her head to the side. Surely she missed something. She blinked again. Yes, he found pleasure. His breath puffed in and out, and his bluish-red penis stood stiff as whale-bone between his legs. Amazing. Strangely the sight aroused her. Her eyes widened. How could she like watching such an act?

She tried to take in the whole scene, but she couldn't stop staring at both men's sex. The man who knelt possessed a long narrow phallus, much narrower than the two of her experience, but a good thumb longer than Simon's.

The other of her comparison was a vague memory of beauty and satiny skin, to which neither of these could compare. Her heart sped and her skin heated as she remembered her youthful hand trembling, rubbing down the hot skin and plum-shaped head. She shook herself and pushed the pleasant memory from her mind.

WHACK!

Hannah flinched. She couldn't imagine Simon finding pleasure from a spank, but then again nothing she did pleased him, so maybe she was wrong. He only found excitement in his whores and at his clubs.

The man moved from the back of the cottage into a better view. Hannah ducked behind the old birch tree and closed her eyes.

God, she was mad. She gasped for air.

The five lonely years since Simon's death had made her crazy with the urge to learn to please a man. First she had lowered herself to purchasing all sorts of bawdy books, books that talked of things such as this. And now . . . Now she ogled Mr. Roland and invaded his privacy.

Her chest tightened. The reality was she would never hold the skill to master such pleasure. God, this was agony. She needed to leave before one of them noticed her. Indeed . . . Her shoulders slumped. Oh poppiedust. She turned and stepped in the direction of Huntington cottage.

"Emma, dear, I want to feel your hot cunt while you frig Kit with your mouth."

Hannah flung around. This she couldn't resist. She read about kissing a man's sex in the *Perfumed Garden* and wondered if men and women truly found pleasure that way.

Emma knelt on cushions on the floor. Kit lay in front of her, his phallus standing straight as the trees that surrounded her.

Hannah's hands brushed the smooth trunk of the large birch tree. Imagining the hotness of smooth male flesh as her hands ran across rough cool bark, she slid her hands out to the edges, then up and down. In her mind her hands explored every ridge and vein of his sex. Her pulse increased, and her chest tightened. God, she needed to feel a man again. Her hands trembled. With all the books she'd read, the next time a man joined her in bed she hoped she would have an idea what to do.

Emma leaned down and her tongue traced the head of the man's penis. Kit groaned.

"Umm . . ." Hannah's tongue slid out and traced her lips. She imagined the salty flavor of skin and the tapered shape of prick head as an erection pressed into her mouth. Her nipples peaked hard beneath her corset.

The other man, Rupert, knelt behind Emma. Flipping her skirt and petticoat up onto her back, he ran his hands down the swell of her creamy bottom. "Good girl, Emma. Take Kit in," he murmured, then slid his hand between her spheres. Hannah whimpered. Oh how she wanted rough male hands on her bum again.

"No, Emma. Pleasure Kit. Concentrate on nothing but him."

Kit groaned and thrust his hips up as Emma lowered her head down. Half his shaft slid into her mouth. As she pulled her head up to the tip, his shaft shimmered with her saliva.

Hannah's mouth watered. She wanted this, wanted to be Emma as she slid hot male flesh into her mouth and another man caressed her. She swallowed hard. How scandalous.

Emma's tongue slid out and traced the ridge; she puckered her lips, and slid back down the length.

Hannah could feel the pressure of a phallus as the head slid into her mouth. Saliva pooled and dribbled down the length of the prick as it throbbed and twitched. Her lips caressed the ridge and popped to the tip. Wetness dewed her skin, and her sex pulsed as a moan caught in her throat. She crossed her legs in an attempt to control the building desire and slickness slid down her leg.

Good Lord, she should tear her gaze away. Her chest tightened and her skin tingled. Too many years . . . how she needed a man's touch. She had no prospects, no admirers. This was madness. Her lip trembled.

Kit groaned, and tears sprang to her eyes. She would never, could never, possess the ability to pleasure a man this way, but still she stood and watched. She was a fool.

Tingles slid across her body with every caress the threesome made. Her nipples strained against her corset as Rupert grasped his large stiff prick. He ran his hand along the length, then laid his prick in the crack of Emma's bum. Not between her legs, but in the crevice. He rocked his staff back and forth, sliding the head up and down the valley. His gaze fixed on the sight.

"Oh, Em, you have the most glorious arse." Gripping the base of his shaft, he slid his hand forward and back in the same motion as he rocked.

Simon had never done such a thing to her. In the short month he shared her bed, he always joined her in the same position. Him on top, with her legs spread wide.

Viewing such an animalistic position caused a hunger to seep through her. She could almost feel the hot skin as the head of a penis slid between the spheres of her bum, stretching her sex, spearing her womb. A man's muscles shaking against her bottom as he pumped into her like an animal in the fields.

Her sex spasmed and she arched her back in search of the imaginary prick. She wanted Rupert's penis to fill her, to bring her the blissful release she only created with her fingers on her own, but there was nothing there. She gritted her teeth.

Oh how she wanted to diddle a man in that position. This man. Shifting her stance, she gasped, and her nubbin throbbed.

His hands flexed, gripping Emma's bum and she imagined his fingers on the soft flesh of her bottom, gripping her hard. His arms jerking her back into his hips with controlled precise moves as his penis pushed into her sex again and again.

The delightful friction of her flesh stretching to fit him as he mated with her made her knees weak. One of his hands slowly trailed her hip to her stomach and then dipped to the curls at the peak of her thighs. Forging through the coarseness he fingered her dripping flesh and touched where they joined.

Her entire body trembled at the thought of touching the spot where they fused together. Slick and wet as he thrust into her, she would drag her fingers across his smooth burning skin and caress his sack as it hit her bottom on each thrust.

She clamped her leg muscles tighter trying to capture the sensation in her mind, and the delicious ache between her legs spiraled. *Good Lord.*

Emma continued to devour Kit's penis. She licked and sucked until on a groan Kit thrust his hips with abandon. Her mouth slid farther down his length, and he cried out in pleasure. His hands gripped Emma's curly hair as his face contorted in ecstasy.

Pain ripped at her heart and she closed her eyes. *Please let me have the chance to make a man cry out in pleasure the way this woman did.*

Her eyes fluttered open. Oh! Juices slid down Hannah's leg as Rupert slid his prick into Emma from behind. Blast it. She wanted to feel the delight they shared, but the only way to do that would be to touch herself. Trembling, she tried to restrain her hands as they slid down her dress. Her sex pounded with the beat of her heart as her face flamed with heat. What if someone saw?

Rupert pumped and flexed his ass as his penis speared into Emma between her bum cheeks. She could hear the wetness as he slid in again and again. Her fingers found the place between her thighs and pressed her skirts between them.

The fabric of her shift dampened and clung to the lips of her sex. She wanted to feel their slickness with her bare touch, but she didn't dare lift her skirts in the open and touch herself.

Imagining her fingers were Rupert's, she caressed the swollen folds through the muslin and brushed over the hard bud between. Lightning shot through her body and a groan bubbled up her throat. Every muscle in her body strained for release.

Rupert's breath labored and Emma whimpered with each stroke. His phallus shimmered with wetness and the head and skin shone an intense red each time his penis pulled out.

Hannah pressed the fabric into her opening, mimicking Rupert's stroke, and rubbed hard against her blissful nubbin. Her eyes barely slit open, she watched as Rupert grew closer to spending in Emma.

Rupert grunted, then cried out a deep thrilling sound that was music to Hannah's ears and body. Splendid contractions wracked her, starting from womb and spreading through her entire being. Her knees weakened and she braced herself with her shoulder against the tree. How she wished this magic coursing through her was created from his prick.

Kenneth Walker plodded down the path toward the river. He refused to stall any longer. They needed to be ready for the members when they arrived for the masque. The masters would be excited about the event and ready for bawdy play. If they weren't there to greet them when they arrived, things would get out of control.

Damn Rupert for not restraining himself until the festivities for a bit of nifty. Last night finally proved to Kenneth that he preferred his loving one-on-one. Emma had favored him, much to Rupert's annoyance, then all but wrapped her legs around him this morning before the group could rise.

He refused to be any woman's plaything. Just the idea that Emma was Rupert's and preferred other men made his skin crawl. Out of respect for Rupert, he let this morning's flirtation pass without comment.

Memories of his father's sobs in his aunt's library as his mother coldly told him she would not give up her lover chilled his spine. His jaw clenched and his cheek twitched. How she reduced the powerful Duke of Deventon to a slobbering lump still puzzled him. He shook himself to rid the thought.

Never, never would he let himself fall prey to that kind of humiliation or, more precisely, to that kind of woman for more than one night.

He rounded the turn in the path, and the summerhouse lay ahead.

"Emma, dear, I want to feel your hot cunt while you frig Kit with your mouth."

Shit. He stopped in his tracks. So much for his dallying. Turning toward the river, he beheld black hair and a deep blue dress peeking out from behind a white birch tree.

Well, well. His lips curved up. Someone peeped on Rupert and his games. He held in a chuckle. If Rupert knew, he would perform to the fullest and probably spill his seed within a second.

The woman's face slid out from behind the tree and gazed into the summerhouse. Her hands slid up and down the rough bark as if she stroked a large cock.

Damn, what a pretty thing. And oddly familiar. He glanced at her hands again as they clenched the edges of the bark. His chest tightened. Could it be? He stared back at her, black hair and a round face with pale clear skin.

God, that tiny nose and those lush lips occasioned his dreams. A groan caught in this throat as he stiffened. What stood behind that tree would be just as magnificent as it had been twelve years ago. Even better, she would have matured into a woman, soft, with flesh in all the right places.

Hannah Hay, the Marquess of Wolverland's eldest daughter and the first woman to touch his cock, stood watching his friends as she stroked a tree-sized prick in her mind. Only her imagination could make such a leap. His smile grew bigger and his cock throbbed. Lulling his head back, his fingers found the ridge that pressed against his buckskins and he stroked.

Hannah's hands had been so small and soft against the tender flesh of his youthful prick. His body shook. He had longed to touch her for weeks. When she finally consented, he had been so aroused that he spent after one stroke of her silky hand.

His fingers tightened upon the ridge of his straining shaft, and he forced his eyes open to watch her as she spied on Rupert in awe and fascination. Her face was still so easy to read: curiosity, pleasure, and arousal showed clear as day on her china-doll features.

Her pink tongue slid out and traced her lips, then her mouth opened as if taking a prick between their fullness. Damn, those lush lips would feel amazing on his cock. Wetness seeped into his pants and his prick strained. Closing her eyes, she sucked in the sides of her cheeks.

Good God! Without a doubt Emma sucked Kit right now, and Hannah wanted to suck someone too. Raw need flooded his body, and he stepped forward. He would walk to her and offer his body like he did all those years ago.

His boyish voice came back to him. *"Come now, Hannah. Let me tickle you."*

She had been awkward then, just as he had. His mouth watered as he touched his boyhood tongue to the crevice at the base of her throat and tasted her skin. She would taste the same. He knew it.

The smell of her perfume and the sound of her laughter. Shaking hands, trembling bodies, and sloppy, urgent kisses. His throat constricted. God, the way she had looked at him and gently touched his face. No woman since had been able to measure to her genuine kindness when his world shattered. This time what they shared would be different; no one would force him to leave. This time he would bed her and bed her well.

"Ahhhha!"

The cry of passion snapped him back to the sight at hand. Emma moaned and whimpered. Kit surely spent and now stroked her as Rupert had his way. They would be done soon, and he wanted Hannah to know he watched her watching them.

He cleared his throat loud enough for Rupert to hear in the cottage.

Hannah did not budge, but her hands slid down the front of her dress.

He shook his head and smiled. Just like her to be so absorbed. She probably wouldn't notice if a herd of sheep wandered through. Bending down, he picked up a stick and tossed the twig at the tree she stood behind. The foot-long branch hit square against the trunk and she jumped. Her gaze flew to him as he stood in the path to the summerhouse. He grinned. *Yes, dear, someone is watching you.*

The trail was the only way she could go. If she went past the summerhouse, Rupert would see. She glanced at the house, then at the path. Her face flamed crimson.

Ah, Hannah, how you flatter me. He did not know there were still people around who blushed at such things. With her head lowered, she turned on her heel and cut through the trees to the riverbank.

Oh no, you don't, my sweet Hannah. In five long strides, he came up behind her and clasped her arm.

She pulled, but his grasp held firm. "Let go of me, you beast!"

"Sweet, sweet Hannah . . ."

Hannah's eyes widened. "Do I know you, sir? Please unhand me." Yanking her arm again, his grip eased but did not fall from her body.

Her heart pounded so hard the beat made her hands shake. How could someone have seen her? Good Lord. This was the man Emma mentioned when Hannah first spied on them. He knew what she watched. Her cheeks grew hotter. She averted her gaze to the riverbed and stepped away from him.

"Not so quickly, sweet." His hand stroked her arm, and lightning slid through her veins straight to the place between her thighs. *Not now, blast you, damn body.* She closed her eyes and tried to quell the shiver his caress caused, but failed. His muscles stiffened in return.

"Don't say you don't remember me." The man shook his head at her as she tried once again to yank her arm free.

"Damn you, sir, let go of—"

"I believe I was the first man to ever touch you."

"P-pardon?"

He inclined his head and raised his eyebrows.

Her mouth dropped open. "Kenny . . . Kenny Walker?"

He smiled. Then laughed. "Haven't been called Kenny in ages, but, yes."

Was this truly him? The young man with whom twelve years ago she had spent her most memorable summer. They had run through the woods, played hide-and-seek, and swum in the lake with her sisters and his brother. Her first infatuation, her first kiss. Good Lord. The young man who by just saying "Hannah" had made her heart pound and heat grace her cheeks with wicked thoughts.

She searched his face. His strong straight nose, angled cheeks, and dimpled chin were the same. His eyes, the same smoky brown that you could get lost in, stared back at her with intense heat. Her body dewed, remembering all that that hungry stare promised.

She studied his body. Oh my! His shoulders had broadened, and his chest, encased in a tight-fitting coat, left little to the imagination. Her breath hitched at sculpted thighs encased in tight buckskin breeches. A lump formed in her throat, and she swallowed hard, envisioning those legs tangled in hers.

A very fit, attractive, and well-muscled man stood before her. God, he was much taller than she remembered. Her memories . . . oh. Her eyes closed. His fingers as they slid up her skirts and into her wet folds, making her tremble in such a way she thought she would die.

Kenny gently stroked her arm and with his thumb traced circles in the fabric of her sleeve. Her nipples ached, pebbled hard, wanting the circular motion.

His hasty departure from his aunt's after a summer of friendship and flirtation and his last words "*I will bed you one day, dear sweet Hannah*" slid through her mind.

She stared at his breeches where his erection bulged. He didn't even try to conceal his arousal. He journeyed to the summer-house today to have relations with his friends. He, like her husband, was a rake, with a bad enough reputation that she had heard of his adventures.

A deep rumble of a laugh came from him, and his erection twitched beneath the leather of his pants. Her cheeks grew warm, but she was unable to pull her stare from the bulge. All she wanted was to touch that ridge. God, she was mad.

"Let me tickle you, my sweet," he said as he slid his finger beneath her chin and raised her eyes.

Eyes blazing with need met hers. Her sex clenched and she groaned. His words, the same he used all those years ago. She bit her lip. Her body knew the promise in those words. But what if she was as bad as her husband claimed? Kenny had been with many women since their encounter . . .

"Hannah? Please . . ." His voice, filled with raspy desire, caressed her nerves. She needed to be touched, and who better to touch her than the man who initiated her to the act of coitus?

"Yes, Kenny, touch me. Touch me."

2

Deeds

Hannah slid her hands under Kenny's coat as he pulled her to him in an embrace that turned her limbs to pudding. His strong muscled arms squeezed her, burying her face into his waistcoat and crushing his starched white cravat. He smelled the way a man should—clean spice soap, leather and sweat, or arousal. The hair on the back of her neck prickled, and her body trembled. She inhaled again and sighed. It didn't matter that this was scandalous, she yearned for him to touch her, and he was willing to oblige.

"This way." He released her from his hold with a groan, laced his gloved fingers with hers, and pulled her along the riverbank. Reaching the grass pasture, he pulled her up the grassy slope without saying a word.

What a striking man. As a boy, he was handsome, but now he possessed the power and presence of his father. Only a powerful man would contemplate slighting him.

Her sister, Louisa, wrote once to say she sighted him at a ball. The gossips were all a-wag about his exploits. Apparently, he was very selective about the women he propositioned, and when he did find a lady he fancied, he would make her an offer of only one night.

His brown hair blew in the slight breeze and stood at awkward angles. Her knees weakened, and she wobbled. He looked like a god, Hercules or some such. A woman would have to be mad not to accept such an offer from him.

A grin crossed her face.

She stared at his bum as he stopped and glanced around. What a beautiful backside. Under the tails of his coat, she could just barely see the rounded flesh. Firm in his breeches with a slight squared edge. In her mind, her hands slid across the smooth hot surface, the tiny down hairs tickling her hands as he slid into her. Oh. Her hands trembled as wetness coated her sex.

He stopped abruptly. "This will have to do, sweet." Dropping her hand, he shucked off his coat and gloves, then placed them on the grass. He stared at her and smiled; sexual heat radiated from him.

This tall powerful man meant to touch her. She couldn't believe it. He would touch her in a way no other man had ever come close to. She bit her lip and feared she would never live up to his experience.

His waistcoat landed next to his coat on the grass as smoky eyes slid down her length. Yes, indeed he wanted her. She couldn't allow herself to disappoint him. Good Lord, please don't let that happen.

With trembling hands, she unbuttoned and removed her gloves. She needed to feel his hot skin beneath her bare caress.

"Come." Kenny held out his hand and pulled her to him. His body, so firm and strong, pressed against her soft curves.

Yes, this was happening. She would—

His lips touched hers, feather light. She couldn't breathe. The warmth settled again and pressed firmly, opening, pushing teeth against softness. She froze. If Simon was right and she was horrid, her dreams of this man would be shattered forever. Kenny stiffened and pulled back.

No, don't do this to yourself. You waited too long to prove you are desirable and that you can give pleasure. Be bold. Follow your body's desires.

She lifted her shaking hands up his chest and pressed onto her tiptoes, her tongue slid out and licked the clef in his chin.

Kenny groaned and tightened his grip on her.

See, you can do this.

"Sweet, sweet," he whispered.

His lips trailed back to hers and fused with urgent, intense heat. Her tongue pushed into his mouth, tasting coffee and spice. God, it had been too long. The determined tangle of his tongue with hers made her heart race. She needed more. She needed it all. She stepped forward and forced her body into direct contact with his length.

Growling, he rubbed her belly with his hips. Good Lord, his prick. Her whole body trembled. The large line of hard flesh pressing into her was unmistakable. Waves of pleasure spiraled from the spot filling the tender flesh between her thighs. Juice dripped down her leg as she imagined his large phallus filling her. She wanted this act with him, but would it happen or would he become disgusted with her before it came to the tickle?

His hands slid to the swell of her bottom and cupped her, spreading the spheres. A large male thigh slid between her legs, pressing against her sex. She moaned. Heat raced through her veins as her hips arched into him. So good . . . The sensation felt so good.

Her hands slid down his belly, and his muscles jumped and tensed. Reaching the waist of his breeches, her fingers slid down his hard phallus.

"Umm." His encouragement vibrated through their dueling tongues. She wanted to see the ridge of flesh, not just touch the skin, to compare his full-grown sex to the beauty of his youthful prick. Finding the buttons to his flap on the waist of his trousers, she popped one from its home.

Kenny pulled from the kiss and placed his forehead on hers. "Good God, Hannah, this is too much." Kissing the tip of her nose, he lifted her off the ground. "I'm certainly dreaming." He spun her around, laid her in the grass atop his clothes, wedging a hard leg between her thighs.

Bolts of lightning slid through her. Soon he would wedge his entire body in that spot, sliding his prick into her as she writhed beneath him. She studied his face; only desire resided in the depths of his eyes. There was no anger, no disappointment. She could do this; she would pleasure him.

Her hands clenched fistfuls of shirt. Oh how she wanted to run her hands up his naked back and clasp his clenching bum, to wrap her hand and her tongue around his throbbing staff.

To make him cry out.

She never felt so wanton in all her life.

"Kenny. I . . ." God, how did she ask if she could lick his prick? If he said no, she would feel like such a simpleton. Her cheeks warmed, and she closed her eyes.

"Yes, sweet?" He placed a kiss on the exposed skin of her neck. His soft hair brushing the tender skin beneath her chin. He kissed her just thus all those years ago. She trembled at the memory of what came next.

His tongue slid and swirled into the circular crevice at the base of her throat. A groan crept from deep within her chest as she imagined his tongue licking the rest of her, the moist heat circling her breasts, her belly button, and her sex. Oh God. She needed this. She needed him. Her hands gripped his shoulders, then trailed to his neck, searching for bare, hot skin.

"Hannah?" His mouth pulled from her flesh, and her eyes fluttered open. He stared at her. "What do you need, sweet?"

"I . . . I want to see your prick," she blurted.

Please, please don't pull away from me. Her breath hitched as his muscles tensed and he pushed away from her. His brows drew together, and he stared at her with an amused smile. He wasn't displeased. Thank goodness.

He sat back on his feet and pulled her up to kneel beside him, grinning. "Do you?"

His hands busily worked at the last two fastenings of his buckskins, then he reached in and slid his phallus out. Her breath caught. Beautiful. More beautiful than she remembered. His prick jumped in his hand, and as he gazed back at her, the corner of her lips turned up. "Can I touch it, Kenny?"

"Yes," he said, and closed his eyes.

She scooted forward so that her legs touched his, and trailed her fingers about the smooth shaft. A deep groan rumbled in his chest.

The blazing heat of his prick seeped through her icy skin. The head, the shape of a plum, with a deep ridge where the shaft connected, made her mouth water. Her lips would fit in that indentation.

Closing her fingers about the shaft, she could barely circumference the girth. She placed her other hand above her first and gripped him. Amazing, room still resided between her hand and the fat tip.

She wanted to lick the heated skin. To taste his satiny smoothness. Her tongue slid out and wet her lips. Glancing up, she met black pools of heat.

He licked his lips, gritted his teeth, then nodded. "Lark me with your mouth, Hannah."

He knew what she wanted. She wet her lips again as he reclined farther back and outstretched his long legs.

Please let me do this right.

She stared at the round plump head—*Do just as Emma did* —then leaned in and placed her pursed lips on the tip. His body jerked and his breath caught.

The hot tip tasted of salt, and the flesh smelled deliciously sweet and spicy. Sliding her tongue through her lips, she licked the eye at the tip.

His hand fumbled, pushing up her skirts, and slid up the length of her leg. She jumped at the intimate caress, and wetness flowed from between her legs. He was going to touch her weeping flesh. Good Lord, yes. She wanted his touch *there*. Her thighs parted to welcome him.

His large hand seized her bum and sensation seeped through her. She paused to savor his heat on her skin. If she disgusted him before this was through, she would have this moment locked away for her lonely nights.

His fingers probed between her bum cheeks, pushing into her wetness. Oh! Her sex throbbed. Her breath jittered with each stroke he made. She needed to return the sensation. She slid her lips down the sculpted taper of his phallus to the deep ridge, swirling the edge with her moisture.

"Damn, sweet." His hips jerked up, and a finger curled into the opening of her sex.

"Uhh . . ." Her hips pressed down against the invasion. She wanted him deeper within her.

"Take more, my sweet, please. Lick the head . . . suck me into your mouth . . . like you wanted to when you watched."

Good Lord, he saw that. It didn't matter. She wanted to lick his prick, suck his hardness, and taste his seed.

Placing her hand at the base of the staff, as she had read in one of her books, she slid three inches of hot male flesh into her mouth. "Umm." Her tongue rubbed the underside, feeling the raised veins and sucking back to the tip. Kenny groaned deliciously and breathed in, clenching his teeth.

She sucked him again and again, each time achieving the same result. Each groan from him melted her reluctance, emboldened her actions, and made her body hum. His fingers slid in and out of her sex. As her hips pressed down, his thumb pressed into her bumhole.

Her entire body tensed. "Ahh." What a strange sensation. The pressure turned pleasurable as he moved his fingers, and the bliss intensified.

She continued to suck to the top of his prick, then swirled the fat spear with her tongue. The saltiness of his skin turned tangy, and she could feel his sack tighten under her hands.

"Good God, Hannah. I'm about to discharge."

Indeed, she wanted to taste him. Placing her other hand fully on the sack, she massaged as she descended.

"Hannah . . ." His hips rose again, and she slid him farther into her mouth. Fingers laced through her hair, grasping her head. She sucked back to the tip. His hips thrust up, and she slid down.

"Oh . . . uh . . . by God, H-Hannah!" he shouted, clenching her head as he thrust his hips. His penis slid in and out of her mouth and gush after gush of hot custard spurted into her. His hips settled back to the ground, and she slid off his hard phallus. Swallowing the tangy fluid, she smiled.

She enjoyed the taste of him. Her tongue traced her lips. Even more, she enjoyed pleasuring him. She did it. She pleasured him. A grin spread from ear to ear. She wanted to get up and dance a jig around his spent body.

There was no way he could say otherwise. He had cried out, and she had caused his delight.

His chest rose and fell with labored breaths.

She sat back on her feet and stared at his penis as the flesh shriveled. Her hand trailed up the inside of his thigh and traced the base of the rod with her fingers. The hairs created a black nest for his manhood to lie against. Could she arouse him again? She glanced at his face. A small smile curved his lips but he still didn't move. She bit her lip and stared at his flaccid sex, then wrapped her hand about the prick.

He chuckled. "Not yet, sweet." His hand possessed her wrist. "Come here. My turn."

He rose up on his elbows with lazy, passion-filled eyes, and yanked her atop him. Rolling, he pinned her beneath him. Face-to-face, chest-to-chest, and hips-to-stomach, her legs so wantonly wrapped about his. He was so large. With the tip of his finger, he traced her cheekbone.

"Umm." Kenny shook his head, leaned down, and licked a trail to her ear. "More beautiful," he whispered. Twinges raced through her, and gooseflesh scattered on her skin. The situation was the same as years ago, except this time they both wished to take things to full coitus.

"Kenny."

"Shh, my turn, sweet."

He leaned back and wedged his leg between hers. Lifting and shifting himself, he freed her skirts from his legs and laid them upon her stomach. He did not touch her, and her legs spread farther in seek of his touch. Still nothing. The muscles of her sex grasped readily at the air, trying to find any part of him to ease their desire. She leaned up to see him staring at her sex. Why was he doing that? "Touch me, Kenny, please. I'm about to burst."

"Shh, sweet, I know."

The backs of his hands feathered the inside of her legs. Her muscles jumped and clenched, hips rising in invitation for the touch that would not come. Her legs trembled. His fingers gripped the bare skin of her bum and lifted, tilting her up.

"God, you're beautiful. Deep crimson. With black lace." His thumbs traced her bumhole, moving up her slick lips and spreading them. She groaned so deep the tenor vibrated though her womb. The sensation contracted her sex, and she arched her hips to him.

"Please, Kenny . . . please," she whimpered.

Warm wet tongue traced her slit, back to front, flicking that special place.

"Kenny!" she cried out. Her muscles spasmed with such intensity, she screamed again. Tears streamed down the sides of her face, and her breath jittered with each hard contraction from her womb.

"Better, sweet?" He leaned forward and gazed into her eyes.

Good God, she was a wanton. One lick and she spent for him.

His finger traced the line of one of her tears. "Can you take more, Hannah?"

All she could do was nod.

"I'm going to make you scream twice as hard. It is the most beautiful sound." His voice was a raspy choke.

She nodded again, wanting his hard prick to fill her, to stretch her and make her release.

He leaned back, grasped her bum in his hands, and swirled her blissful place with his tongue. Her whole body trembled, and the muscles in her womb tightened. Good Lord. Each stroke of his tongue probed and laved her slit, tightening her muscles lick by lick.

She couldn't stay still; she needed to touch him. Her hands wandered to his hair and let the mass of tangled strands run though her fingers. A deep groan came from between her legs, vibrating her sex. The bliss built higher.

He braced his shoulders against her knees, spreading her wider. Touches ran down the curve of her bum and into her slit, parting her flesh so his tongue could explore. His tongue worshipped the lips, the blissful place, and the space before her bumhole.

Her hips arched and wiggled as she tried to get him to enter her. With the next lick, his tongue pressed in.

"Oh God, Kenny!" Her body arched off the grass, and she screamed, locking him to her as he probed in and out through each contraction. She collapsed in exhausted bliss as he lowered her bum back to the earth.

Kenneth shifted, spreading her creamy white thighs. So full

of life. So full of passion. He couldn't wait to sink into her and make her scream again. As her eyes fluttered open, he grinned. "Sweet Hannah." He had dreamed of this, and so far the act surpassed his maddest dream. His cock strained and he placed the tip at her slick wet cunt.

"Well, well, what have we here?"

Hannah screeched and tried to roll onto her side, away from the intruder's voice.

"Go away, Rupert," Kenney growled, and pinned Hannah to him.

"Tsk, tsk, I thought we all shared."

"To the devil," Kenneth said, and Hannah buried her face tight into the pit of his arm. He glanced down at her trembling in his arms. He would not give up her identity. He shook his head. Cursed again.

"Well, if you aren't willing to share, our company has started to arrive, and I know they won't mind."

"Leave, Rupert," he said through clenched teeth. Damn him and his blasted curiosity.

Rupert laughed. "Sure will, chap. Sure will."

The sound of crunching leaves and grass signaled his retreat.

Hannah pushed hard against Kenny's chest. He sat back so that she could sit as well.

"Is he gone?"

Kenny realized she was not about to let this continue, not now. Fuck Rupert. He couldn't blame her. He stared at the clearing where Rupert walked into the trees.

"He's gone." His cock throbbed, longing for the slickness of her heat. He shifted and cringed. He would be sore after this. Bloody hell. Rupert would pay. He hadn't held in a spend in years.

"Hannah." He reached out and cupped her face, trailing his thumb along the swollen lips of her mouth. "God, Hannah. This is too much like last time."

"I know." She smiled. "I'm sorry, Kenny. I have to go. I have been away much too long." She scrambled to her feet, her dark blue dress falling in a swoosh around her pale white legs.

Grrr. Legs he had almost wrapped around his waist in blissful fucking.

His cock throbbed again at the memory of her mouth sucking the very essence from him.

"Kenny." Her expression pained as she stared at his rampant erection. "I—"

He clasped her waist and crushed her to him. His face buried in her breast, he inhaled the smell of her again.

"I know, sweet. Go. I'll be fine."

She pulled from his arms, turned, lifted her skirts, and ran off in the opposite direction from Rupert. He watched her go as she darted into the trees.

Hannah. He knew she was married. His muscles clenched. She was no virgin, and Lady Hannah would never have given that up without a vow. But who was she married to?

Bloody hell, she was on her way home to a man who would have every right to fuck her as she walked in the door. A growl ripped from his throat. The thought of another man sinking his cock into her after . . . Shit. Shit! His fists clenched.

He couldn't let her go now that he found her, husband or no. He would bed her. And what would bring her to him? The masque. The party Rupert and he worked so hard to pull together. Rupert would know who she was; he knew every woman in the vicinity. Surging to his feet, he picked up his coats, tucked his cock in, and headed to the manor. He would send her an invite, and sweet Hannah would be too curious not to come.

3

Anticipation

Mr. Rupert Roland and Friends Invite
Mrs. Hannah Rosworth to Attend a Masked Evening of
Beauty and Sexual Intrigue This Thursday at Nine in the
Evening. Costumes are required but please leave all
proper clothing and morals at the door.
Mr. Rupert Roland

No respectable lady would consider attending this event. Hannah's hands shook, clutching the invite as she ascended the stairs to the great manor. She didn't care. Society didn't see her as proper. She was an outcast. It didn't matter that her father raised her to be a proper wife. A lady by all standards. They saw her through suspicious eyes. Eyes that condemned her the moment Simon died and no one but her was there to blame. This was her chance to mingle with those in society who had somehow gained the ton's scorn.

The event appeared a normal masque. No naked men stood on the stoop. No strange erotic decorations. But she didn't know what she had expected.

The guests arrived wearing heavy cloaks and masks. The footmen all dressed in the Brummelton livery of red and black. Not a hint of human flesh anywhere. She frowned with disappointment. Inside would be different.

A line of guests at the top of the steps brought her to a halt. How odd. Only one guest or couple entered the manor at a time; then the door would close, reopening after a few moments, allowing the next guest to enter.

Her heart pounded. What lay behind those doors was not a normal masquerade but a sexual one. She gulped. She would enter next into the world of the erotic unknown. Her stomach fluttered and she smiled. Tonight she would learn more than she ever thought possible, with a man she'd thought she'd never see again in her life.

The door opened. She hesitated. *Go on, you ninny.* Straightening her shoulders, she stepped into a small entry hall, and the doors closed behind her. A single candle lit the small space. Blast, she could barely see.

"Good evening." A man with dingy hair came out of the shadows. She jumped and gooseflesh pricked her skin.

His cheeks were sunken, and he held out a crooked hand. "Your cloak."

Goodness, he looked dead. His gnarled knuckles clutched the air as he waited for her to turn. *He is not about to hurt you. Give him your cloak. Relax. He is just the butler.*

She glanced around the enclosed entrance. No one else resided in the room. Shadows played across the floor, and her knees trembled. *Think about Kenny. You will be with him soon.*

With shaking hands, she untied the ribbons that held her cloak together. The butler's bony fingers dug into her shoulders as he lifted the warmth from her body. Ouch. *Kenny's brown eyes . . . Kenny's beautiful behind . . . yes, that's it, relax.*

Maybe this was not the kind of party she thought. No. Just foolishness. Nothing bad could happen to her here. Moreover, she did just see others enter the house. She would not be alone with this strange man for more than a few ticks of the clock.

Shivers went through her body as she stood in a short robe that just skimmed the tops of her stockings. She had searched for hours for an acceptable costume and decided to shorten her Grecian robe and wear a white feather mask. She stood here as Artemis, the Greek goddess of the hunt.

Though Artemis was not particularly pretty, she was strong, and Hannah needed that boldness. Especially now, as she stood alone with the Brummeltons' eerie butler. Dressed as such a powerful woman made it easier to play the role, to be the huntress, and learn all she could from this event. She hoped Kenny liked the costume. Her hands ran down her curves.

"Your invite?" the man said, and her heart pounded.

Blast it, Hannah, there is nothing to be afraid of. Kenny and Mr. Roland were decent, though a bit wicked.

Wickedness.

She came to learn to be wicked, to pleasure a man. Kenny's groan as he spilled his seed into her mouth filtered through her mind and she grinned. Without a doubt she would do that again.

She held out the invite, and his bony hands grasped the paper. Smiling, he revealed a mouth with two teeth. Hannah grimaced. Who would hire such a butler? She quelled the urge to flee. Just a few more moments and she would be out of his presence and in Kenny's arms.

"This way." He turned and walked to the door that led to the rest of the house. Hannah held her breath, eager to see what lay behind those doors. In her mind, a line of naked men and women waited to pick a partner for the night, and as she entered the hall, Kenny would claim her, wrapping his strong arms about her as she squeezed him tight. Her muscles trembled.

The door opened and deep blackness stood beyond. Not

one single candle. How odd. Her shoulders tensed. This wasn't right. She peeked through the door. At the end of the corridor, golden light streamed into the darkness like a ray of sun illuminating the tiles.

"Where is everyone?" She frowned. There were no naked men. There was no Kenny. Her heart sank to the soles of her feet.

"In the parlor, miss," came the man's scratchy voice.

The parlor. Yes, that made sense.

"And why are there no candles?"

"His lordship is away. He prefers us not to waste 'em, and Master Rupert doesn't mind the dark." He stared at her from the corner of his eye, and Hannah held still.

Why did this man unsettle her so? Things would get better when she reached the parlor. She breathed deep. The sound of a glass knocking on wood down the hall, followed by a loud laugh, made her breath come out in a rush. Thank goodness. She couldn't wait to be with the others.

"This way, missus."

As he stepped into the hall, Hannah rushed close on his heels. Paintings hung in thick gold frames all along the corridor. How she wished she could see them. Art always inspired her. As she stepped into the column of light, she stopped. Beautiful.

A painting of a woman hung on the opposite wall. With black hair loose, she stood in a field of flowers. The wind blew her hair out behind her, eyes closed to the world, arms outstretched as she tried to catch the breeze. Breathtaking. Hannah smiled. She could actually feel the warm breeze tickle her hair, the sun warm on her face. The woman's mouth formed the most content, happy smile. She seemed truly happy. Hannah sighed. She had never experienced that kind of contentedness in her adult life.

The warm breeze tickled her neck again, and her brow knit. That was real. She turned her face in the direction of the air and jumped at blue eyes behind a black mask, mere inches from hers. A man. His short blond hair shone like a beacon in the dreariness of the hall. A handsome man.

"Glad you could join us." His calm voice slid down her spine. Her shoulders relaxed. Another person in a mask for the party. Thank goodness. She wanted to throw herself into his arms and kiss him.

"W-who is the woman in the painting?" Her voice trembled with each word. Blast, where was her fortitude?

"I'm not sure. She is pretty, though, like you." His hand reached out past her to the man with no teeth. "Thank you, Guss."

"Master." He bobbed his head and disappeared back toward the front of the house.

Hannah stared after Guss, thankful not to be in his presence any longer. Yet, he called this man "master," and he was not Rupert. "Are you related to Mr. Roland?"

"No."

"Why did he call you master?"

"Shall we?" The blond man held out his arm to her and she started. He was naked. A red feather covered his phallus and nothing else.

How did she miss that? And how did that feather stay on?

She tilted her head to the side, looking for an attachment. The plume stood straight up his belly in an arc and touched just below his chest. If a feather touched her there, her skin would tickle. However, this man did not flinch as the plume brushed back and forth with his movements. He cleared his throat. "Miss?"

You ninny. You did receive an invite to a sexual intrigue. You are about to see more naked flesh.

There . . . The feather was secured to his body with leather around his bum. Her fingers itched to trail that thin piece of leather, to touch his firm and dimpled ass. She couldn't help but stare as her cheeks grew toasty warm.

His long legs, sprinkled with blond curls, flexed as he turned. Beautiful. Glorious. A god. Biting her lip, she forced her head up to meet his gaze and smile. She would truly enjoy this evening.

As she placed her hand on his bare arm, hot male flesh warmed her chilled skin and shook off the last of her unease. Her heart thudded hard as her hand glided up and down his forearm. Fingers lingering, her touch caught curl after curl of the dark blond hair. Umm. She never thought she would feel a man again, and in the last day she had touched two. She grinned. She was wicked to find pleasure in such a situation.

As they entered the parlor, the men in the room stood. *Oh my!* Her eyes widened, taking in every detail. Twenty guests sat about the room, the men all dressed in the same fashion as her escort, with black masks and red feathers covering their sexes. The women wore some type of scandalous costume and mask, each one different from the next.

One blond woman wore nothing but a red corset and bright red mask. Emma. From the summerhouse. She stood and walked toward them, an easy smile on her face as if she recognized her. Hannah's heart beat so hard in her chest, her whole body pulsed. Had she seen Hannah watching in the woods? Oh blast. It had been daft of her to do so.

Hannah's escort held out his hand and gave Emma her invite. She read the paper and glanced at her. "Umm . . ." Her gaze raked Hannah's form and her lip quirked.

God, she'd seen her.

"Stay with this one." Emma glanced back at Hannah.

Feather Man nodded and guided Hannah to a seat.

What did that woman think? She was a peep, an ogler. Oh poppiedust! Who was she trying to fool? She was, and today she discovered herself to be a tad more wicked than she thought.

Feather Man stared down at her and smiled. "What shall we call you?"

"Artemis," she said with all the strength she could muster. She would not be the proper Hannah this night.

"First time with us, Artemis?"

She glanced up at the blond god. "Yes."

"Good. We need new blood to feast on." His eye winked behind his mask and she laughed. Did he mean to eat her? She didn't think she would mind. How scandalous.

A naked man crawled into the room, and Hannah's eyes gaped. A tray with a steaming kettle and a large wooden bowl perched on his back. He stopped in front of Emma. She picked up the kettle, poured the steamy clear liquid into a bowl, and stirred.

"My guests." She waved her hand in the air. "The time for preparing has arrived. Come now and drink my brew."

"Come." Her host held out his hand and she stood.

"What is the brew?" Hannah whispered to the blond god who she now stood beside.

"It is a kind of tea."

"Tea?"

"Yes. To relax you." A hot finger pushed a curl of her black hair from her face, and she bit her lip at the gentle caress.

"You mean for the blood drinking," she said, half in jest.

"Yes." He smiled. "Precisely."

Hannah approached the man kneeling before Emma, who held out the bowl. The man stared only at the floor. His shoulder, round and muscled, held the tray with ease. How odd that a man would put himself in such a position. To be . . . a servant? He served Emma and the guests in a primitive form. Like what she imagined a Greek goddess might have owned ages ago before tea carts and clothes. She stared at the human tea cart again. She would take a naked man instead of cold wood any day.

Gripping the bowl in her hands, Hannah raised the brew

and inhaled the spicy-sweet scent. The clear liquid smelled of basil and raspberries.

She placed the rim to her lips.

"Take a good swallow," Emma said.

She drank, the horribly hot fluid flooded her mouth, and her lips puckered at the tangy rancid flavor. Yuck. Her tongue pressed the roof of her mouth, working to expel the liquid, but she managed to swallow. Shuddering, she turned to the next woman, who grabbed the bowl from her hands.

"Good girl," Emma said.

Hannah tried to smile as her throat tingled. What did she just drink?

"Come," her escort said. "We will venture to the ballroom."

"How awful a tea." Her hand covered her mouth as her stomach rumbled.

"I know. Worse than blood." His lip quirked.

"Oh good, I hoped blood would taste better." She grinned.

"Much. You will start to feel the effects soon."

Leaving the room, he availed himself of a candle from the table before the door. They entered the hall, and she wanted to run ahead to the ballroom, to find Kenny and start turning this night from strange to wonderful.

Her heart beat wildly in anticipation as they entered the ballroom. Warm light poured around a black curtain hung two paces inside the room. She couldn't see a thing beyond that drape, but Kenny would be there. She was certain.

The smell of sweet smoke filled the air, and her body hummed. Warmth seeped into her veins in a wave of tingles that caressed her muscles and dewed her sex. How wonderfully delicious a sensation, yet strange. Surely her nipples peaked hard beneath her robe because of the brew. Her mind slid into a slight haze and the room spun. She clutched at the hard male arm beneath her fingers, and her breath hitched.

"This way, Armetis."

He pushed her against the wall and dropped to his knees, pressing his lips to her stockinged leg as if worshipping her. Waves of pleasure pulsed through her. His hands clasped her slippered foot and slid her shoe from it, then he placed her foot on the cold tile floor. Her muscles jumped as iciness crept up her leg. His lips moved against her thigh and heat spread down to her toes. Knees shaking, her hand slid into his hair, gripping his head for support.

"What . . . What are you about?"

"Preparing you." His lips curved against her flesh.

"Oh, it is delightful."

"You may wear only a robe and mask. Nothing more."

She nodded and leaned her head back against the wall as he raised his hands and undid her garters. Delicate caresses slid her stockings from her body, and her muscles bunched as she groaned.

"How do you like the brew now?"

"Mmmm."

Moist kisses slid their way up her naked legs to the apex of her thighs. Placing his lips to her curls, his tongue slid out along her slit and back in one slow lick.

"Oh!" She closed her eyes, her sex clenching.

"Anything you wish of me, you need only to ask." He stood.

I want you to tongue me. No, I want to lick you. Her face grew hot and she nodded. What a wanton she was.

"This way." He offered her his arm and escorted her to the edge of the curtain.

Naked flesh, both male and female, was everywhere. She glimpsed a breast with a rosy nipple peaked as a man cupped the mound—her breast swelled at the sight—then a bare shoulder blade and a bare ass. Her body tingled everywhere her gaze rested, the images emblazoned in her memory in short little bursts. It was beautiful. Mesmerizing and like nothing she ever dreamed of seeing or feeling in her life. She wet her lips.

From the ceiling hung swaths of dark cloth, which made the room more confined. Along the far wall, more cloth hung to create compartments that housed low mattresses strewn with silken colored pillows. Men and women lounged about the beds, drinking wine and smoking what she imagined were hookahs. Her heart sped and her nipples pebbled hard as she imagined Kenny's hands caressing her on that mat. Her body trembling as her slit dripped, and he pushed into her. Other faceless hands caressed her. What a scandalous thought.

This room was an erotic, exciting, fantasy world. Masked, one could do and be anyone they wished—the hunter or the prey. She would be bold, strong, erotic, a seductress. Yes. She would do what her body and mind wished without the social strictures society demanded of a female. She would learn what men desired. She would please them.

Her blond god's fingers tickled her palm; delicious gooseflesh raced across her skin and she shivered. She needed to know what to call him.

"Umm, who shall you be?" Hannah asked.

"Call me Timothy," he said, and turned her to wander the room. "Prey to all things beautiful." He smiled.

Prey to me. She could be his huntress. Or his prey.

"There is more to see. Any pleasure you might wish can be found here. What are your deepest desires, Artemis?"

My deepest desires? No one had ever asked her that. Kenny. She wanted Kenny. Kenny possessed a power she didn't understand. When he touched her, her body did things, felt things, she only dreamed of.

Yes, that was her desire, to pleasure him, to prove Simon wrong.

Her feelings were foolish; she should be running in the opposite direction, but she couldn't. Rake or not, she wanted his hard prick to sink into her. To writhe beneath him and coat his penis with her juices as he spilled his seed into her womb. She wanted to experience all of this night with him. Touching him, pleasuring him.

He would surely be here—she glanced around the room—somewhere.

"Let me show you what is offered. You may find a delight you fancy."

Ugh. Kenneth reached up and ran his hands through his hair. The sharp pain in his head beat a tattoo against his skull. What the hell? He moved his tongue and dry flesh scraped against teeth. Groaning, he squeezed his eyes shut.

A drug of some sort caused this. One glass of wine never did this to him. He rolled to his side, his muscles aching in protest, and slit his eyes open.

Shit. Pitch-black stood beyond his window. What the hell time was it?

He struggled to sit up. His muscles resisted and lagged in response. Bloody hell. Straining, he flung his legs over the side of his bed and stood. His knees wobbled and his head spun; he sat back down. Damn.

He could hear laughter and groaning through the window. The party was already under way. Hannah. Shit.

The sound of her scream of rapture this afternoon rang in his head and eased a bit of the pain. He would bed her this night. His blood heated remembering the taste of her sweet cream on his tongue. But nothing swelled. He let out a long breath through his teeth and glanced down at his flaccid member. The devil, the drug did more than make his head split.

Emma did this with one of her brews. When he asked for

Hannah to be invited, she certainly saw the desire, the pure elation in his face when Rupert said she was widowed.

He closed his eyes and pushed himself back to standing. The world spun, and he forced himself to stay still.

They both would find this situation incredibly funny and too irresistible to pass up. Walker succumbs to a female, a widow. A femme fatale. One of them gave him herb, he knew it. He stepped forward on wobbly legs.

Where the hell was Jerome? His valet always woke him. He staggered to the dressing room that joined his room and flung the door open. Light flooded him. Damn. Pain sliced through his head. Knees wobbling, he squinted and leaned against the doorjamb.

"Jerome?" he bellowed, then winced at the pain throbbing in his head. The door that led to the hall flung open.

"Yes, sir. Sorry, sir. I . . . I'm not well, sir."

"What the hell is going on?"

Forcing his eyes open, Jerome stood in the same state.

"Bloody hell. Give me my tan robe and black mask."

"Yes, sir."

"How much of the party have I missed? Has selection begun?" His fists clenched. Bloody hell, if he missed the chance to bed Hannah tonight, he would go mad. No, he would kill Rupert.

"I don't know, sir."

"Hurry, man, we have no time to lose."

His valet came toward him and pulled his shirt over his head with a wince. "The woman you asked about is here. I checked with Guss on the way up."

Ah, sweet Hannah. He closed his eyes as Jerome held up his robe, and he slid his arms in. She came. Of course she did. He smiled. She couldn't resist.

Good God, he was going to enjoy watching her as she awakened to what the underworld of society did with their free time. He had to see. Her curiosity, so great, so genuine, amazed him. He wanted to teach her everything he knew.

Now, if he could only get himself to the ballroom before selection and get his prick fit enough to serve her. He looked down. Grr. He may need help with that.

4

Priming

They turned into the hallway, and a tall man dressed in a red robe stepped in front of Hannah.

"Mrs. Rosworth, enjoying yourself?" Rupert's baritone voice skittered down her spine.

"Yes, thank you for your kind invitation." His emerald eyes stared down at her. He smiled wickedly, and her cheeks grew toasty warm. This man saw Kenny between her legs that afternoon. Good Lord. She lowered her head and tried to feign indifference she didn't feel.

"You may leave, Timothy. Meet her at the stage in quarter an hour."

Timothy bowed down deep, knelt, and placed his lips to the bare flesh of Rupert's knee. Hannah gaped. A somewhat odd display for a man to give another man, but Rupert's hand slid into his hair. A gesture that showed he didn't mind.

Timothy stood. His warm fingers touched her arm, and gooseflesh washed across her neck.

He bowed his head. "Artemis."

"Timothy." She inclined her head.

He turned and his beautiful dimpled ass disappeared into the crowd.

"Take a turn with me." Rupert offered his arm.

His long olive-skinned legs stood wide, partly covered in a dark red robe. A red robe that bulged at the apex of his thighs. The image of his prick sinking into Emma from behind flashed through her mind, and her heart sped. He found pleasure in watching a man receive a spank. Did he also enjoy receiving one?

His emerald eyes continued to stare at her, and a flush heated her skin. *You ninny, speak to him.* "I would be delighted." Her breath hitched as she placed her hand on the back of his.

He walked with catlike grace, padding through the crowded room, head held high. An amazing man. His assurance, his presence, made people move out of his way without even noticing.

She stared down at those beautiful artistic hands she had wanted on her body so badly that day by the river, her hand so small next to his. His raw virility coursed through each motion he made. She was small and piffling in comparison.

When he reached the side of the stage, he stopped. Turning her, he backed her against the hard wood.

"May I touch you?" Though phrased like a question, the words were a demand.

Her body trembled, as his thumb drew circles in the back of her hand. Breath hitching, she stared at that spot.

"You already are." Heat spread in a slow wash up her arm, and her breasts peaked.

"Indeed I am. Would you like more?"

God, yes. The urge to please him sparked strong and blazed, pulsing through her from the inside out. She was losing her mind. It was scandalous to accept advances from two different men in one day; it was wrong. She came here tonight to pleasure Kenny. For some reason she didn't care. She wanted Rupert's touch. Wanted to please him, and to please him, he needed to touch her.

She stared at his graceful hands and nodded.

"Ah." He dropped her hand, and his touches traveled slowly up her arm. Sensation shot straight to the flesh between her thighs.

"Oh!" She closed her eyes. This was so wrong, but oh so good.

"Mmm." His finger brushed the side of her breast, trailed to the already hard peak, and pinched. Her back arched, filling his hand with her breast as he squeezed.

"He has excellent taste. Always has."

Her eyes shot open and settled on his chin. He kneaded again. "W-what?"

"No wonder he was in a panic to find out if you were wed."

"Kenny?"

"Kenneth. Yes."

Kenny wanted to know if she was married. Her heart sped. Everyone in this vicinity knew of her scandal. The widowed Mrs. Rosworth, suspect in her husband's death. He wanted her and she allowed his friend to take liberties. What was she doing? She shouldn't be doing this, but something in her couldn't make Rupert stop.

The brew. Panic possessed her and her throat constricted as sweat slid down her back. The brew was affecting her mind, her desires, her actions.

Her body trembled, and pain throbbed in her temple. She needed to stop him, to tell him enough. Raising her hands to his chest, she pushed and jerked away as he pinched and massaged her nipple. Pulsing pressure slid through her womb with a need for release. She shook her head as her vision grew soft. Oh, all she wanted was his touch.

Rupert's hand slowly trailed up the hem of her robe. How sinful. Just as she thought his caress would be. Her skin heated with dew.

"May I?" he said in that deep voice that made her tremble. Yes, indeed he could have anything.

"Umm-hmm." She nodded and closed her eyes. His hand slid to the curls of her mound. Lightly flicking, he slid one long finger into her slick folds.

"Oh." The most exquisite sensation. Her hips pressed forward into his hand. Two different men had had their fingers in her today. So thrilling. Cream drizzled and her sex clenched about his finger. Her mind wanted to recoil from this illicit act, but her body wouldn't let her. Never in her life had she acted such.

"He is so right to have craved you for as long as he has."

"Craved me?" she whispered. Another finger slid into her wetness, circled her weeping flesh, then pulled back out to tap her blissful spot. What was she thinking? Oh yes . . . He could have anything, anything he wanted.

"Indeed. As I do now."

His hand left her breast and circled her wrist. Her eyes fluttered open, and she watched his hand pull her touch to his firm, hard phallus. Gliding her fingers along the solid flesh just beneath the thin robe, her touch traced the width, the length, then circled the head. If she straddled him and rode down on his prick, would he growl in pleasure?

"Ah." His finger circled that spot between her legs, and her eyes shut. Every muscle wound tight as her need built to have him between her thighs.

Warm breath spread across her ear. "She is pretty, isn' she?" a feminine voice purred. "A fine choice for him."

Hannah's eyes shot open.

Emma stared at her with a wicked smile, then glanced at Rupert. "I need you, master. There is a problem only you can solve."

Rupert stared at Emma and blew his breath out.

"You are ready, Mrs. Rosworth. Pardon me." Rupert's fingers slid from her sex, leaving a blazing ache. He turned and left with Emma.

She wanted to drop down on her knees, as Timothy had, and crawl behind him, to please him in any way she could, to beg him to touch her again. Hannah shook herself and breathed in raggedly. How odd. She always wanted to learn to please a man but not like this. The pressure building within her made her feel as if her body would burst if she didn't please.

Glancing around the room, Timothy stood gazing at her with heavy-lidded eyes. A smile touched his lips as he pushed from the wall and strode toward her.

"Artemis." He offered his arm.

"Timothy."

Good Lord, what did she just do? Heat washed her cheeks. She shook her head, mortified and demeaned by her urge to please. Her legs shook as she stepped with Timothy into the crowd.

Rupert could have made her do anything. Timothy steered her to the edge of the room. The urge to please Rupert still pulsed through her. This madness had to be the brew, but shouldn't the urge to mate be greater than the urge to please?

Kenneth left his room, his head spinning. Damn. What the hell did he ingest? Wheezing, he tried to pull air into his lungs and clear his head. He would go outside and enter the ballroom on the far end. The crisp air might help shake loose the cobwebs.

Striding across the lawn, the cold night air pricked his skin, and he shook his shoulders. *Come on, old boy. Clear your head.*

If he wasn't there to protect Hannah, anything could happen to her. He hastened his pace, and his heart pounded; he hoped the selection had not begun yet. Bloody hell, he would kill whoever did this to him. He had planned to meet Hannah at the door and keep her in his sight as she was awed and fascinated by what went on around her. Then he would have eased the brew's effects by teasing her and fucking her all night. He blew out through clenched teeth.

Hopefully Emma gave her one of the seasoned hosts. Cool sweat touched his brow. Every woman reacted differently to Emma's brew. One woman had spend after spend just by having him blow on her sex, but other times the women became so aroused they actually experienced pain with the need for release. He didn't know how the brew worked, but if eased properly, the effect always resulted in a more sensual experience for both man and woman. The brew pushed their innermost desires to the extreme.

Whatever trait the brew heightened, he hoped Hannah's host had experience and could ease her before pain arose. If he used the wrong ease or did nothing, things would slowly get worse. Shit. The idea of Hannah in pain because of him . . . He closed his eyes. He couldn't handle that. Piercing pain sliced through his temple.

He needed to see Guss. The old gardener would know an antidote to whatever the hell he ingested. He was no good to anyone in this state. He clenched his fists. He was going to kill whoever did this to him.

Glancing into the ballroom through the sea of bodies, his body heated. In the midst of all that debauchery stood a slice of angel he intended to savor.

Red cloaks bobbed among the field of naked flesh. They were readying for the theatrics the selection would follow.

Half an hour, no more, and the ceremony would begin. That

wasn't a lot of time. Guss would be in the kitchen on the opposite end of the house. Shit.

He reached down, rubbed his hand along his cock, and called to mind Hannah's deep crimson cunt with black lace. His tongue ran along her flesh as he lapped her juices, her sweet aroma filling his nose. His mouth watered. He needed that smell on him again. On his cock, on his hands, on his mouth. Damn, he even wanted the scent on his toes. He squeezed his crotch and gritted his teeth. Come on, damn it. All he needed was a slight rise.

Stroking firmer, he recalled her sweet exquisite scream, her body quivering, as she locked her knees to his head and spent. Bloody hell. Not a damn thing. If he entered the ballroom now, he would be no use to her. His cock would not stand. He turned on his heel and ran for the kitchen.

"Wantons and Wickeds, the festivities are to start with an instructional theatric of Aretinian postures of pleasure."

The first of the entertainers—a young couple—wandered out onto the stage. Timothy stood beside Hannah and watched her intently. The woman, dressed in a long white silk robe with black hair that hung loose down her back, smiled at her partner. The man, one of the striking hosts who escorted women into the masked event, flexed his arms and shook out his legs.

Before tonight, Hannah never knew sexual events like this existed, and now she and fifty or so other guests would watch instruction on how to mate. How to pleasure. She shook her head and blinked. She really was here watching this. Heat seeped through her body as the man turned, and the woman untied the feather covering his sex.

His short phallus, covered with thick veins, jumped as she stroked the length with her hand. Then the woman placed a skin on the tip of the man's sex and rolled the letter down. So that was what a sheath looked like. How strange. Would a man's heat penetrate that skin? The man then helped the woman disrobe.

"Position fourteen," Rupert called out.

The man lay down on his back, then pushed up onto his hands and feet. Hannah could see under his back and bum as he created an arch.

His ass clenched in the most fascinating way, like what she imagined it looked like during futter. Hannah's hands fisted, as she squeezed his bum in her mind. Her nectar dewed her sex and her flesh throbbed. She gasped as the woman straddled the man facing away from him, then slid her fingers around the man's hard phallus and pulled his prick toward her bum.

"Don't pull the cart, dickhead of Cupid."

Hannah jumped and sighted a second man speaking on stage. He read the Italian text from the *I Modi*.

"Because I want to enter by way of the pussy, not in the rear," continued the man onstage.

The woman placed the phallus between her engorged red nether lips and sank down on the man. Everyone moaned. Applause rang through the room, snapping Hannah's attention to the others in the room. This couple on stage pleased the entire crowd. She closed her eyes as her chest tightened, the ache within her homing in on her blissful place. Her hands slid down her body to between her thighs. She needed to ease the ache. Her finger slid easily into wet and engorged lips.

Hannah's body tingled painfully. The words combined with the sight caressed her. She longed for Kenny's phallus to spread her sex as slickness slid down the hard shaft and he filled her, pressing deep. Like the woman onstage, she would ride him until they both cried out in pleasure. Her fingers slid into her opening. Why wasn't this working? Instead of the pleasure she created when alone, pain filled her womb and burned her skin.

Timothy's mouth twisted in what looked like concern, but he did nothing but watch her.

The other guests fondled each other. From the corner of her eye hands groped, cupping breasts. Mouths fused in kisses. Pain shot through her womb, and she breathed in through clenched teeth. Hunching, she pressed her hand to her stomach as her pulse vibrated through her. Each thrust, each groan, tightened her like an overwound violin, stretching her need to the point of pain, to the point of breaking.

Her legs trembled as her breath puffed in and out with the rhythm of the mating onstage. Blast. Where was Kenny? She needed him. Why hadn't he come for her?

"Oh, Ass of Milk-White and Royal Purple, if I weren't looking at you with such pleasure, my cock wouldn't hold up worth a measure," the man on stage called out.

The woman bit her lip and whimpered. Her body convulsed as the man groaned and thrust up hard once more, his hips pulsing as he spilled his seed.

In her mind, gush after gush of Kenny's hot fluid coated the walls of her sex. Hannah's sex contracted and crippling pain shot through her womb. Blast, she needed to leave.

This wasn't right. Something was wrong. She reached out for Timothy's arm and glanced around the room.

"Artemis!" He grasped her.

Where was Kenny? Where was he? Only he could ease her desire, ease this pain. Pain sliced though her body. Good Lord. She doubled over, her fingers digging into the flesh of her rounded stomach. Timothy lifted her into his arms and darkness met her.

5

Declaration

"I use it myself. Makes the limpest of man hard as a bull," Guss's voice crackled as he stirred the steaming broth.

Kenneth chuckled. "The maids all flock to your room, Guss. You have no need for such an herb." He shifted his stance and leaned on the rough wood table in the large kitchen. *Make haste, Guss. Make haste.*

The old man handed him the cup and raised his gray eyebrows. "Precisely why I need it. You think a man as old as I can stay up all night on his own. Things work differently when you age, and this cures any cock stand ailment." Guss winked.

Kenneth's smile broadened—*Randy old man*—then he stared into the cup filled with green herbs and steaming water. Any woman Guss bedded ran giggling back for more. Maybe these herbs were the reason behind his legendary staying power.

He raised the cup to his lips and in one swallow drank the sweet anise-flavored liquid down. Disgusting. The fluid stung his tongue and burned a trail down to his gut. He shoved the cup back at the old man.

"Now what?"

"Now you get back to the festivities so you can enjoy your new strength." Guss turned back to chopping herbs on the kitchen table.

His new strength? Hannah. Kenneth turned about with haste to head toward the ballroom. She needed him. "Good night, Guss."

Guss grunted, but Kenneth paid him no mind.

He left the kitchen and ran down the darkened hall, his heart pounding in his chest. The serum would be the only reason he would make it.

Hopefully.

Not quarter an hour passed as he traversed the black halls, back to the main ballroom.

A woman groaned as he passed a couple deep in futter in the darkness and his cock tingled with warmth. Thank God the herbs worked. He picked up his stride . . . Hannah . . . and bloomed in his pants.

The agonizing ache spread through his head, and the burn in his eyes lingered, but his cock could perform, and that was what he needed to ease her with.

A smile curved his lips. He would finally sink into her velvet warmth. His loins grew heavier. Oh what a sensation.

Please don't let her be in the first group.

He skidded around a corner. If she was . . . Good God, he didn't want to think about another man fucking her. The idea of a husband bedding her drove him mad. For a man who had less right than him to touch her . . . Shit. To feel the clasp of her velvet skin . . . He shook himself. No, he couldn't allow another to fuck her.

Turning the corner, he stopped. Chants came from the ballroom, and the sweet smell of incense hit him. The selection had already begun. His stomach twisted. Please let him find her well. Well and unselected.

He straightened his shoulders and entered the room. First he needed to find Hannah; second he would find out who had drugged him.

Everyone faced the stage. The masters formed the circle for selection. Bloody hell. Hannah knelt in the circle while Greyington paced her. Damn. He was too late. His heart lurched in his chest.

His fingers dug into the flesh of his palm. Shit. Shit. He ground his teeth together to hold back a frustrated scream. Who did this to him?

He inhaled and skirted the edge of the room, muscles tense, ready to pummel anyone who got in his way. Hannah was not only the first person he invited, but she was the woman who had never left his thoughts for twelve years. And someone snatches her from him. Fuck. Why would someone do this?

Greyington's tastes in women ran the same as his; a night with a woman on occasion connected them. He couldn't blame him for wanting to taste Hannah's charms. But she was intended for him. Greyington didn't have the personality to dose a member. He was not his delayer.

A tall blond woman stepped in front of him and dropped to her knees. Clasping his foot, she placed her lips to his thigh.

"Master, how may I please you?"

Bloody hell. He couldn't deal with the formality of the selection right now. Hannah knelt as Greyington chanted and dropped wax in a circle about her. He needed to reach Hannah. He couldn't let Greyington have her, not this way. Glancing down, he met blue eyes staring up at him beneath blond lashes.

"Good evening, Jennifer. Please rise; there is no reason for you to yield to me. You are not mine." His teeth clenched tight.

"But I could be." Her lip jutted out in a pout as she unfolded herself. As she stood, her touch trailed up the sensitive flesh of his thigh. His hand shot out and snagged her wrist, stopping her from reaching his cock.

"Good God, woman." He pushed her hand away from his

body. Jennifer had been pleasant but by no means his best. Though she seemed to think she was the cat's cream. She, like his mother, only found bliss going from one man to another. One man alone would never satisfy her. She thought he could.

On the other hand, one man would satisfy Hannah. He needed to get to her. His shoulders tensed, and he shook off the exclusive thought.

Jennifer ran her finger up his arm. "But—"

"You were a delight, dear, and you agreed to my terms when I took you to my bed. Once and only once." He inclined his head. "Have a good evening." He stepped away from her, breaking the contact of their skin. She cursed under her breath.

He strode up the steps and made his way to Rupert, who stood in his dark red robe at the head of the ceremony. Heat flooded his tense muscles, and his blood boiled.

Anger, disappointment, and guilt twitched his limbs. Rupert had better have answers, or he would strangle him. The muscles in his cheek jumped as he came up alongside him.

"Where you been, chap?" Rupert glanced at him, then back to Hannah in the circle.

"To the devil, Rupert," he ground out, wanting to shake him—no, wanting to punch him. But he held back; otherwise, half the masters in the room would be on him. He needed to figure out a way to get Hannah. "You even put her in the first pod to make sure I had little chance."

"What are you talking about, chap?"

"Hannah, she is in the circle with Greyington." The selection rituals said that once chosen, you belonged to that person until they said otherwise. Nothing. No holes. It could be hours, days, weeks before Greyington gave her up.

He closed his eyes. Good God, he wanted to fuck her for weeks, for longer. Never to let her go. Cool sweat ran down his back, and his heart beat wildly. Bloody hell. He wanted her wholly.

No. He rolled his shoulders. It was just this situation. He couldn't possibly want to give a woman the power to turn him into the slobbering lump his father had been when his mother left. His hands fisted.

But Hannah was different. He hadn't been able to shake her from his mind for years.

Rupert turned to him. "Greyington did her a favor. He chose her because of the pain."

Pain. His gaze shot to her. Her eyes closed, a pinch between her brow. Lips that were usually in a smile now frowned. Bloody hell, she was so white. How could he have missed . . . His stomach tightened and sweat pierced his brow. He caused this. If he hadn't invited her . . . His breath hitched and his stomach rolled.

"Shit. What the hell happened, Rupert? Why herb me? You knew I wanted her."

"I didn't dose you, chap." His green eyes softened. "I don't know what happened to you, but you can still claim her. Just intervene. Make a declaration."

A declaration. He closed his eyes and sighed. It was the only way for him to get her now. If he declared her his, the group would bind them. Forever.

A wife. A partner. A slave. And he hers.

He would have every right to fuck her as she walked in the door. His cock stiffened, tenting his robe.

God, could he do it? His shoulders tensed.

The commitment would mean no other woman, none without Hannah's participation. There was so much they did not know about each other. Would she want to stay?

He wanted to know her, to hear about the years they spent apart, and to tell her of his. She would want to listen to the hell his mother put his family through when she left.

But would she care she was bound to a bastard? His cheek

twitched. He had never told anyone that, and he wanted to tell her. His chest swelled.

She was not his mother. Quite the opposite, in fact, and he wanted her despite all the pain she could cause him.

Hannah whimpered as Greyington pricked her finger to let her blood flow. Kenneth winced. Bleeding her would ease her pain by letting the brew out. But, not enough. An intense spend would be the only way she would find peace, and he couldn't sit back and watch another man sink his cock into her velvet warmth.

Not after dreaming of her, wanting her all these years.

Declaration, it didn't matter if she left. He would have her. Hannah knelt on the stage, arms trembling as her blood ran down her fingers.

"Rupert, what is her desire? Do you know?"

"To please."

He closed his eyes. *Sweet, sweet, Hannah, I never intended to hurt you.* He ran a hand through his hair and breathed out through clenched teeth. "Bloody hell."

"Yep, the declaration ceremony could put her in further pain. The level of pain all depends on *who* she is with. Can you make worshipping her pleasurable to you? More so than it is for her? I say, a fitting challenge for you, chap."

Of course he could do it. Pleasuring her would be the most exquisite thing he had ever done.

Kenneth stepped forward into the circle, and Rupert smiled. Whether Rupert dosed him or not, it pleased Rupert that he decided to make this transition. He and Emma both urged him to go to the next level of sensuality, and he couldn't go there without a declared partner to experience the ritual with.

Hannah knelt in the circle, unable to move. The pain slicing through her womb stole her breath and made her legs shake.

Why had Kenny not found her, come for her? She did not know. This pain needed to stop, and Timothy said the only way was to follow her urge. To please a man.

Then she would leave. What a fool she had been. Her eyes squeezed shut on tears welling to the brim. Why would she think any man would want her more than once?

Kenny had his taste just as her husband did, and that had been enough. God, he probably lay in one of the special rooms with a wench who did exquisite things to him.

She was inexperienced. She closed her eyes. Too inexperienced.

You're a passionless fuck, Hannah. I made a mistake marrying you. Simon's voice rang through her head.

Oh God. A passionless fuck. She cringed. It was because of her aunt's instructions: *Lie passively, dear; don't move, don't make a sound or your husband won't like it.*

What did she do wrong? Following that instruction with Simon hadn't done her any favors, and following her body's desires hadn't helped with Kenny either.

It was surely her screams. Simon always told her to be quiet. Her body shook. She would never achieve giving a man pleasure. Burning pain pierced her stomach and darkness loomed again. No more. No more.

Chants went on around her as the man with black hair and soft caring eyes knelt. He wanted to help her. He realized her pain. "Please," she whimpered.

Warm fingers wrapped about her hands, which were clenched to her stomach, and pulled them from her. He ran his finger up her hands and gripped her trembling middle finger. Gold metal flashed in the light as pressure traced a line into the flesh.

Her eyes bulged as he pinched the flesh, and warm red slid down and dripped to the floor. *He cut me.* She yanked at her hand, but he did not release her.

Her muscles tensed, awaiting more pain, but it never came. Warm tingles of pleasure swept her. Her womb tensed, then eased. Amazing. Letting her blood flow eased her. The blood ran off the tips of her fingers and spattered on the floor. Her heart pounded, and her body trembled as desire flooded her anew.

His lips moved and he stood, dropping her hands. What did he say?

Blood rushed so loudly through her veins she had no idea. A sharp twinge slashed through her. Oh please. She dug her fingernails into her palms, and warm stickiness coated them.

She ground her teeth together at the pain, and a groan crept up her throat. If she could only hear him, the ache would go away. Listening to him would please him. She shook her head and strained to hear.

"Greyington, leave." Kenny's voice slid down her body in a wave.

Oh! She squeezed her eyes shut, and her body jerked as she tried to breathe. Did he actually come for her?

His voice came from behind her, and she couldn't move. Her body quaked as she struggled to hold back tears. She wanted to stand, to go to him and let him take her from here. But did he want her? Another agonizing twinge hit her womb and she flinched.

The black-haired man who slit her fingers stared past her and mouthed something.

"I said step away. She is mine." Her heart lifted. He did want her. She did please him. Soothing warmth slid through her belly, easing the pain and peaking her nipples.

"Master." The black-haired man stared over her other shoulder.

"Walker, are you declaring?" Rupert's baritone voice said from the other side of her.

Declaring. What did that mean?

Another twinge hit her, and she sucked in a breath through clenched teeth. When would this end?

"If you are, say so. Otherwise leave," Rupert said with the same command he had in the cottage that day.

Good Lord, what was declaring? Please don't let him duel for her. Oh, the ache would only get worse if that happened. She couldn't handle more pain, even if Kenny regarded her. Tears swelled in her eyes, and her lower lip trembled. She wanted to throw herself into his arms, but she couldn't move.

"Ah, sweet, are you all right?" Kenny asked.

No, I'm not well. Her whole body heaved on a sob. She tried to hold back the tears and gulped for air. Impossible, they tumbled down her face.

"Shit."

"Walker. Declare or leave," the black-haired man said from in front of her. He kneeled and clasped her hands. Turning her palms straight up, he slit her index fingers. There was no pain as new blood dripped down her hands. The ache in her stomach eased, and she could breathe again. Good Lord, this was too strange. Make him come to her.

"Move, Greyington." Kenny's large form appeared beside her, and tears ran down her face. Kenny was here; surely he would make things better.

Heat radiated from his body and she shivered. She was so cold. She wanted to curl into him, and breathe in his scent as she wrapped the warmth of his skin about hers. Her body was shaking—she couldn't control her limbs—as he placed his hand on top of her head.

"I, Kenneth Walker, declare this woman mine."

She was his, whatever that meant. He would take her, and she could please him to rid herself of this ache.

He reached into his robe and pulled out a similar gold knife. What was he doing? Placing the blade to his hand, he slit both his index and middle fingers, then pressed blood from the cuts. Her eyes gaped. He didn't even flinch. Grasping her hands, he pressed his cuts to hers.

"As one."

Then he raised them to his mouth and sucked each one into his wet warmth. The pressure made the blood flow. Warm tingles spread up her skin, and wetness pooled between her thighs.

Thank goodness the pain almost disappeared. Wrapping his tongue around each finger, heat as warm as a wool blanket swept her chilled body. His eyes, smoky black pools, stared back at her as he slid her fingers from his mouth and raised his to her.

"Open, sweet," he whispered.

She opened her mouth, and he placed his cut finger against her lower lip. He wanted her to drink his blood as he did hers. The idea of tasting another person's blood should make her cringe, but this was Kenny. His blood was a part of him, and she craved his intimacy.

He dragged his touch across the dry skin of her lips. Her tongue slid out, wrapped about his finger, and pulled it into her wetness. Sucking, salty warm bitterness swirled in her mouth and she swallowed. Blood did taste better than the brew.

Kenny growled and her heart sped. What a wonderful sound. Tears slid down her face as a smile tugged her lips.

"It's all right, sweet." He ran a finger down her face, tracing her tears.

People moved about them, and his finger slid from her mouth. "This is just the onset. I cannot ease you just yet." He touched her temple. "Hannah, I'm so sorry."

She nodded. Everything would be well; he was here now.

His arm wrapped about her, and he straightened, pulling Hannah to her feet. She pressed her length against his, and heat from his body seeped into her icy skin.

Good Lord, the smell of him . . . that spicy scent. She rubbed her face in the opening of his robe until her nose caressed the curls of his chest. Mmm . . . Her knees wobbled, and her hunger for him blazed. Arching her body, she pressed her breasts into his hard flesh.

"Bloody hell." His arms tightened about her.

Oh how she needed him. To feel every ounce of his hard body pressed naked, flesh-to-flesh. To have those hands—that now soothingly rubbed her back—brush her bare skin. He placed a kiss on the top of her head.

"Don't worry; everything is set. She will be fine," Rupert said.

Hannah stiffened. Did he mean for Kenny to leave her? No, Kenny wouldn't do so. Her hand slid from his sides in search of his warm bare skin. Finding the part in his robe, her fingers delved beneath. The coarse curls caressed her. Magnificent. Hard muscles beneath hot skin.

Her hand massaged through the sea of curls to the hard button of flesh while her lips circled, licking and flicking the other through his silk robe.

He grunted and blissful sensation ripped all the way to her toes. Soothing heat spread through her womb and liquid fire dripped between her sex lips. She closed her eyes to savor every sensation. God, she needed more, needed his hands on her bare skin. With haste!

"Rupert, give us a moment." Kenny's need-filled voice sent her nerves ablaze. He wanted her. She pleased him.

Yes, Rupert, leave. Her chest rose ragged and fell as she drifted in blissful light-headedness. She would not let him go. The pain in her body had eased, but she needed to please him or the pain might return. His fingers plucked her hard nipple.

"Uhh." Her eyes opened and settled on his full luscious lips, moist with dew.

A kiss. Yes.

A kiss would pleasure him. She rose up on her tiptoes and

trailed her hands up his robe. His muscles jumped in a wave beneath the thin cloth. The need to hear his labored breaths and strangled moans of pleasure gripped her.

His head bent down as hers tipped up, and hot breath met smooth, wet flesh, pressing firmly. Their lips gently caressed and nipped. Her hands slipped under his robe and pushed the tan silk wide to explore.

Strong powerful hands slid down her back to the swell of her bum. His fingers kneaded and separated the spheres, pulling the short fabric of her robe up so his bare flesh met hers. Good Lord, lightning slid through her body.

A finger slid into the dewed crack until the touch rested against her bumhole. Her whole body quaked, wanting his fingers probing in and out of her sex and her pucker. He tapped lightly and pressed into her bum. Cream drizzled down her legs.

He groaned. Yes, that was the sound she craved. Her body hummed.

Wetness traced her lips, and she arched her trembling body into him. She wanted to catch his prick in the crease between her thighs, to make him scream out his pleasure as he spilled his seed into her warmth. The walls of her sex quivered.

His chest labored in and out under her hands, and with a jerk of his hips, his sex slipped into the crease of her legs.

"Oh, Hannah." His hips pressed forward.

Yes, he desired her too. His entire body radiated lust for her. She thrust her tongue and hips into him. The engorged folds of her sex clenched his hard prick and coated his length with her juice. The sensation . . . oh God. She moaned. His skin was so hot as his prick parted her folds as if melting butter.

Rupert cleared his throat.

A tremor hit Kenny's body, and he jerked his lips from hers. Her eyes fluttered.

"No!" She snagged his robe and tugged, needing his lips

back on hers. He slid his cock from between her thighs. She didn't care if the whole world saw them mate. She had waited twelve years for this, and she would wait no longer.

"Rupert, I won't leave her." His voice, deep and raspy, vibrated through her.

Thank goodness. Her muscles relaxed, fingers sliding down his taut stomach. She circled his penis and stroked the hot satiny skin. The tip, so hot, scorched her skin. Wetness drizzled from the tip, and his breath whooshed out. She wanted to taste him again, to feel his prick twitch and quiver in her mouth as his seed began to rise.

"Sorry, chap. You know the rules of the ritual."

The ritual. That was why he needed to leave. The declaration.

"Let me ease her prior. Nothing says she has to start the ceremony in need."

Hannah glanced at Rupert from the corner of her eye. Her head rose and fell with each labored breath Kenny made.

He nodded. "Make haste, chap. Once she is eased, come to the stockroom."

"Right."

Kenneth reveled in the feel of her small hand as she stroked his hard cock.

"There is a small room down the hall that is more private. I will ease you there."

"Yes." One hand clutched at his robe; the other stroked his heated stiff skin. *Touch all you want, sweet. This time I'm not about to stop.*

A long breath of air whooshed out of him. He would finally bed her. He slid an arm beneath her knees and lifted her. Cradled her against his chest as her hands explored.

So light, so perfect. She fit him.

6

Pleasing

Gliding his lips across hers, he walked through the parting crowd as her tongue slid into his mouth. Sweet and warm, it swirled around. Damn. She made it hard to breathe.

She shifted, wrapping her legs about his waist. Her robe crept up, and his hands slid to the naked swells of her bum. The skin was so smooth; he couldn't wait to taste it, to run his tongue along every inch of her as she screamed with release.

Holding her hungry body, he sought her wet flesh. His touch slid into the folds and probed her soaking sex. Good God, her cunny scorched with heat. His prick pulsed with the beat of his heart, muscles clenching tight. He needed her hot cunt around his cock.

No, she needed this slow, to prove to her how beautiful and desirable she was. To keep the need at bay. To show her how much she pleased him.

Her tongue thrust in and out, tangling with his as touches slid, cupping and kneading his flesh beneath his robe. His head spun. Flesh against flesh. The fervor of her ardor broke what little restraint he possessed.

His cock jumped, brushing the heat of her bottom. Her arms tangled about his neck as her kiss turned harsher, stealing his breath and giving it back. His fingers dug into the tender flesh of her ass, clasping her as she rocked against him. His pulse raced, skin tingling everywhere she touched.

Damn, twelve years was too long to crave a woman he never expected to get. The urge to sink into her here and now . . . oh God. He had to wait, just a few more moments and they would be in the room.

Arching her back, she rubbed her breasts against him and moaned.

His cock touched the silken oil of her slit, and he gasped, needing more of the sweet sensation. He slid back and forth in the crack of her, and his sack pulled tight. Shit. His desires were against him. He would not make it to the room. The need to sink into her heat overwhelmed him.

Stumbling into the hall, he pressed her up against the opposite wall with a thud. His hands separated the velvet folds of her cunt.

One taste of her silken oil, then he would take her to the room for a proper fuck. He shifted his fingers into her humid flesh; slick cream coated and scalded his hands. God, she was so wet, so ready for him.

She arched, frantically rubbing herself against his belly. "Oh, yes, Kenny." Her teeth grazed his neck, and his muscles strained for control.

Bloody hell. The room, so close yet too far away. He needed her now.

"I can't wait." His fingers left her drenching sex. Shit, he was about to bed her in the hall like a dove in the street. She deserved better but he could wait no longer.

He shifted and spread her farther. She reached down, wrapped her fingers about his stiff shaft, and guided his throbbing head into her folds. One thrust of his hips, and slick hot flesh stretched, engulfing and caressing his cock.

"Oh! Oh!" Her cunny muscles spasmed as he fully sheathed himself.

His eyes closed, and he shuddered. Teeth clenched, he struggled not to spill. She was so damn hot.

"Good God, Hannah."

He kissed her neck and her cheeks, unable to get enough of her salty sweet skin.

"Tight, so tight."

She whimpered and wiggled, fingers digging into his shoulders. His shaft throbbed within her, begging him to move. Oscillating her hips, her mound rubbed against the rough hair of his sex.

"Thrust . . . please . . ." Muscles tightened in a wave about his cock. "Mmmmm."

The sound, so exquisite, made him grind into her swollen flesh. Her inner muscles quivered, and a gasp of sweetness pressed to his lips.

He pulled his lips away. "Open your eyes, sweet. Let me see you as you come for me."

Her eyes slit open. The blue, a thin sliver about the passion-filled black.

"Oh, Hannah."

Instincts so powerful possessed him. His hips slid back as he withdrew to the tip, then thrust back in. Hot oil slid down his hardness, clasping him, pulling him deep. Her face contorted as pleasure built.

The slap of flesh on flesh, flesh on wood, and wet hot cunt drove him. Fingers scratched his skin. Teeth bit his lips. She whimpered, then screamed, grinding into him. The muscles of her cunt convulsed, clasping each thrust of his shaft. His ass tingled, and his stomach clenched tight. A grunt ripped from his throat as his cock burst forth, spilling his seed within her smoldering wetness. Knees weakening, they toppled to the tile floor.

Hannah could not believe the intensity of her spend. Every muscle in her body clamped tight around Kenny's penis. He lay atop her, phallus lodged inside her, panting heavily. Their passion was wonderful. Heavenly. She wanted more.

His hands cupped her bum. Her legs wrapped wantonly around his hips, her hands tangled in his hair. So intimate, so amazing. Tears welled in her eyes as she felt every muscle, every bone, every breath of him. She wouldn't change this first with him. Even with the pain from earlier, she would cherish this act.

"Kenny?" Leaning forward, she nibbled the soft flesh below his ear. "Did I pleasure you?" She needed to hear him say yes, even if the pain no longer resided in her womb.

The air swirled and feet padded past them. They behaved like animals. Her cheeks grew warm. It felt good to let her body follow her own desire.

"Good God, sweet. What do you think? We are lying on the floor in the hall." His head lifted from her, and he grinned with lazy eyes.

"Yes!" She couldn't contain her smile. He enjoyed her. A tear slid from the corner of her eye and down her cheek, and her lip trembled. She pleased him. She could please a man. Simon was wrong.

"Yes," he said between pants. "I want more, Hannah." His finger brushed away the tear. "I want this all night. After the ceremony, will you allow me?"

What was the ceremony? She didn't care. "Yes, oh yes!" That was why she had come.

7

Confessions

Kenneth carried a sleeping Hannah into the stockroom. Rupert would be angry, but damn it, he didn't care. He would not let her out of his sight. Not even for the short amount of time for them to prepare.

Someone dosed him tonight in an attempt to keep him from Hannah. He would kill before he let anything horrid happen to her. An irrational emotion, but he couldn't help the powerful urge to protect and possess her. Humph. Possessiveness, like his father, because of a woman. Maybe he was his father's son.

Rupert strode toward him, a frown on his face; but his eyes smiled. He wouldn't give him much grief for Hannah being here.

"I want her to be prepared in the same room."

Rupert stopped in front of him and glanced at Hannah, who dozed lightly in his arms.

"Is that so?" He pointed to the other side of the room where three women stood. "Guessed that would be the case, chap."

Kenneth's muscles tightened as he beheld the tall blonde who waited with Emma. "Why Jennifer?"

"Sorry, chap. You know the rules. One of your formers needs to be present to witness your devotion."

"What about Emma? I have fucked her too."

Rupert's head shot up. "Emma is mine. If I had not consented, it would not have happened."

Shit. "Sorry, Rupert, I didn't mean to offend."

"I know. This is a big step for you."

Kenneth placed his lips to Hannah's temple. "Sweet, time to wake."

"Umm." She snuggled her head closer into his chest, and he sighed, his cock swelling. Damn, everything she did aroused him. He smiled into her hair. He would enjoy being bound to her.

He strode across the room to where the ladies stood.

"Emma, Mary, Jennifer." He bowed his head. "Take care of her."

Emma smiled at him, then reached out and touched his arm as he slowly lowered Hannah from his hold. Hannah visibly trembled as his hands fell from her body; she swayed into Emma, who braced her. She would be fine. He trailed his fingers across her cheek. God, he didn't want to leave her. He inhaled in an attempt to control his desire. They would be apart for only a moment. She gazed up at him with sleep-laden eyes.

"Sweet, sweet. You will be fine," he said, more for him than for her. "I will leave you in their care." Bowing his head to Hannah, he rolled his shoulders and strode back to Rupert.

He stared at her from across the large room. For some, the brew held strong for a day or more. For others, the effects lasted only a few hours. She had fallen into a light slumber as soon as he'd scooped her off the floor. The pain was gone. He hoped the reprieve would last. With the battle her body and mind had gone through, the last thing he wanted was to cause her more pain.

He strained to hear her conversation as Rupert and Jerome slid his robe from his body. He sighed. Thank God. He could hear them. He wanted to know how she was feeling, and at the moment, hearing her talk was the closest he could get.

"You are the one who performed the theatric," Hannah said to Mary. "How do you learn such complex poses?"

Kenneth held back a chuckle. Truly amazing. He doubted a question existed she wouldn't ask. When they were young, she'd been the one to ask him what a kiss felt like. Gazing up at him with those wide desire-filled eyes. He'd groaned and then covered her trembling lips with his. Her first kiss, his first feel. Damn, she was still the same Hannah in so many ways.

Emma lifted Hannah's robe from her body. His eyes widened. Large, deep-rose-colored nipples stood erect. Wonderful. Beautiful. He had known but . . . good God, what glorious breasts. His mouth watered. He couldn't wait to taste them.

"There's a book with pictures in it and with a bit of practice . . ." Mary shrugged her shoulders. "I was supposed to do one more posture, but the selection started early for you." She continued to rub oil into Hannah's stomach.

Kenneth's heart constricted. That was the reason he was late to the selection. Rupert started early because she was in so much pain. When he found the person who tried keeping him from Hannah this night, they would end up in as much pain as she went through.

"What was the other position?" Curiosity poured from Hannah's voice, and he couldn't help but grin.

Jerome, his valet, poured oil into his hands and began to rub the slickness into his thighs. Burning tingles, changing to cool tickles, spread in his hands' wake. His muscles jumped.

"What is in that?" he asked Rupert, who stood setting candles into a candelabra.

"It is a mint oil. Good, isn't it?" The corner of his lip curved up. "You will enjoy using it in your play."

Jerome continued to massage, and Kenneth turned to face the ladies again.

Hannah's eyes were wide; her body leaned forward trying to absorb every detail of her conversation. The same curiosity and awe on her face as ... His stomach clenched. Damn, that look. *Sweet Hannah. After tonight, I will awaken your mind and body to pleasures you don't know exist.*

"Sir, lift your arms please." Jerome shook his head.

His body tingled as the oil rubbed up his underarms. With the friction from Hannah's body, this oil would be maddening.

"How ... umm ..." Hannah paused, waving her hands in the air as her hair tumbled down in a rush. A curtain of black velvet. Beautiful. He groaned, imagining the soft strands tickling his chest as she rode him. "With all your amours, what would you say brings a man the most pleasure?" Hannah's voice hitched in pain, and her hand spread across her belly.

Sweet Hannah. He closed his eyes. Shit. The urge to please still pulsed strong. He sighed. He had hoped the brew's effect was fading. He would do his best to not cause her further discomfort. Warmth spread through his muscles as he imagined her pleasuring him till he couldn't move. His lips quirked. After this, she would do it too.

"So you stretch before every encounter?"

"Sure do. Most of my amours like to watch." Jennifer brushed a white cloth across Hannah's breasts. She was being nice to Hannah. He worried about that.

"Amazing. I ... I never would have thought." Hannah's hands clenched. Kenneth blew his breath out. Her pain increased.

"Ah, you know men. They like to look at anything naked that has a fine shape." Mary ran a comb through Hannah's mane.

"So true," Emma said.

"You have a lovely form, so tall and lean."

Hannah glanced down at her body. "Me ... well ... I ... I'm quite short." She inhaled. "My husband always said I was much too s-short for his liking."

Kenneth's muscles tensed at the anguish and uncertainty inflected in those words. She was perfect. What kind of cork brain would tell his wife she was too small? His teeth clenched as anger flooded him. Ah, Hannah. What did your husband do to you? The bastard. Her strong urge to please came from something that bugger did to her.

"But look how well put together you are. Fine hair and eyes. You are quite pretty." Mary smiled.

Yes, she was, and more, and he intended to prove how much she meant to him. Hannah bit her lip, eyes big and round, uncertainty and pain written plain as day on her features. He would show her in every action how much she pleased him. That was what this event was for. To worship her, to please her, and in the process to show her his pleasure.

"Do you need anything else before the ceremony begins?" Emma's eyes sparkled with . . . glee?

Hannah watched her, unsure what to expect during this event. A twinge hit her stomach, and she bit her lip. Not again, please. Her hand pressed into her slick, oiled stomach.

"The ceremony is intense. You should relieve yourself if you have to." Emma waved to a door down the wall. "Jennifer can assist you. I know Kenneth does not want you to be alone."

"Yes, thank you."

Hannah walked into the room with the tall, elegant Jennifer. Her legs alone came up to Hannah's stomach. Those legs had been around Kenny. She was sure of it. Just as she was sure Emma's had.

You ninny. Does the fact that he futtered many women matter?

No. She didn't care. Kenny focused only on her. For now. That was enough.

The skin on her arms pricked, and a giggle caught in her throat. She wanted to cross her arm about her nipples. This woman caressed her stomach only a moment ago, yet an embarrassed heat caressed her skin at her stare. She could not piddle with the way Jennifer watched her. She needed a distraction.

"Tell me about this ceremony. What is the declaration?"

Jennifer stepped forward and pulled Hannah's hair away from her body as she squatted over the pot.

"I'd hoped to be in your place." Anger poured from each word. Her fist clenched Hannah's tresses tighter, and pins spread through Hannah's scalp.

Ouch. Hannah stilled, leaning her body in the direction of Jennifer's hands. Why was she angry? And what place did she want to be in?

"You're hurting me." Tingles touched Hannah's neck as a chill swept her.

"The pain is worth what you will have with that man." A jealous lover was the last thing she needed tonight. But Jennifer didn't say Kenny's name. Did she want the ceremony?

"Tell me, Jennifer, what is it that I will have with him? This is my first time at this event. I have no idea what this group does." She would never trade Kenny but . . . She turned her face to see Jennifer's; her lips formed a deep tight frown, and her eyes narrowed in smoldering heat. A growing unease slid through Hannah's veins, and her hands began to shake. She truly intended to harm her.

Jennifer's hand jerked her hair, and pain shot through her scalp. Blast. What did she think she was about? Kenny stood right outside this room waiting for her. She was daft in the attic. She needed to find a way to calm her.

"W-what would please you, Jennifer? Do you wish to trade places with me?" Her voice firmed and her teeth clenched. For twelve years she had wanted a man to touch her the way Kenny had. Her frustration made her blood boil. No way would she let this act push her to flee.

"Oh yes. I would be delighted to. But you have exchanged blood. You have tasted each other. Even if I wanted to, I could not step into your place."

Thank God. Hannah wouldn't let her anyway.

"I never thought he would declare himself for you. I risked a lot in drugging him. I don't understand how he can know he wants to forsake everyone for a woman he just met."

She drugged him? That was why he arrived late. Hannah's heart sped. How could Jennifer do something . . . something so devious? She was through being polite. Hannah reached up, placed her hand on her hair between Jennifer's fist and her scalp, and pulled. Catching Jennifer off guard, her hair came free of her clutch and she turned quickly away from her.

"Ah, that is where you are wrong." She stared at Jennifer. "Kenny and I have known each other for years. He was my first love." Yes, that was true. She had mourned when he left his aunt's so hastily. She never told him of her regard, but her heart had ached for months.

Jennifer stared at her hand that had been in Hannah's hair. Her lip trembled. "I will help you no more." She spun around and left the room before Hannah could say another word.

Hannah leaned against the wall, the pain in her womb increasing. Good Lord, this night . . . what madness.

Jennifer had said Kenny wanted to forsake everyone for her. Like a wife? Her heart lurched and her lip quirked. How odd, wonderful, and utterly terrifying!

Could she keep him?

She wanted to cuddle with Kenny in her bed with his arms wrapped about her, to awake in the morning with no more pain and the knowledge that she had pleased a man enough to make him stay.

* * *

Where was Hannah? Jennifer left the door to the retiring room, but Hannah was not in her wake. He stepped forward and strong fingers wrapped about his arm.

"Don't, Kenneth. Give her a moment. She needs time. Tonight has been too much."

He jerked from Rupert's hold. "How would you know? I need to make sure she is well."

He stepped away from Rupert. Rupert stepped with him.

"Give her the moment she needs," Rupert said firmly. "Are you ready for this commitment, chap?"

"Rupert." His friend didn't understand what Hannah meant to him. But how could he explain?

Rupert's eyes softened. "I know she is the one, chap. The one whose name you call out at night. The one who makes you rush out to find cunt after you dream about her."

Good God. He knew that? "Rupert—"

Rupert held up his hand. "I know you won't let her go. All I'm saying is this is a big step. She is in pain. I could see the effects coming back as she entered the retiring room."

Bloody hell. He knew about Hannah. All these years and Rupert knew. He stepped forward and gripped Rupert's shoulders. The familiar scent of sandalwood caressed his nose. "Damn, Rupert. Why didn't you talk to me about this?"

"Nothing to discuss. Our group has never been exclusive." He pulled back with a soft smile on his lips. "We have enjoyed our follies, but you and I both prefer cunt. This was not intended to last." Rupert patted him on the shoulder. "You have a second chance. If you don't think you're up to this, let Emma give her the dose. She will sleep through the rest and you won't have to commit yet." He squeezed his shoulder once more and left.

Bloody hell. He closed his eyes. He had shared women with Rupert off and on for the past four years, and he never once told him he knew about Hannah.

Hannah.

Without a doubt, he was ready for this. More ready than he would have guessed yesterday. He wanted Hannah more than he wanted any other person.

But did she want him with the same ardor?

8

Worshipping

Hannah exited the room and pitch-blackness met her. She only hesitated an extra moment. Had the ceremony begun?

Her breath caught as shuffles of feet and heavy breaths sounded all around. The door closed behind her, extinguishing the only light. She couldn't see. A warm breeze blew her hair back from her body and she shivered, gooseflesh rising on her skin. The breeze was faintly familiar . . . Oh. The woman from the painting in the hall. Hannah smiled warmly as the breeze blew her hair.

"So enchanting." Kenny's voice seemed to come from all about her. "Beautiful. Passionate. Wanton." Light touches feathered her body, making her tremble. "The best combination."

She reached out in the direction of where the voice came from, in the direction of the touch, but clutched nothing but air.

"Where are you?" she whispered.

"All about you. In you. A part of you."

Light cool silkiness dragged down her stomach. "Stay absolutely still." Warm moist air dragged past her ear. Her body trembled at the desire washing through her skin. Nipples peaked hard, her skin tingled everywhere.

"Kenny." The light caresses—a feather— trailed down her back. Her chest swelled, and her bum cheeks clenched. "The ache is returning."

"Not for long, sweet."

Hair brushed her thighs, and her hips jerked forward. Warm lips traveled up both her legs. Good Lord. Her eyes widened. Someone else caressed her. Kissed her. "Kenny? Who is with you?"

"We are all here to serve you. To worship you." His breath caressed the heated skin of her thigh.

"I . . . I—" A tongue brushed the curls at the apex of her legs, then pushed into her slick flesh, probing and seeking the entrance to her womb. The other lips traveled up her stomach to her breasts. Groaning at the intense sensations, she squeezed her eyes shut. She shouldn't enjoy this, but it felt so good.

"Mmmm. The most exquisite taste," Kenny said as his tongue left her mound. "You are so wet for me."

"Yes." Fingers probed her slit. Lips suckled her nipples. "Oh, Kenny!"

"So hot."

"Yes."

Warm fingers slid over her body, probing, stretching, sliding fingers in. Her hips pressed forward, opening her thighs farther for the caresses.

A finger pressed into her bum. Oh! Her muscles spasmed, and bit by bit, the digit sunk fully in. Her breath caught as pressure built, and the finger buggering her picked up the same rhythm of the fingers probing her sex.

Oh so . . . she gulped for air . . . shockingly exquisite. More touches rubbed her blissful place and her body jerked. Her breath puffed in and out as warmth spiraled her muscles, tightening, bliss just on the horizon. But she didn't want to shatter this way; she wanted Kenny's hard phallus buried deep as she made him scream in pleasure. Her heart sped and a gush of wetness seeped from her.

Kenny moaned as fingers wiggled between her legs, then thrust back in.

The moan, pure delight, wound the rapture higher. She bent her knees and rode down on the fingers frigging her. Good Lord, she wanted Kenny's prick sliding in and out of her womb or her bum.

"Kenny, I . . . I need you in me."

"Patience, sweet. There is much more delight to come."

Fingers that couldn't be Kenny's circled her breasts. Nipples tingling, she gasped. Oh, the sensation was exquisite.

She owned engravings where multiple partners touched and caressed each other and always wondered what different touches would be like. Now she knew why people enjoyed such acts.

"Yes, that's it, sweet. I want to hear more gasps. I want to hear you scream. Like you did at the river."

Did he want her to scream in rapture?

"Truly?"

"Oh yes. It is the most maddening sound."

Heavy breaths and the sounds of wetness scattered about them. She inhaled and could smell sex and cunny. Her body trembled. Others were mating about her.

"Listen to the sounds around you." Kenny's breath heated the curls on her mound. "What do you hear, Hannah?"

"Umm, mating." Fingers pinched her nipples, fingers caressed her stomach, fingers smoothed down the swell of her bum. Her breath puffed in and out as her body shook with arousal.

"Just futter? No more?"

What did he mean? She tried to calm her beating heart and listen. "I hear wetness."

"Yes."

"I hear motions." She inhaled, trying to pull her mind from the sensations assaulting her body and comprehend. "I smell cream."

"Yes, they are all in the air. But there is more. Feel it, Hannah."

Her body trembled as the murmurs of love endearments from both females and males came from all about her. They whispered to each other, so softly that if you didn't really listen, you would only hear them as moans. They did not just mate. They loved.

Her breath caught. Her body trembled. Did he mean he loved her? Was that what he wanted her to hear?

"Kenny?" The fingers stopped their caress.

"Yes, love." His breath caressed her ear, his heat radiating down her entire back. "What do you hear?"

"I . . . I hear lovemaking." Her lip trembled in the dark.

"Yes." His tongue traced her cheekbone. "My goddess, I—"

"What are you saying, Kenny?"

"I love you. I always have." His lips pressed to hers. And her knees wobbled. "Let me worship you with my body."

"Kenny." Tears ran down her face.

"Hannah." Strong naked muscles wrapped about her. "I want you to see how I love you."

A candelabra lit, flickering in the room. In front of her stood a mirror, no more than an arm's reach away. In the reflection Kenny stood behind her, hands wrapped possessively about her stomach. Two forms brought a large stool out of the darkness and placed the bench behind Kenny. He sat, pulling her with him. Lodging his legs between hers, he spread her wide.

She could see her sex in the mirror, the deep crimson lips engorged and shimmering, her nubbin poking out, pebble hard. She bit her lip.

"Yes, you are beautiful. Every part of you."

Kenny's hand splayed across her stomach and pulled her back tight against his prick. He rubbed his phallus on her bum, his coarse hairs tickling her aroused skin. Male heat and the smell of spice enfolded her body. Trembling with intense lust, she groaned.

"Sweet, sweet Hannah, I'm going to slip my cock in here." His hand slid to the apex of her thighs and dipped into her slick flesh. Finding her opening, he curved a finger into her.

"Kenny." Her hands grasped hard thighs, and her head fell back as she slid her tongue along the rough skin beneath his chin. The masculine texture sent shivers cascading down her spine.

His finger probed in and out. "Watch the mirror, love. Watch how I love you." His hand rubbed the sensitive nub, and her hips arched into his hands.

Forcing herself, she turned her head back to the mirror. Kenny's fingers slipped into her glistening sex and spread her. Good Lord. She could see his motions. Could feel his touches. Hannah's eyes gaped. Never had she seen the female sex, so open, so exposed. Watching her folds part as fingers slid in and out was the most erotic thing. She trembled.

"That's it, love, see how I'm loving you."

She whimpered, but she wanted more. Needed more.

Abruptly, his fingers slipped from her wanton flesh, leaving her open and empty. She squirmed and rubbed her bum against his erect shaft. Her body needed him, needed his phallus to stretch her slick flesh as he sunk all the way in, warming her from her core to her toes.

Demanding more, she whimpered as his hand continued to rise to his lips. Slowly his tongue slid around each thick finger in a caress she wanted on her body, and sucked her cream from them.

"Umm, so wonderful, love."

She needed his mouth. Arching against him, she kissed his chin, sucking the rough stubble and spicy scent. Her hand reached between her legs, following the scalding heat of her sex to his sack. She massaged the marbles, and he rewarded her with a groan vibrating through his chest. Her pulse soared and she grinned. Yes. She could please him.

His hand slid down her arm and gently removed her grasp from him, then trailed back up the slick core of her and pushed their fingers deep. Juices flooded out of her, coating their fingers, as he thrust them in and out. She had never been so wet or touched herself so deep.

Pulling her fingers from her cunny, he raised them to his mouth. His tongue swirled each finger, lapping every ounce of cream from them. Oh, that tongue. What she would give to have him licking deep in her womb where she just touched. Her body shook with need.

He shifted his hips and his prick popped in front of her. Gazing down at the plum-shaped head and large shaft, her mouth watered.

"I . . . I want to suck you, Kenny."

"Not yet, sweet. It is my turn." Grasping his sex, he shifted and lifted her, pressing his prick into her slick folds. She breathed in through clenched teeth. "Watch, love."

The head of his prick parted her folds. Barely entering her body, her flesh stretched. The walls of her cunny burned as his large swollen head disappeared into her glistening sex, spreading her wide.

She panted, her heart hammering in her chest as her muscles eased to his penetration. His fingers spread her folds along the edges, tracing the engorged flesh for a better view.

So good . . . so good . . . His hot flesh probed her and her insides quivered. This was what lovemaking was supposed to be. Not the hasty hard mating her husband had done, but slow sensuous caresses. Loving with one's complete being, not just their body parts.

Watching each movement in the mirror, she groaned.

He nudged up. She sank down.

Their breath caught, as bit by bit his hard shaft parted her soft flesh, disappearing into her wetness. A gush of fluid coated the walls of her womb, and her cunny muscles clamped tight about him. Hannah groaned again and again, unable to stop herself, her eyes fixed on their joining.

Warm caresses slid up her elbow to cup her breast from behind. Sliding her nipple between two fingers, Kenny pinched the peak, then rolled. A sharp delicious pain swept her, and her breath rushed in through clenched teeth. "Oh my!"

Moist heat fanned her neck and ear. "Beautiful. Perfect in every way." His tongue tickled her.

"Ahhaa." Her knees shook as his legs spread her wider. Gooseflesh pricking her skin, her cunny muscles tightened. Eyes half closed, she watched as the couple in the mirror continued to grope and plunder each other. The same sensations happening to her. She was the woman loved. He was the one providing the caress, the emotion.

The red head of his phallus disappeared into her body, then reappeared shimmering with her cream. With each slip of his prick, they groaned and sighed, muscles straining. Their slow love played like a fine piece of music; it soothed, heightened, and tightened the need coursing through them.

He made love to her. She trembled and tears pricked at her eyes. Emotions and passion washed through her so intense she wanted to sob and scream in ecstasy at the same time.

The strong muscular thighs that bunched and clenched beneath her belonged to a man who declared his love for her. His phallus pulled to the tip of her folds, then thrust back in, and she saw his sack tighten.

"Good God, Hannah."

Her gaze jumped to his face and her breath caught. He stared at her with such vulnerability, such caring and love. Her cunny muscles spasmed, clamping hard about his shaft. "Oh . . . oh . . . oh my!" she screamed. Her whole body convulsed, milking his seed, as gush after gush of hot fluid filled her womb and spasm after spasm racked her.

"Good God, love. Kiss me," he panted. "I need to taste you."

Hard and firm, his lips met hers. His tongue thrust in her mouth and twined sensuously with hers. Tears spilled down her face. A smile curving her lips, Hannah sighed.

Kenneth woke the next day to hot oiled velvet sliding down the length of his cock. He groaned. Sweat beaded his body and his teeth clenched hard. He neared discharge. How long had Hannah been riding him in his sleep? Her tongue traced her lips. Arms trembling, she slid her entire body along his, caressing every nerve. Damn, those full round breasts rubbed his chest.

Her thighs clamped tight about his sack, an exquisite pressure. God, she was beautiful, her skin rosy with passion. Passion she spent on him. His hands gripped her fleshy hips and guided the rhythm.

Tremors rippled his stomach. "Good God, Hannah!" His cock quivered deep inside her silk.

He was about to spill. He couldn't hold back.

"Yes. Indeed." A smile touched her lips as she pressed hips to hips, increasing the friction.

Hot velvet slid rapidly over his staff, milking his very

essence. With each caress, his prick never leaving her hot hold. His hips thrust up hard, body shuddering as his sack contracted. "Ooh . . . damn . . . " Burst after burst, his seed spilled into her womb.

"Kenny!" She rubbed frantically along him as the walls of her womb clamped tight about his spent prick in wave after wave. Her arms collapsed. Her head plunked on his chest. They panted as one.

Her lips curved against his skin.

"Sweet." He ran his hand through her dark hair. "There is no better way to wake up."

"I know. You called out my name several times this morning and were stiff, so I . . ." She raised her eyebrows, staring down at him.

"Scandalous."

"I guess I did take advantage. I couldn't resist."

He sat up and pulled her with him.

"It is all like a dream." Shaking his head, he pushed her thick black hair over her shoulder to nibble her neck. He kept thinking she would disappear just as he put his arms around her.

"This is real." She placed her hand on his chest. "I love you, Kenny. I have since the summer we spent together."

He flipped her, wedging himself between her legs.

"Do you? Hannah . . . I am not who you think. You deserve so much more than a man whose mother does not know who fathered him."

Her blue eyes, filled with compassion and heat, stared at him. "Kenny, I have no doubt who your father is. You are the mirror image of the lord Duke of Deventon. Either way, it does not matter. Not to me. I love you."

He smiled. "Love." Such a strange all-encompassing passion. She had held his heart since boyhood, and now that he had hers, he would never let it go.

Shifting his hands, he cupped her bottom and lifted her to

gaze at her beautiful full nether lips, swollen from fucking. There was nothing more beautiful. He wanted to massage them with his tongue. His cock stiffened; he would never get enough of her.

He leaned in to worship his love as she deserved.

Checkmate

1
_____

R*AP... RAP...*
RAP...

The hard wood stung through Cora's gloved hand as the door to the large servant's entrance jerked open, revealing Lord Nottingland's cook, Jan. The woman's churlish eyes narrowed upon seeing her and scrutinized Cora's cloaked body.

"Yes, dear Jan, I still look as handsome as ever." She pushed past Jan and into the kitchen. *What a jest.*

Cora slid her hood back from her face; Jan still frowned at her. She no doubt noticed her jest in the wrinkles at the corner of her eyes that increased in length and width at each visit. No amount of cream could conceal them or the beginnings of gray that tinged her hair.

Jan's master would soon tire of her fading looks, as would all her protectors, and loneliness would be her fate.

The frown that graced Jan's face showed no compassion.

Disgust radiated from the plump woman's body as fevered

as any lover's passion. Jan despised her and the men she still attracted.

"I believe your randy master is expecting me." Cora raised her eyebrows. Jan's eyes widened in shock, and a grin tugged Cora's lips. She couldn't resist flustering her.

Allen's valet entered to escort her to his chambers. Smiling once more at Jan, she winked, clutched her satchel to her body, and followed him to his master's suites.

She entered the dim, royal-blue bedroom to find Allen stretched out on his ornately carved dressing couch. His robe lay open, displaying naked hairy legs, a typical scotch in hand. To think his title made him a catch on the marriage mart. If the ton could only see him now. She stifled a chuckle.

"My dearest." He inclined his head. "I beg your pardon, but I am not up for our appointment this night." Dark black bags hung beneath his eyes, his complexion sullen as he gulped a mouthful of the amber liquid.

She sauntered to him without saying a word, straightened her shoulders, and dropped her valise to the Oriental carpet. "Ah, but, Allen, I am the one who decides what we do."

Inside, a smile lifted her heart at the thought of lounging by his side. It would be nice for a change to break from crops and whips, the tools Allen so craved.

"Indeed, that is true, but I am the one who pays for your service. I have no vigor after last night's debauchery. You would squander your fortitude this night, and you deserve the pleasure of making me squirm."

If only he knew she didn't enjoy it. Well that was not entirely true. She did, just not the way he thought.

Her protectors were, well, not men she naturally found attractive. She chose them with the strictest of care, ensuring not one of them could overpower her.

"Very well, Allen. Tell me of your fun and share your scotch."

She forced her lip to protrude out into the pout he liked, and inwardly sighed. This aspect of Allen she enjoyed; he truly knew how to relax after an intense night.

He slid his legs to the side and she sat, grasping the glass from his hands.

" 'Twas the most amazing night, my dear. To say I saw and did things I only dreamed of would not boast enough. The Hell Knights—"

The Hell Knights. She closed her eyes. Yet another of her clients that couldn't keep up with the infamous club's antics.

The Knights were everything she avoided in her career. Powerful, handsome, and ruthless in the carnal desires. The kind of men who made her blood heat simply by standing in the same room with them. A tremor raced through her muscles as she imagined a large powerful man licking his way across her dewed skin. Oh how delightful.

Several members approached her over the years, but she always turned them down. The risk of letting her emotions, her desires, get in the way of her profession was too great.

She'd made the leap once—her heart constricted at the memory—to catastrophic consequences and still had the scars to show for it. Her fingers slid over her stomach and the prominent line of flesh beneath the cloth. Though—she scrutinized Allen's slight form and crooked smile as he spouted on and on about his follies—it would be nice to do the act of shame with a man she fancied. She bit her lip. Perhaps one night she should indulge herself. Pins pricked up her neck. For just one night.

The carriage swayed and rocked as her stomach rolled. Bile rose in her throat, and her hand shot to her mouth. She wished the carriage caused her stomach's unease. She swallowed hard.

She swore she would never do this.

Her hands trembled, nerves raw. As she closed her eyes, the carriage rolled to a stop.

It was one night. One night she hoped would change her life forever.

Heart in her throat, she grasped the bottle of bourbon that sat on the brown velvet seat next to her. Raising the decanter to her lips, she gulped one last long swallow. Yes. The liquid smooth and strong scorched her throat and burned through her limbs.

Much, much better.

Her hand shook as she placed the decanter back on the seat.

This night was the thirty-sixth anniversary of her birth. Tonight she would indulge her desires and experience all she wished before her beauty faded and the world shunned her.

The door to the carriage opened. The misty weather beyond the coach didn't invite her out into the night. She bit her lip, her skin turning clammy. She needed to do this.

Her footman held out his hand, and she alighted on wobbly legs. The plain brick terrace house and warm candle glow cast from the windows did not intimidate her, but the members within the walls quaked her to the quick.

It was late evening and the street stood quiet. How foolish she acted. Once she had decided to attend, she washed and dressed in half the time she normally required but couldn't sit still and wait for the minute to arrive.

The past hour she rode the local rain-soaked streets waiting for the required time like a girl anticipating her first ball. No doubt she was the first to arrive.

Her lips quirked. The infamous, hard-hearted, Cora Durand eager to engage in a sexual matter? No one would recognize her by this attitude.

The man at the entrance stood a head taller than her. Shoulders held broad, he dressed impeccably in all black. A beaver hat sat atop his head, which upon closer inspection, was bald.

Eyes, a deep gray, fixed on hers, never wavering as she ascended the steps.

Indeed, he was fine. Powerful. A lord in the animal kingdom. Chills pricked her skin, her gaze trapped in his. *Lower your eyes, you goose, before you trip up the steps.* Her knees shook as she lowered her gaze to his tight-fitting black trousers.

If no one inside possessed the ability to quake her, this man would do; although the members who had approached her earlier in her career all possessed the ability. No doubt they still would. Tonight she would let down her guard and feel all these potent men could offer.

"Good evening, ma'am," his cavernous voice boomed. "Tigers in the jungle . . ."

"Eat their prey." Her voice shook as she said the password to enter; then she forced a smile.

He opened the dark green door, and she stepped past him into a large entrance chamber. Warm spiced scents filled the air, putting her at ease. A grand candelabra hung overhead, and the walls cut of coarse sandstone radiated warmth and richness.

This was a club of money.

Three naked men approached her, each one a different shade of tawny. Their chests broad and sculpted, free of any hair, led to rolls of muscle and proud stiff staffs.

Her eyes gaped. Amazing. Not one ballock between them, yet their staffs still stiffened. Never in all her career has she seen such a sight, and there were *three* of them. Where did they come from? And who cut off their sacks?

She reached for the ribbons that held her cloak closed. Just amazing. She shook her head.

Their hands raised and brushed hers aside. Her muscles tensed. *Oh no, you don't.*

She would undress herself. Her hands rose to slap theirs away, but she quelled the urge. No, tonight was different. She was different. She stilled her hands in midair. Tonight she would let her true self come through, allowing others to tell her what to do, to touch her without permission.

No control. Her muscles relaxed and she sighed. For once, someone else would make the decisions. Not knowing what would happen to her felt edgy, exciting. Emotions she had not experienced in years.

Her hands dropped to her sides as her cloak lifted from her body. One of the men worked the tiny row of buttons to her dress while another hiked up her skirts and undid the garters about her knees, sliding her stockings and shoes from her.

Within a matter of moments, she shivered naked in front of the three. Her nipples pebbled hard in the air of the entry.

Without saying a word, they stepped toward her. Fingers wrapped about her arm and more fingers pressed to her back as they spun her about and pressed her hard up against the sandstone wall. Her heart leapt. Her face turned to the side, breasts pressed firm to the cool rough texture.

What were they doing? Her skin tingled with excitement.

The masculine fingers worked her flesh. Her arms rose, and a wide leather strap slid about her wrists. They tied the tether firm, holding her hands spread high and wide.

Warm hands wrapped about her legs and slid them apart as a piece of leather slid over her eyes and part of her nose.

She jumped as they cinched the strap tight. A sliver of light came from the crease of her cheek, and the hairs on her neck stood.

Nothing of any significance would she see. Strapped to a wall, she would do nothing but feel.

Pulling on her arms, her muscles shook as she tested the strength of the straps. They held firm. There was no going back. Her chest rose and fell, and her lungs constricted as she labored for breath. She couldn't do this. She swallowed convulsively, her heart beating in her throat.

Would it be different this time? She was older, wiser, she'd been on the other side. Her emotions were not engaged with any of these men. She just didn't know if she could trust a man who could force her to do as he pleased. Icy sweat slid down her spine.

Relax, good God. No one can harm you the way he did.

Her hair fell loose down her back, tickling the sensitized skin. Fingers laced through and lightly tugged her tresses.

Yes. She closed her eyes. She could do this. She needed this; anyone could touch any part of her, and she could not object. Her throat tightened.

Only her voice could protest.

No matter what happened, she would not talk back. Well, she would try not to. This night, strapped to this wall, she would overcome her past. Tremors shook her body.

She would give control to take back the type of man she desired.

The three men receded from her, and she leaned against the rough stone wall, head spinning lightly. Every move of her body rubbed the flesh of her tingling nipples into the sandy stone wall.

The door to the street opened. A blast of frigid winter air sent shivers along her skin as the temperature changed from steamy to cold and back to hot again.

"Good evening," the man at the door boomed.

"Well, well. You have snagged a prim pretty for your entrance decoration this night." Was he referring to her? He obviously could not see her age. She held still, listening to the rustle of cloth.

Warm hands spread over the small of her back to her hips. Her muscles tensed and jumped, pulling her body away from the startling caress.

Blast. What was she about?

"Tsk, tsk. There, pretty. Don't you know not to move?" His hands left her body.

The blow was coming; she tensed, waiting for the crack of flesh on flesh. To feel the sting of his hard hand against her tender skin, to know if she didn't move, he would touch her kindly. Nothing happened. Her breath came out in a whoosh of disappointment. Maybe she was wrong about—

WHACK!

A large male hand hit her backside hard, sending pins and heat through her. Clenching her teeth, she forced herself not to make a sound.

Warm air caressed her ear. "There, pretty, let's try again."

His touch rubbed the burning brand his hand left, and wet warmth traced the heated flesh, soothing the redness. Lips kissed the mark as another gush of crisp air washed over her.

"Good evening, my lord," came the greeter's voice.

Another man. Her heart sped to a gallop as she imagined the feel of two pairs of male hands caressing her skin. She tried not to respond in any way to indicate her desire, but a small moan crept past her lips.

More cloth rustled and then male murmurs. The man who kissed her flesh with lust trailed his hands up and around to her sides. As he gently caressed her breasts, tingles circled her flesh and peaked her nipples hard against the stone.

"Till later, pretty." Warm lips pressed the side of her cheek, then disappeared.

Where was the other man? No one approached her and the room stood silent. She pulled on her arms and tried to shift, but the straps prevented her the slightest turn. But she could move her feet and her legs.

Frigid air again caressed her.

"Good evening."

The door closed and the warmth seeped back in.

"Do you think Lord Brummelton will be attending this night?" a woman's small voice asked with excitement.

"I'm not sure, but we know his brother Rupert will be. He

always attends and they do like to share so . . ." The woman's deep sultry voice faded.

Blast . . . damn . . . Her eyes squeezed shut. That voice. Maybe she wouldn't notice. Every muscle in her body tensed.

"Look what we have here, Janice. And the first one to show, no less." Rustling cloth indicated clothing stripping away.

"Holy crow. It couldn't be, could it, Mary?"

"Ah, Janice, I do believe it is. My question is, what would cause Lady Strike to lower herself to such a wanton display?"

Cora went rigid. Just her luck her former teacher would attend. Biting her lip, she held back her typical stinging retort.

Small dainty hands ran up the inside of her thighs.

Damn. Straining, her muscles jumped and heated. She would have to touch her, wouldn't she?

Light touches smoothed the swell of her bottom, sending gooseflesh in its wake. The small feathery fondle slid to the red mark on her bum, then traced. Cool fingers pressed the heated tissue, arousing and taunting her to respond.

"It seems someone has already tried to put her in her place."

Trembling, Cora's arms shook against the restraints as Mary's fingers pinched the red welt and held the skin.

"Well, Cora, how does it feel? Are you aroused by this change of role?" Her teacher's breath tickled the hair at her ear.

"Ah, holding your tongue, are you? Very well, I can find out on my own."

Mary's delicate hand traveled to Cora's spine and into the crack of her bottom. Her sagging breasts pressed against Cora's back as her nimble fingers slid into the all too telling slick folds.

"Umm." Mary licked Cora's shoulder and wiggled her fingers.

"Well, how is she?" Janice's voice grew nearer.

"Wet as the rain, dear Janice, wet as the rain."

Mary's fingers slid into Cora's pussy, and she tightened the walls around them.

"Good girl," Mary soothed as her other hand wrapped around Cora's hips. With a jerk, she pulled Cora's lower half from the wall, pressing into her for better exploration.

Years had passed since a woman had caressed her body, the gentleness foreign, yet exciting. Dew sprang across her skin, heart pounding, her hips pushed back into Mary's probing hand.

"Yes, she does like it, does she not?" Janice's voice squealed by her ear.

Her hands, smaller than Mary's, slid to her breast; fingers slipping between the wall, one on top of her nipple and the other below, Janice pinched. Mary's expert fingers slid from her flesh and circled her button with moisture. Sensation seeped like a slow breeze through her muscles. She had missed this.

Mary slid back into her sheath and Cora's hips jerked. Muscles tight and trembling, she tried to hold back a scream of delight.

"Well, well, dear. It is good to see you have put the past behind you," Mary whispered in her ear. "Lord Dranger was a rascal not worthy of your fast."

No! Cora's eyes squeezed shut, her whole body tensing at the mention of Matthew. The scar on her belly prickled beneath Mary's arm and she wiggled. The wound always did that when she thought of him.

She hoped to get through this night without the reminder, or worse, actually seeing him. Though, that was a bit of a dream now that Mary was here. Mary would not let her hide from or forget her past.

Mary's fingers slid from her wanton flesh and back up the crack of her bum, spreading her cream about her skin. With a quick harsh pinch to her nipple, Janice turned away. Mary's hand caressed her bottom, then with a deep throaty chuckle, left her. "Good to see you again, dear. About bloody time."

* * *

Rupert's body hummed as he watched the new lovely writhe beneath the ministrations of the two women. Her hair, a mass of tumbled dark corn, crashed in a storm of waves on her shoulders as she tried to contain her scream.

He craved these moments when no one knew he watched. When people did what their bodies and instincts wanted, to hell with the consequences. If she would only give in and scream. He was sure it would be the desperate sound to send his vigor soaring.

His face pressed harder to the two slits in the wall. He inhaled, trying to smell her arousal, but nothing reached his nose.

The older woman, Mary, rubbed her hand over the spherical surface of the blonde's arse, then laughed and left the entry.

The woman, who stood strapped to the wall for all to touch and see, sagged against the leather restraints. Her back expanded as she inhaled a deep shuddering breath. Did she weep? No. His eyes narrowed. She tried to contain some emotion. But what? Desire. Fear. Or sadness. Maybe a mixture of all three.

The door opened again, and a woman and man stepped into the entrance. As the woman slid back her hood, Rupert cringed. Emma.

The damn woman tried to cuckold him with an attachment to Kit. How could she choose a scrawny man when she admitted Rupert was the better lover time and time again. Sure Kit's hands knew how to rouse pleasure and pain, but . . .

He is accessible. His heart is not tainted. Emma's heated words filled his mind as he remembered shoving her out of bed for once again favoring Kit.

Blister it. He had a heart, even if he hid it away beneath his fiery skin, kept only for himself to see.

Jealousy wasn't an emotion he possessed.

How could one be the jealous sort when his deepest pleasure came from watching others, friends he cared about, pleasuring each other?

Emma had wanted proof he cared. He shrugged. He couldn't give it, not the way she craved. Their connection he had severed over best of a year now.

No pain came from seeing her. He still watched her, watched her pleasure Kit as he always had. The only change was he no longer had the right to sink into her wet warmth once aroused. It didn't bother him. Someone else was always willing to oblige.

Emma approached the woman stretched on the wall, her fair curly hair shining in the candlelight.

Holy hell. He blinked and blinked again. How did he misjudge that hair?

Hair washed in a bath of raspberries that stained her very core. He had thought the strands as blond as Emma's but, no, her locks held a touch of fire.

Only one woman had hair her color. He groaned as his body tensed and his groin grew heavy.

The woman tormented him in years past by turning down every advance he made. Cora Durand. Why was she here? Had she changed her mind?

No, she would still find him repulsive. All of her protectors were the opposite of him, of everyone he knew. But then . . . *Good God, woman, what have you come here to find?*

2

The straps about Cora's hands loosened, and strong warm touches squeezed and rubbed the muscles of her shoulders as her arms lowered. Prickles of blood flooded her veins. A delicious arousal seeped through her sore muscles as the large, long male fingers continued to massage and comfort her kindly.

She rolled her shoulders and staggered back from the wall, slamming into a broad, heated chest. Strong arms wrapped about her waist and steadied her. The smell of leather and sweet smoky honey radiated from him, calming and arousing her like nothing she had ever experienced.

"Come with me." His voice, deep with a slight growl, skittered across her skin, bringing the image of a large ape to mind.

His fingers lightly gripped the sensitive skin just above her hip, twinging her. Would her fading looks hold any sway with this man? Her body hummed at his touch. She wanted him to want her. How strange to desire something, someone, she couldn't see.

"Where are you taking me?" She stepped forward to see if he would guide her. His feet stayed rooted to the stone floor.

"What the hell are you doing here?" he breathed in a deep raspy choke.

"What?" *Do I know him?* Her muscles tensed. It was possible. She had deliberately erased every introduction to a powerful man from her mind. "Why I'm here is obvious. I want to experience all this house has to offer." His fingers drew small circles around her hip bone. She did arouse him. His raspy choke played in her mind.

"Not so obvious, considering your clientele."

His fingers stopped and gripped her hip as he dragged his tongue over her right shoulder.

Delicious. Her body trembled, nipples hardening further to painful peaks.

"You have me at an advantage, sir." Thank goodness her voice held firm and hard; only her body betrayed his effect on her. His size, his smell, quaked her to the soul. She needed to know who the man was who pulled at her. "Tell me your name, sir, or remove my veil."

A deep resonating chuckle burst from his chest. His breath, warm and moist, caressed her neck. The walls of her pussy swelled with moisture, longing for him to touch her delicate flesh.

"Someone you do not wish to know. Now, tell me what you desire here."

Damn and blast. Who did this man think he was? She reached for the ties of her hood. She had every right to know who handled her with such expertise, whose touch stirred her like nonesuch in her life.

"Not so quick, woman." His hands possessed her wrists before she could reach the hood, and she squirmed. How dare he. Her heart pounded, and her teeth clenched tight.

Well, if she couldn't find his identity that way . . . She arched her spine and rocked her bottom into his hips. Her hands, held firm in his grasp, lowered and brushed his thighs. He wore clothing. The smooth fabric of his trousers brushed her bottom and her fingertips.

His breath grew ragged, and he released her hands. Wrapping an arm about her belly and snagging a fistful of her hair, he yanked her head back to place hot wet kisses along her jaw and neck, fluttering his tongue over her pulse in the column of flesh.

By God, he was good. A tremor wracked her body, and her knees weakened. The fact she could barely stand spoke of years of wanting just this, of denying herself the pleasure of a physically powerful man.

"Don't toy with me, woman. Don't play games. I'm not your kind." Sultry breath rasped across her ear. His tongue circled into her ear's crevice, and her legs parted involuntarily.

Oh, how he was wrong. He was exactly the type of man she craved.

A restrained tremble ran through the muscles of his arm about her belly. He was not immune to her. She was certain.

His tongue swirled just below her earlobe, and shivers slid from that spot to her pussy, wetness slicking the folds. The aroma of her arousal was so strong in the room she could fairly taste the heady scent.

"How can I know if you are my kind if you won't acquaint us?" She wanted to introduce his prick to her dripping flesh, to writhe against him as he fucked her none too lightly.

His breathing deepened and he growled, pulling harder on her hair and nipping the flesh of her neck. The hand about her stomach trailed fire to the curls at the apex of her thighs. She stilled, heart pounding, as a long finger slid into her and tapped her wet flesh.

"Oh." Her hips arched into his hand. With each tap, her pussy reached for the contact, spending more and more fluid on his fingers.

His strong muscled arm anchored her to his body. He pulled

her head back, arching her to him like a bow. His steamy mouth and tongue kissed and sucked the flesh of her neck.

She was helpless to this man's strength and will. Yet, he did not frighten her. If he would only tell her his name. Her body shuddered, wanting any part of him to bring her release.

"Hmmm. Your body responds to my touch." His finger tapped into her flooded flesh with different degrees of force. Each stroke was audible, and the air dripped with the scent of her.

"Quite," she rasped. She wanted to beg him to enter her, to fill her wanton body with his and diddle her until their bodies spent in exhaustion. But she couldn't, not until she knew his name.

"What do you want here, Cora?" The tip of his finger slid into the opening of her pussy.

She bit her lip, whimpering as if she'd never been touched.

His teeth scraped her neck. "Answer me."

"I . . . I . . ." His fingers left her pussy. "No." Oh, he possessed her. She tried to pull her mind from the sexual web he had created. To stand on her own.

"What do you want here, Cora?"

"I . . . I want to experience what this house has to offer," she blurted.

"Which is? There are many things here, dear. Do you know what you have ventured into?"

No, she didn't, not entirely. She only knew what Matthew and Mary had hinted at before she left them and what her clients confessed when they squirmed.

The members of this hell used her protectors as playthings. When one of the men wanted a taste of a male, one of her clients would be invited. She knew that. But she never got out of them what exactly went on with them or what this place was.

"As I thought. Shall I enlighten you?" His tongue slid once again into the cup of her ear. "Any form of stimulation you might crave exists here. Any form." His hand returned to between her thighs and tapped her already-sodden flesh. An unrestrained moan burst from her lips.

His breath caught and he shifted his stance. He was just as affected by her. The idea that a woman as old as she could create this intense passion in this powerful man overwhelmed her. Her body shook. They were a burning flame flickering. All he needed to do was take her and their fire would engulf them both.

"What you do—your flogging and making men squirm—only begins to touch what happens in this house."

She no longer cared what happened in this hell. She wanted to know what he fancied. Why he was a member.

"And what excites you, sir?" she asked in puffed breaths, trembling, unable to control her body and the emotions this man created in her.

He didn't answer, and all his movement stopped.

"Sir?"

"I watch," he whispered, deep and sultry, as he wiggled his fingers between her legs.

"Watch?" The words barely passed her lips when his muscles shook with restrained force. "Y-you mean you don't participate in any extreme wickedness?"

"I do," he said gruffly.

Ah, he liked to watch others in wicked acts until he was aroused. Then he would take his pleasure.

"Do you watch all forms of wickedness?"

"No."

"What, then?"

The thickness of his erection grew larger beneath the fabric of his trousers.

"Nothing you need to know." His body hardened and doused his flame. "Are you sure you wish to enter the remainder of this house?"

"Nothing can sway me."

His arm loosened in her hair and about her stomach.

"No, don't!" *Don't leave me.* The need to feel this incredible connection for a bit longer shocked her.

"Don't what, Cora? You don't give orders here. If you came to try to order one of us about, you had best leave before someone takes you for jest and forces you."

"No, that is not why I am here. Tell me, sir, what do you watch?"

"Women. Men. Doing whatever brings them pleasure."

Oh. Wetness flooded her sex, and her muscles tightened at the idea of this man, whoever he was, watching her as someone brought her pleasure.

He strode forward, caging her against the wall, pressing her breath from her body. "Ouch." Her hands braced the stone to push away. "How dare—"

Fevered hardness smothered her. Pinning her to the wall, the scalding thrust of his prick slid between her thighs and parted her aching flesh.

Oh yes. He wanted to join with her.

She pushed her bottom against his hips and delighted in the contrast of his brand probing her legs and the roughness of his trousers.

His knees bent and clasped the outside of her legs, winching them about his stiff staff. His erection, round, thick, and oh so delicious, pulsed between.

He groaned and she tightened her thighs about the burly prick. Exquisite friction raced along her slit, and her inner muscles clenched tighter. Yes, yes.

His heat scalded her back from the tip of her head to her toes, pressing her against the chilly wall in tactile opposition. He possessed her every pore.

Her hands slid to his hips and bum, and held him as they

rocked together. Their breath deepened in unison. Her insides began to quiver. Rubbing her legs together on his length, more cream slid down her thighs and coated his phallus. A powerful bliss built with each grind of the hot head of his penis against her slick clit.

"This is mild, Cora." He pulled her hair again, arching her farther against him as he groaned. His tongue traced her cheekbone, his hips rocking faster and faster.

"You desire me."

"Yes. What have you come here for?" His metallic words hissed out through clenched teeth.

"To experience this and more with a man like you." Her body trembled imagining this man, this aristocrat in the jungle, mounting her as another man suckled her breasts and pressed fingers into her bum.

His lips kissed her shoulder, and he grunted. Warm wetness traced down the curve of flesh as his hands clenched her hips, increasing the stroke of his prick trapped between her legs.

She wanted to separate her thighs to ride down on him. For him to impale her against this wall, just as he rode her trembling legs now. He gasped for breath, shuddering behind her as his muscles tensed, slowing his strokes. He would spend soon and she needed to know.

"Who are you? Let me see your face. I wish you to fill me—"

"Good God, woman. No!" His staff pulsed as he slid forward. His entire body shuddering about her as burst after burst of boiling seed sprayed her swollen clit.

"Oh! Oh!" Her pussy convulsed on top of his shaft. Fingers digging in to the cloth of his pants, she held him to her and screamed.

Her body trembled in rolling waves as the intense bliss grasped her. His seed dripped from the lips of her sex, thighs, and the wall as she collapsed panting against him.

"Damn it." His body shuddered as he pushed from her. Warm lips lingered on her shoulder and then everything vanished.

She spun around, panting for breath. Reaching out for him, she shivered at the loss of his heat and body contact.

"No! Wait! Don't leave." Her hands flailed through the air. She tore frantically at the strap covering her eyes. The leather slid loose, and she spun around in the entry. She stood alone.

3

Rupert cringed as he entered the game room from the hall. Damn woman. He never lost control; he always asked before he touched, before he took.

He owned few principles, and he had plowed straight through them at the sight of her. He shouldn't have touched, let alone frigged her, knowing she disliked him so.

The desire to rut with her pressed against the wall overtook him, and he barely managed to stop himself from shoving his cock into her scalding cunt. That would have been disastrous, even if she begged for such.

Devil help him, he did have some pride, and joining with a woman who found him repulsive went against all of it.

Her skin, so soft. And the smell of her arousal . . . He closed his eyes. Blister it, why was she not attracted to him? How could a woman of intense sensuality only desire the dandies who protected her?

He wanted to fuck her. Even more he wanted to watch her. Watch her being brought to discharge by, well, by someone. He groaned as his cock stood stiff from his body.

Damn it all to hell. Why did she have to come here tonight? He didn't like feeling as if he had commited a lewd act, an act against someone's desires. But . . .

They both found release, and he now had the memory of her sweet slender thighs squeezing him to an uncontrolled spend.

To sink into her would have meant the end of any control where she was concerned. He could feel it . . . uncontrolled desire, the want to posses her, to make her beg him to fuck her hard, while knowing fully who and what he was.

To watch her pleasure and be pleasured by another, only to be the one to bring her the ultimate release. He closed his eyes and dragged a hand through his hair. She was here for a man like him. Did she mean it?

He had tried a dozen times over the years to get Cora to consider him. Each time she turned him down without a second glance. If only . . . No, he wouldn't think of that.

Striding to the wall just inside the room, he turned and waited for her to emerge. The faro and whist tables held no sway for him this night; his entire body was focused on the woman who would walk through that door.

Her beautiful naked body appeared, turning the heads of most men in the room. If she came to him or considered him with her stare, he would pursue her. But he would not, could not, approach if she once again lifted that pretty head of fiery hair and stared down her nose at him.

Cora. The epitome of woman: long legs and sensuous curves. Yet in her naked form, the light showed a large scar across the smooth swell of her belly. A frown creased his brow. Did she enjoy pain? She enjoyed giving punishment, but . . .

She regarded the room, looking for him most likely. Though, she wouldn't know him when she saw him. She turned toward him and inspected his length as he leaned against the wall.

Ah, those breasts, small swells of flesh with peach-tipped nipples covering a good third of them. His mouth went dry.

Her gaze locked with his. His did not waver. The corner of his lips turned up. *Yes, Cora. Watch me.*

She stared down his naked chest, then lower to his black trousers and bare feet. *The same as your unidentified lover.*

He shifted as his cock swelled his flap. Her pink tongue darted out and licked the corner of her lip as her gaze locked with his again.

Shit, she was a siren calling him home. Maybe she'd grown bored with her scrawny fops. Well, he sure as hell would find out.

Another naked woman, much older than Cora, padded up to her side. Cora turned away from him. Ahh. But not once had she stared down her nose at him in disgust. He would have her yet this night.

"Well, Cora." Mary slid an arm though hers. "What do you think?"

Cora couldn't believe it. Few of the guests in the card room wore nothing. A few women, a handful of men. Some had shirts off, but most of the gentlemen dressed as if at any other club in London. She frowned.

"A bit disappointing, Mary." Surely, the Hell Knights was more than the typical club.

A wicked smile curved Mary's lips. "You were just a living hors d'oeuvre, and this is only one room of many in this house."

Violin strings strained in the small card room.

"Ah, the vices shall begin." Mary winked.

The man Cora watched bowed his head to her with indifference and turned toward an open door. A delicious flicker of emotion and sensation lifted the hair on her neck. Her eyes widened. What was that?

Mary chuckled. "A fine catch you have made, my dear. Not here an hour and you have the master drooling to bed you."

What? She studied Mary. "He didn't seem affected by me." Her gaze turned back to the door and the man's retreating muscular back. His arms were incredible. The sensations lingered, caressing her skin as a feather would.

"That is Rupert Roland. Cool control. I have never seen him act impulsively. But underneath all his restraint, I think he is special."

Rupert Roland. Of course she knew of his name. Who didn't? But she never allowed herself to become familiar with his face or his physique. From his reputation alone, he was everything she had avoided over the past years.

Mary's hand rubbed her arm, stroking her as warmth spread to her stomach, to her heart. The arousing, soothing sensation brought tears to her eyes. She missed Mary.

"Rupert had one bound to him for many years, but she never understood him or wanted to take the time. You two may be just what the other needs."

"He is as bad a scoundrel, if not worse, than Matthew. I could never connect myself to a man like him."

"Oh, sweet girl. All of the men in this club possess some of the qualities of that bumpus Dranger. That is why you are here."

Mary continued to lightly stroke her.

"I'm not sure why I'm here. I know I want to experience a powerful man again. Just not one who is as controlling as—"

"As Matthew. Well, I don't think Matthew's control frightened you, dear. If I remember correctly, you enjoyed that aspect."

Mary was correct, of course. His rages, his possessiveness, ended their love. Never would she put herself in that position again. To be owned to her soul. She would find a man who desired her, but not to the point of not letting her talk to another. Touch another.

"You're right, Mary."

"Well, then Mr. Roland just might do."

"No, he is too controlled."

"Ah, in search of a bit of passion, are you? Well, no doubt you will find plenty. The men here are known not only for their control and vices, but also for wonderful fucks."

"Mary," she said in mock outrage.

"Well, it is true, dear."

Cora giggled, feeling like the fresh-as-grass girl she'd been when Dranger introduced her to Mary. Once again, she wanted to tell her everything. To have Mary mentor her, guide her back to this world.

"The man who let me down in the hall was just wonderful, Mary."

"Oh, do tell. Which one of the masters untied you?"

"That's just it. I . . . I don't know."

"Well, dear, your senses will tell you. Only the masters are allowed to untie."

"Where is my dear girl Janice?" Mary glanced around the room, then guided Cora toward the door.

They walked through together, and Cora stopped still to gawk at the room. Now this was what she had in mind. This room dazzled from fantasy.

The walls, a rich shade of deep emerald green, depicted colorful men and woman in all sorts of vices in broad strokes. Strokes she could feel. There was flogging, buggering, a man in chains, and several pictures of multiple men and women engaged in different positions of the act. The images themselves were not shocking, yet wetness pooled between her legs at the scent of honey radiating throughout the room. Her mystery man.

White Corinthian columns stood proud around the edges, and the floor was open. This room no longer hosted the fancy dancing of a ballroom. Instead, the room was for strategy, control, and wicked desires.

An alternating pattern of black and white tiles formed a square in the center of the floor. A chessboard. Around the edges, naked men and women gathered as human pieces.

Rupert stood in the center and conversed with two other men. One of them bowed his head and left. Then he shook hands with a man with the same dark hair and chiseled chin. A striking resemblance; surely they were brothers.

"What an entertaining game this promises to be. Rupert will play his brother."

"Being brothers, wouldn't they have played previously?"

"No doubt. They enjoy sharing. It is said Rupert was introduced to woman by his brother's mistress, but . . ."

"But what?"

"Rupert *never* plays. Not here anyway. I bet he is counting on you, my dear, to join his set of pieces. I think he wants to see how obedient you are."

Hmmm . . . She bit her lip, taking in his muscular torso and arms as he gestured and quietly talked. Shivers raced across her body, remembering the arms of the man in the hall. Rupert's arms fit the description of what she remembered. He could be the man who pleasured her so thoroughly in the entry. The man who she wanted to complete what he started.

"Does he normally watch?" She held her breath. *Please let her say yes.*

"Everyone watches, dear. Who couldn't?"

She bit her lip. Even if Rupert wasn't her mystery man, the man from the entry enjoyed watching. What better way to allow him to see her than to play a game everyone watched?

She would do it. The idea set her skin tingling. She had found a man who not only possessed a great presence of command, but also managed to show respect and kindness. That man was in this room; she would be a simpleton not to try and attract him.

She stepped forward into the ballroom and froze. No! Why did this have to happen? In front of her stood the reason she shunned men of presence for so long.

He hadn't noticed her. Had he? She could leave. Her body trembled as it always did when she glimpsed him. Next her lungs would lock and she would flee like the coward she was. She turned around, but Mary stood on her heel.

"Put him behind you, dear." Mary brushed her hair over her shoulder. "It is time for you to face Dranger, to show him he has no power over you."

She was right. Cora closed her eyes. She was too old to pique his interest anyway, so she had nothing to fear. The hair on her neck stood and her hands shook.

"If you wish to show him he is mud to you, play on Rupert's board. He will not approach you. And if Rupert is interested, he will not allow Dranger near you."

Icy sweat slid down her back unrestrained by clothing. Mary's sultry hand slid down in its wake. Settling on her bum, her delicate hand massaged. The touch, so caring, reassured and emboldened her.

You can do this. You are no longer emotional about him. You are strong. You can put him in his place if he does approach.

"You are right. I came here tonight to enjoy myself." She nodded her head and continued down the ballroom floor to the gathering of people who lined up on each side of the checkered floor.

Rupert regarded her. His brows drew together, and a frown crossed his lips. What did he see in her face? Could he see her fear?

She glanced to where Matthew had stood. He was gone. Her shoulders relaxed. Thank goodness.

Rupert now conversed with his brother. What handsome men they both were. Though Rupert's height and some unnameable quality said, *Respect me and mine or you will pay*. What would it be like to be with a man like him? All precise control.

She shook her head. She was not after unflappable desire. The raw carnal need she experienced in the entry this night is what she craved. Whoever her mystery man was, she would find him. Or more likely he would watch her play this game and then possess her.

4

Each brother selected their pieces from those willing to play. Rupert chose her with barely a nod.

How frustrating. He did not speak at all!

He couldn't be the man who possessed her in the hall, much less be interested in her. Her shoulders slumped, and she shifted her feet from side to side.

Many of the men assembled around the checkered floor easily fit the description her body remembered—tall and lithe. But would a master who possessed the ability to quake her also have the ability to take orders from another man? Doubtful. Surely he watched from the sides.

Rupert pointed to four men and four women and waved them to step forward. His eyes narrowed in concentration, sparked and glimmered with control she wanted to shake.

Would their offspring have the same brilliant green eyes and dark hair?

Damn, what a stray thought. Without a doubt, the sight of Matthew caused it. She shook herself and pushed the painful emotion down.

Stop staring at him. She forced herself to glance about the room. Matthew stood on Lord Brummelton's side of the board, leering at her. His narrowed gaze caressed her body, leaving bitter sweat in its wake.

She would be damned if she let him see her fear. Forcing her lips into the sultry smile she used with her protectors, she inclined her head, then tore her gaze to the pieces on the board.

That was easy. See, you can be in the same room with him and stand on your own. You have had nothing to fear all these years.

The air swirled past her as Rupert guided a selected piece to the board and placed him on a square, alternating sexes, male then female. They were his pawns. She regarded his taut bottom, a firm rounded swell encased in expertly tailored black silk trousers. Why did she keep staring at him? He did cut a striking figure, but his indifference ground her teeth.

She forced her attention back to the game and watched his brother fill up the first line on his side of the board.

One man and one woman received white lengths of silk, and Rupert placed them on the board as his bishops. Two others received long thin birch switches, his knights.

He turned back toward the remaining pieces, and the corner of his lips curved into a wicked smile that sparked his amazing green eyes. Sinful. His legs moved in easy languid strides as he approached her. Her heart jumped in her chest. He was coming for her.

She clutched her hands together in front of her and bit her lip, stomach fluttering. *Relax. You would think a man had never touched you before.*

He reached out, snagged her hand, and turned it palm up. Her arm trembled as the tips of his fingers found the pulse on her wrist and gently circled the beating skin. Pinpricks raced up her arm, and her eyes widened as jade flashed, his gaze catching hers.

Oh, he had plans for her; this eyes told of intense wickedness and desire. She couldn't breathe. He did want her. Her gaze dropped to his firm full lips, and her tongue traced her own. She wanted to spear her tongue into his mouth and taste him.

Icy smooth stone was pressed to her fingers, and she closed them about the object, her gaze snapping back to his. He turned abruptly and strode to one of the males who remained.

A white marble dildo, half a palm's breadth wide and as long as her forearm, lay in her grasp. Her fingers ran across the frosty smooth surface. Rupert stared at her as he passed to position the man as his rook on the board's far corner.

Her body trembled. In her mind, Rupert's hands eased the cold hard prick into her until the tip pressed to her womb. Rupert's hands . . . Her chest tightened. Could Rupert be the man who liked to watch?

He returned to her and dragged his fingers along the scar on her belly to her hip. The muscles of her torso tensed and jumped. Oh indeed, her body knew that touch. Or did she? The control that oozed from him was opposite from what she experienced in the entry. Yet, that power shook her just as much.

When he placed his hand on the small of her back, spirals of warmth radiated from the contact up her spine and her lungs locked. Yes, indeed it was he. That soothing heat.

Her body remembered and the sensation gentled her. The strength of the irrational emotion was unexpected and a bit frightening too. Was she sure? Or could she be so hungry for a potent man's touch that any man who touched her would do?

She wanted to turn around to look him in the eye and see if that same intensity sparked his soul. Her heart beat through her limbs.

He guided her to the closest corner black square, placing her next to a knight, a man of equally impressive stature as Rupert's, and behind a woman, a pawn, who she stood a head above.

His hand left her, and he strode to the last woman who re-mained—a pretty, short, auburn-haired girl. Handing her a rid-ing crop and a length of leather, he placed her on the board as his queen.

Cora narrowed her eyes. If Rupert was her watcher, shouldn't he place her in that important position, his queen on the board?

Her body might have been wrong. Damn and blast. If only he would speak, she would know for sure. The last man, a big stocky fellow, became his king.

Rupert strode down the line of pawns and stopped in front of the woman who stood before her. His hands ran down the woman's hips. Squeezing, his long fingers slid up the insides of her thighs, then disappeared, reappearing at her sides about breast height. He leaned in, his head dipping below the woman's shoulder, and suckling sounds ensued.

Cora stood on her tiptoes, but blast it, all she could see was the dark hair atop Rupert's head. The woman groaned, her head tilted back and her shoulder blades shuddered.

Her teeth clenched and she tore her gaze away as envy seared through her. She wanted his lips on her skin, sucking her breasts.

As his head rose, green dilated eyes met hers and he winked. Winked. Good Lord, he possessed no compassion. He damn well knew he affected her, and he taunted her with it.

He continued up the row of pawns, sucking and pinching each woman until they groaned. Caressing and rubbing each man's prick until they grew stiff. Then he came down the back line.

What would those graceful hands do to her when he touched her? The carnal animal in her cried out for his hands on her body, to control her as he so effortlessly did everyone on the board. Her muscles grew tense with desire for a man she didn't know. How terrifying. Two men? Hmmm . . .

His brother aroused his power pieces first and now ended

with his pawns. Placed in the far corner of the board, she would be the last piece Rupert touched. Was that significant?

She tried to behold anything that made his actions toward her seem like that of the man in the hall. There was nothing. *Foolish girl wishes. You are certainly no longer a girl.*

Did she think that finding the man who touched her soul would be that easy?

He approached her, his eyes heavy, pupils dilated in arousal and a happy cat-that-ate-his-cream grin on his face. Any man would be elated to have a harem of men and women to order about and touch sexually. She rolled her eyes at him, and he chuckled as he stepped behind her. Her breath caught at the deep tone and extreme closeness of his body. He had not stepped behind any other piece on the board. His steamy hands squared her shoulders to face the opposite team.

She imagined his gaze running down the length of her spine, stopping to caress the swells of her bottom. He inhaled a choppy breath as his fingers slid down her collarbone to the top of her breasts, then flexed.

Gooseflesh raced up her arms, and he wrapped his hold about her shoulders. Fingers slipping lower, he pinched her straining nipples.

Those hands. She sighed.

The scent of warm smoky honey slid through her nose, and she groaned deep and low in her chest. Warm breath wafted her ear.

"Who am I, Cora?"

A wave of heat washed over her at the sound of the deep voice that had caressed her so thoroughly in the hall.

Without a doubt, it was he. The smell, the sound, the touch, all the same.

His hands slid farther down her stomach to the mound of hairs that covered her sex.

"Yes."

"Who am I?" His finger lightly pulled, pinching the hairs.

"Mr. Rupert Roland, the wicked scoundrel." *Who knows exactly how to touch me.* Yes, oh yes. Her knees weakened. She wanted this man.

"How astute. Is there more?"

One of his long fingers slid into her slick folds, and she whimpered, holding herself still.

"N-no." Oh indeed, a lot more. Her eyes fluttered shut. He pressed his erection against her bum, and a groan puffed past her lips.

"Do you desire me, Cora?"

Her insides quivered. Couldn't he tell? She was a puddle on the floor. Trembling gooseflesh primed her skin. His finger circled her clitoris, and her hips arched into his hands.

"You need to ask?" A gush of wetness seeped from her body, showing him without words. She moaned.

Grunting, he trailed his tongue down the line of her neck. He slid his fingers from her tingling flesh and, trailing them back up her stomach, released her.

She turned her head toward him, and he ran a finger coated with her cream across her lips. Her tongue slid out and lapped her scent from him. His eyes flashed with desire at the sight. He turned and left her to make his opening move.

She closed her eyes as chills of excitement chased up her arms. Not only would this man watch her, but he would also put her in situations he desired. Her skin dewed with moisture.

What would the wicked Mr. Roland have her do to titillate him?

Rupert's muscles clenched hard as a rock. His heart beat triple time, a reaction he had not experienced because of a woman in ages.

She desired him. Knowing who and what he was.

So why had she turned him down so many times? He had

not changed in physical appearance . . . well, except for a bit of gray in the sides of his hair.

It was a question he needed answered. None of her being here tonight made sense to him. The fear he glimpsed on her face on occasion compounded his bafflement. With her strength, her experience, this game, one of the club's milder events, should be tame to her. He hated to see those heart-shaped lips frown. A pout—that was one thing, but a genuine frown made his gut clench.

His brother stood across from him and nodded for him to start the game.

Concentrate, chap. Not only do you want to win, you need to figure out how to get Cora into a taking position.

If he maneuvered her right, he just may get to see her pleasure more than one of his brother's pieces. Rupert strode to the center of the board and leaned down to the pawn in front of his king.

"Move two spaces forward. Rub your hand over your cock but do not spend."

The pawn strode forward to the center of the board; once there, the pawn's hand slid up the silky surface of his prick. Rupert turned to watch Cora.

She stood watching his every move. A lump formed in his throat, and he swallowed hard. Her desire shone in her eyes and in the pretty blush that tinged her skin.

He couldn't believe how beautiful she was. More so than he remembered. Maybe it was because he'd never seen her naked or touched her. No . . . At eighty, she would be more beautiful than most silly debuts.

He couldn't wait to see her face as he moved her into play and forced her to spend. His heart beat a maddening tattoo beneath his chest, his cock stiffer than any erection he had experienced in years.

But who? Emma and Kit were both pieces on his brother's

board. Either one of them would do, but having her fuck the black king in a checkmate would be the ultimate win and a sight to feed his vigor.

His muscles clenched and he rolled his shoulders, imagining her light moans and a spine-tingling scream when she spent. A pearl of arousal drizzled from his cock, dampening his pants. *Randy, chap.* He chuckled to himself.

Well, it was too soon to get lusty for an act that may never happen. He would have to see what opportunities arose.

5

Watching human chess was erotic, so exciting. Cora shifted her stance to get a better view. The control that eased from the players stole her breath. They so effortlessly moved each piece into play. No one hesitated. Not one piece considered the order to self-gratify and arouse themselves demeaning as they were placed into play. They all respected the players and wished to do nothing but what they were told.

Already she had learned Rupert liked to watch the pleasure, the emotions of the pieces through their expressions. If she paid attention, she would learn so much more about how to pleasure this man.

"This is your first time?"

The whisper came from beside her. She glanced at the tall fair knight. He remained facing forward as if he said nothing. She turned back to the game.

"If the master stared at me that way, I would leave the board on my knees to pleasure him and forgo the game."

"Pardon?" She regarded him.

"Master Rupert. He studies you. Your face, your body." He remained facing forward as he spoke.

He was right. She shouldn't move either.

She glanced at Rupert. He studied the board intently. Turning back to the board, she peered from the corner of her eye. Just as the knight had said, Rupert's gaze lingered on her face and then traveled her body. His lips curved into a seductive smile when he caught her gaze.

"He can't keep from ogling you. He enjoys watching. I can't imagine why he is playing." The knight's gaze traveled down her. "Then again . . ." His head snapped back forward.

"Do you always play?"

"Yes, on Lord Brummelton's board. But this time I couldn't resist being on Rupert's. To do as he wishes."

"Oh." She was just another moth snared in his light.

"Not that we have an affinity. We don't. It is just . . . well, look at him. He is nonesuch."

"Quite," she mumbled. He certainly had that presence about him, and he quickly became important to her too. But if he had all this, and so many willing to please him, could she hold his interest?

What an utterly maddening thought. This was for one night, so why did it matter?

Rupert walked to a female pawn that stood in the middle of the board. Cora's body was so aware of him she swore his steamy breath puffed her ear as he whispered his command to the pawn. The pawn sidestepped in front of the black male pawn that his brother first moved and dropped to her knees. A smile pulled at Cora's lips. The futter was to begin.

Removing his hands from his staff, Rupert's pawn sucked the hard erection into her mouth. Her lips fanned out over his stiffness, and the sides of her cheeks sunk in and out. His head tossed back as he groaned, lacing his fingers into her hair.

The breaths of the pieces who fondled themselves labored and muscles clenched as the woman's sucking noises became louder and wetter.

"You would think those in play would spend at the sight," she whispered to the knight beside her.

"Most of us have played for years and know to enjoy the slow build of pleasure. By the end, the taking will last a few strokes and the opponent's piece will fall."

Amazing. They played this game for years and she, who made her living in futter for years, never knew such a game existed.

Men and women stood around the edges of the room watching the play unfold. Rupert stared at the couple in the center, his fists clenched and a furrow between his brows. He should be enjoying this, but he concentrated on the game, not on the pleasure of watching these people mate. That was the reason he didn't play. She understood that now. He wanted to savor the sights in front of him while playing, his attention focused on the game.

The furrow between his brows grew deeper as he assessed his brother's pieces. She wanted to run her tongue up that indentation and rub her breasts in his face. To taunt him and brazenly break his control, his concentration, to release that animal who caged her between his legs in the hall.

She closed her eyes as the sensations flooded back to her full force. Large muscular thighs pressed her legs together, his ballocks caressing her legs with each press of his burly prick into the crease of her thighs. Her nipples hardened to stiff painful peaks and her womb pulsed.

Why hadn't he entered her? She'd asked him. No, begged. Her head grew light. Control. In neither of these situations she had control. Amazing how she had missed the similarities.

Rupert played this game devoid of all feeling, but he did

have passion. The heat of his desire was in the spark in his amazing green eyes. Just one look from him set her whole body quivering like jelly.

A grin turned her lips. She would tie him up and make him say why he did not taken his pleasure as he licked her curls.

No! She shook her head. That was the old her. The new her would simply ask, *"Why did you not take your pleasure in my body, Rupert?"* And if he wished to answer, he would.

Just as she would stand here for the rest of the game and do as he wished. Her skin tingled. She stood here to please him. Her head spun in the heady pleasure of it all. No decisions. Wonderful warmth slid through her.

A loud cry came from the male pawn as he spilled his seed. The woman sucked off his prick, and he walked from the board to recover next to Rupert.

Rupert's brother's move came next. He strode to his male bishop, leaned in, and whispered his command. The bishop wrapped his length of black silk about his hands and strode diagonally to Rupert's knight. Tying the knight's wrists behind the tall woman's neck, he stuck his fingers into his mouth and removed them wet with spit. He ran his slick fingers down the crack of her bum and pushed them inside. The woman whimpered.

Cora gaped. Never had she expected to see a man of this caliber bugger a woman.

One of the servants strode onto the board with a bronze pitcher. Holding it over the bishop's prick, he poured thick golden oil over the erection. The bishop rubbed his hand back and forth over his phallus to coat himself to a glimmer. Then with tiny thrusts, he slid his hard member into the knight's heart-shaped bum. The knight cried out and shifted her stance to adjust to the pressure. He grasped her hips and large male thigh muscles shook with the force of their passion.

Oh my! Cora's teeth snagged her lip as heat shot through

her stomach to the flesh of her sex and bum. Wetness slid down her leg, and she closed her eyes. Once Rupert moved her, a puddle of her cream would remain on this spot. Her eyes fluttered back open and she groaned.

Fully seated in the knight's pucker, the bishop reached around her body and frigged her with his hands. Pulling back his hips, he buggered the knight, her fleshy bum jiggling in waves as their bodies collided. They both shuddered, muscles straining as they tried to remain balanced and joined in the upright position.

Too much time passed since a man desired her that way—the sensation immensely pleasurable, the pressure, easing way to fullness, followed by intense sensation. Oh, she never had the pleasure with men like these and never in the standing position. Would Rupert enjoy it? She would find out all his pleasures. She bit her lip as her heart tightened. Would he be interested in her for more than one night?

She shot him a quick glance and a startled gasp passed her lips. Matthew stood next to Rupert in deep conversation.

He turned his gaze to the board, his black eyes catching her startled expression. She gasped. Blast it. *Whatever you do, don't turn away. Stand your ground.* Her muscles strained with the force to turn, but her will won.

Matthew's lips curved up in the smile that had turned her knees to jelly so many times in the past. Her fists clenched. How dare he use that smile on her now. Anger at all the dreams he shattered flooded her veins. She couldn't stop him from gazing at her. But to use that smile . . . Her teeth ground together. Her hand itched to slap that grin from his face.

"Ahhhh."

The sound pulled her attention back to the play. The knight spent with a high-pitched cry as the bishop heaved and came up her bum. A servant man scurried to them with a bowl of water and cloth.

Rupert paced the side of the board, assessing the game. His long legs encased in black trousers rolled up to his calves showed beautiful hairy ankles and wide masculine feet.

The picture he created set her stomach fluttering. She longed for a man like him—casual, strong, controlled, but kind. Above all, his passion called to her. The way his muscles shook when he touched her. Tingles raced her skin.

He glanced at her and a wicked smile curved his lips. That smile . . . She would give anything to have that smile flashed at her before he possessed her each night.

Rupert winked, then strode past her to his queen. He whispered to her. The emotions that coursed through Cora frightened her. How could she feel this bone-deep connection to a man whom she had barely spoken to two dozen times? She had come here tonight hoping to put her past behind her and to engage in wicked acts with a man she desired once more. Could she have found more? Her chest tightened. That was a scarier thought.

The queen strode to the bishop who had just finished buggering the knight and washed his member in a copper bowl one of the three eunuchs held.

Where did they find these men? She would have to remember to ask Rupert. If there ever was time to ask. For all she knew, he would watch her, find her too old or not arousing, and decide to take his queen home.

Oh stop. You are being utterly ridiculous. Take a step back. He finds you attractive. Quit putting things in your way. This man desires you. His lust for you is in every move he makes.

The knight handed the bowl back to the man. The queen gripped his flaccid prick and wrapped the length of leather around the base of his staff and sack, then tied the cinch tight.

She bent him forward, bracing his hands on his knees and ran her crop across his hardening erection and bags. Tracing the flat leather tip over his thigh to his buttocks, she rubbed the crack of his bum, then caressed the swell of his bottom.

Her crop rose out to the side, and with a flick of her wrist, she snapped the man on the behind.

Not bad . . .

WHOOSH!

SNAP!

Her position was good, but she could have gotten a better sensation from the bishop if she had waited a moment before hitting him again.

He didn't mind; maybe he enjoyed the pain as her clients did. His prick hardened, and with the restriction of the leather tied about it, his stiff staff turned bright red-purple. A beautiful erection. Her tongue darted out and traced her lips, wondering what the sultry skin would taste like. Saliva pooled in her mouth, and she swallowed hard.

The queen placed her hand against the reddened area on his bum, then turned him and ordered him to sit.

She straddled him, placing the riding crop between her teeth, and sank down onto the hard purple penis. The bishop groaned as she rocked and rubbed her sex against him.

The spectators groaned in unison. The sound of her wetness and the smell of arousal in the air intensified.

Cora's body tingled, burning hot, stimulated by the sight. Could a person combust from too much arousal? She didn't doubt they could; if one person touched her, she would melt like butter on fresh toast.

The bishop whispered to the queen, and she grasped his hands and placed them on her nipples. "Squeeze them hard."

The bishop's fingertips pinched her nipples and plucked the peaks. Cora's body jerked. The queen screamed as she spent in his lap. Her head leaned against his shoulder, and he rocked and rocked his hips up against her until he came with a growl.

My, oh my. The smell of cream and aroused sweat wafted through the air, setting constant little contractions to the flesh of her sex. What a fevered pitch she was in. All she could think of was Rupert and her mirroring the actions the couple made, or her performing this act of love as Rupert watched.

Honey dripped from her labia as she drew in two deep draws of air. A fire burned between her legs. She couldn't last much longer. She needed to touch herself.

She shifted her stance, the ache almost painful. The large stone prick lay ready for use in her hand. How she wanted to run her hands down her body, feeling the heated skin, then slip lower to the crisp curls of her Venus and into the creamy wet flesh of her pussy.

She could use the stone staff to push her to the edge and cry out as Rupert watched. But this game was about control of others and strategy of the players to achieve the desired results. She would have to wait until Rupert moved her into play, and then she would spend knowing that the bliss she felt was as he wished.

Lord Brummelton's pawn took one of Rupert's, thrashing her with his switch until her ass was crisscrossed with red marks. Cheers arose from the onlookers. He then mounted her from behind, both of them squatting as he pulled her hair back and arched her to him just as Rupert had her in the hall.

Her body shook with the need to feel him around her again. Blast and damn. Would this game ever end? She would do whatever Rupert wanted her to on this board, but in the end his touch was what she craved, and she wanted it now.

Out of the corner of her eye, she saw a man walk up to Lord Brummelton. Cora froze. Matthew. They talked briefly, and Rupert's brother glanced at the board. He nodded to him, then strode to one of his rooks, Matthew in tow. The rook, a slender yet striking man, bowed to Rupert's brother and stepped from the board. Cora's throat tightened and her stomach clenched. Dranger stepped onto his square.

The next six plays went without a futter. He needed to pull himself together. His brother kept shooting him that grin that said he thought he would win. Not once in all Rupert's years had he ever lost a chess game. Granted, he never played human chess but chess was chess.

The pieces were so aroused, they would achieve petite mort in a few quick strokes if he could get into a taking position.

In a series of swift takings, his knight took his brother's pawn, only to be taken by another of his brother's pawns, which he possessed with his bishop. His brother moved his knight. Ah, there the opportunity was. He would castle his king and rook and move Cora into play.

Rupert strode to his king. "You will cast with the queen's rook. Fondle her with everything but your cock. Make her come as often as she can."

The king nodded.

He walked down the line to Cora. Finally, he would see her face as she discharged. Anticipation warmed his muscles, and he fought back a grin. Then he would watch her pleasure.

Her gaze dilated in arousal, met his. Blister it, the smell of her honey—sweet and spicy—set him hardening further.

"Are you ready to move, lovely?" He held in a groan at the thought of watching her receive her pleasure.

Biting her lip, she glanced across the board. She nodded back at him before he could see who she glanced at. What the hell? A piece on his brother's team bothered her. Bothered her to the point that her hands trembled. He wanted to reach out for them and rub them in his until they stopped.

He clenched his teeth, unable to decipher the emotions that coursed through him. Blister it. He needed to play the game. She was fine. Besides, he was not moving her across the board . . . yet.

"You will cast with *my* king for this move. He will fondle you." *I want to fondle you.* "You will not touch him with any part of your hands or allow your body to arch into his caress. You may spread your legs to him."

She nodded and glanced up the row to the king. Her smile returned and his muscles relaxed. Damn straight. He'd awaited this move all night. He licked his lips as his gaze glided down her body. A light sheen of arousal coated the fur of her sex, and his cock throbbed.

His king was a large man, Damon Cavendish, and someone Rupert considered a friend outside of this realm. Tonight he was a savior. He would give him the pleasure of seeing Cora spend without adding to her distress.

Who the hell on his brother's side did she have a connection with? He had never known her to associate with any of the men in this club. Yet she obviously knew one of his pieces, and that person frightened her. *Come on, chap, don't let this ruin your folly.*

His brother stared at him as Cora walked up the board to his king. He would have an earful tomorrow over his order to Cora and Damon. Normally casting would end in a fuck as his brother made his move. But not tonight. Tonight he wanted to see her thoroughly aroused, and thoroughly spent, and in the end fucking him. His head jerked back and his eyebrows drew together. He rolled his shoulders. Watching her futter was what he wanted, wasn't it?

Damon stood on his square and immediately reached for Cora's crotch. His finger slid into the flesh of her cunny, reappearing wet and shiny. Rupert groaned, unable to tear his gaze from Damon's fingers fucking her sex. He wanted to do that to her. Her flesh had been hot and juicy, and when she tightened the walls of her cunt about his probing hand . . . *Control your-self, chap. You will have that amazing flesh about your cock soon.*

Cora stood motionless, her muscles straining not to arch into Damon's caress. *That's it, lovely.*

Eyes closed, her long lashes fanned her blushed cheeks. Her lips parted on an inhale as her body locked, and she silently screamed.

Beautiful.

His cock pulsed as his seed rose. His fingers circled the head of his phallus, applying delightful pressure as her eyes fluttered open. Everything about her was fine.

"Brother, your move."

Startled, he tore his gaze from Cora's flushed face and as-sessed his brother's play. Damn it all. This was why he didn't play. He wanted to savor moments like that one. Bloody, bloody rules.

His brother had no choices left and neither did he if he wanted this ended with haste. Cora's nerve-filled expression flashed in his mind and his muscles clenched. He would send Cora across the board. In doing so, he would push his brother into a pinch and discover who she fretted.

He strode back to Cora, who recovered from another beau-tiful spend. Never again would he play. He wasn't enjoying any of this. His chest tightened as he searched her face for any hesi-tation. Bloody hell. What was wrong with him? This move was supposed to be even better.

He ran a hand down the swell of her bum and lightly into her crack. Burning heat met his fingers, and he thrust them into her juice-soaked cunny.

His body shook as her neck flexed, and a faint moan came from within her. A siren. Tingles raced across his skin, and he fought the urge to take her, possess her, now, here on the board, and end the game in shame. *Stop it. Where is your restraint?*

"You will take my brother's knight with your tongue and your phallus. Do not find pleasure yourself."

Her eyelids hung low, the fear for the moment forgotten. The devil, the look of a thoroughly pleasured woman. He absorbed every nuance of her face, her flushed cheeks and slight part of her mouth, eyes that were sated but still held desire. He hoped to see that look and more for days to come.

She nodded, then strode forward on wobbly legs. His gaze settled on her heart-shaped swells, flush from spending. He would have to remember to invite Damon into his futter more often; he knew how to pleasure a woman. Partway across the board she hesitated.

Shit, he could not see her face. Who was she looking at? He glanced from one of his brother's pieces to another, but all of them watched her.

Blister it. The muscles of his neck tensed solid. He strode back to the side of the board as she continued across. Who the hell was it! He scrutinized each piece. Nothing. Damn it. Then he came to Emma.

Standing on the same square, Cora knelt and pushed Emma's legs apart.

Cora and Emma.

His hand went to his cock and stroked as Cora licked into Emma's curls. Good God, lovely. Her head wiggled up and down as her tongue glided across her dewy flesh.

Emma cried out a shocked excited groan and slid her legs farther apart so Cora's tongue could explore.

The muscles in his stomach prickled and tensed as his hand worked firmer, faster against the taut skin of his cock.

Emma's hands slid into Cora's hair. Damn, this was better than anything he could have imagined. Cora's body trembled as she licked Emma's sweet juice. She enjoyed the act. It showed in every movement of her being. His lungs locked as his sack pulled up close to his body. *Hold back, hold back.* He slowed his stroke to enjoy this to the end.

Emma whimpered, wobbled, and slid to the floor, arching her hips to Cora's tongue. Cora adjusted her head to the new position and slid her fingers into Emma.

Emma screamed as a powerful spend shook her. Cora licked and licked through Emma's contractions. Beautiful. A groan ripped from him.

Cora stood, licked her lips, and turned back around to face Rupert. His heart beat so fast he couldn't breathe. Absolute magnificence. He couldn't move if he tried.

The arousal that coursed through his veins from the look of delight on Cora's face, and the glistening juice shining on the tip of Cora's nose and mouth, overcame him. Hell, she was the most beautiful woman he had ever known. His chest tightened and his throat constricted as emotion pressed on him. Never had this possession for a woman coursed through him.

Deep down in his soul, she was his next bond or more. His cock strained, pointing its way to the target it sought. He needed to sink into her and now. Blister it. Bloody the game. Emma padded off the board and came to stand by his side.

"So, she is your new—"

"Bugger off, Em." How was he to end this game in haste?

"Shouldn't she be warned about you?"

"What?" he said in agitation. "She already knows all she needs to."

"Does she? She has never been here, and from what I'm told, her only talent besides whatever she did to me out there is flogging foppish men. Is she up for you?"

"What, Em?" he ground out.

"Your inability to show passion toward anyone?"

How dare she . . . He spun on her, ready for her hardened snide expression, and glared down through narrowed eyes.

Blue eyes filled with hurt stared back, dowsing all his anger. She was hurt by his action toward Cora. He blew out through clenched teeth.

She was right. He had never shown her any direct regard besides finding pleasure in her body, and even that had come with controlled precise moves.

"I could never give what you wanted, Em." He turned back to the board.

Cora. She unleashed in him the passion Emma had craved. He fought to keep his controlled façade in place just looking at her. The welling desire boiling through his veins confused him. His mind struggled for control of this strange urge to do nothing but fuck her. He had no idea what or how to deal with it.

6

Keep your eyes on Rupert and breathe. Who cares if he is in heated conversation with the blonde you just pleasured.

Icy chills caressed her back knowing Matthew stood on the square behind her. Her fingernails dug into the flesh of her palms. Musk and juniper flooded her senses, making her stomach twist. He stood within arm's reach. His breath caught her hair, and all she wanted to do was move. She inhaled a wavering breath.

That's it. Rupert. Rupert is why you're here. All will be well.

If Matthew talks to you or touches you, treat him as Lady Strike would and stand your ground.

She could feel his gaze on her naked body and the hairs on her neck stood. Please keep Rupert's brother from moving Matthew to take her. Sweat trickled between her breasts, and she struggled to breathe in the suddenly humid air. That would be her worst nightmare come true.

Air swirled by her sides, washing more of his scent to her. Her stomach rolled. His hands. He swung his arms forward and back on either side of her, hoping to provoke a reaction.

Well she would give him the cut. She pushed her tongue to the roof of her mouth and swallowed the burning bile back down. Didn't he know he was to obey Lord Brummelton? Then again, Dranger never listened to anyone.

"My pet, you're gorgeous . . . for an old dove." His voice was a stealth whisper.

Her teeth clenched as a tremor of rage stung through her body. "Quite, but I am no longer yours or anyone's pet."

An old dove. Her hand rose to touch the wrinkles at the sides of her eyes, but she stopped midair. *He is goading you. Don't let him.*

"You dream of me. Your *young,* slender legs wrapped about me as I fuck you until you scream, imploring me to stop only to make you come again."

"Nightmares." Her body trembled with agitation. The only thing she ever dreamed about was their last night. Damn it all, she wouldn't think of that now.

He clucked his tongue and swung his arms again. A touch grazed her bottom. She jumped and shuffled forward so she stood on the edge of her square. As far from him as she could get without moving spaces.

"Cease! We are not to do anything the players don't wish."

"Ah, but you wish."

Her teeth ground together so hard her jaw hurt. "Never."

Rupert's brother strode toward them, the sound of his bare feet against the tiles rang so loud. He was striding to Dranger. Her hands shook and her vision clouded in. She would not allow him to touch her. She could not! He stopped in front of his queen, who stood beside her.

Cora's knees weakened, almost sending her to the floor. *You're being utterly ridiculous!* The queen padded forward one space to stand one square in front of Cora and to her left side. Her gaze traveled Cora's length, and she raised her eyebrows as she passed.

Surely the other players thought her incapable of obeying. Blast and damn, she wanted to be good for Rupert.

"My pet. You fool. Step back."

She refused to answer him. There was no need. He spoke nothing more than silly flirtations. Therefore, he posed no threat. A smile tugged at her lips. She'd stood her ground. She'd managed Matthew.

His brother took too damn long in making that move. Rupert strode to Cora, his cock straining. Would anyone care if he took her on the board? *Hold tight, chap. You don't want to lose status in the club.* The Hell Knights allowed him to be whatever he wished. Only a half-wit would risk their censure.

She stood with a smile tugging her lips as he ran a finger across her stomach. Blister it, he couldn't keep from touching her. His control frayed and she taunted him.

"You find this humorous?"

Her eyes widened, then lowered to his straining erection. "You lust for me, and you can't act on it . . . yet."

Her eyes sparkled at *yet,* and he fisted his hands so as not to grasp her and act on that lust.

"I find that funny for a man who is always in control."

His teeth clenched. "I am in control." He was, damn it.

"Well, sir, make your move."

Blister it. The move he wanted to make was to slide his cock into her and she bloody well knew it. Wait . . . Did she just tell him what to do? His blood boiled and scorched through his veins straight to his phallus. A smile sprang to his lips. She wanted to play, did she?

He gripped her hip as he had in the hall; slowly circling the silken flesh over the bone, he puffed a breath across her ear.

"So what should my next move be, lovely?" His heart leapt in his chest, waiting to see what she would do.

Her body trembled and she shifted, parting her legs for him. "I . . . I don't know, sir. I have never played chess."

The smell of her juice tickled his nose, and he pressed his erection against the crack of her bum. "Ah, are you sure you don't want to make the next move?"

Her hips rocked, picking up the gauntlet he'd thrown down. The velvet flesh of her crevice slid along his shaft, expending a pearl of wetness, drizzling his want onto her skin. Her breath whooshed out and her shoulders jerked. "You know best, sir."

"So true." He leaned in and pinched her rigid nipples. She cried out. A sound so enticing his body caught fire. Her head tilted back to lean on his shoulder. His lungs locked. He flirted with a siren. A siren who no doubt would be the death to life as he knew it. But he didn't care. He wanted her in his bed, in his life, like no other woman before her.

He ran his tongue along her jaw, reveling in the salty aroused taste of her skin. "So lovely," he whispered, and dropped his hands from her. *Finish the game, then you can have her.*

He studied the board. Would she enjoy this command? "Go all the way across the board and stand by the king."

Nodding her head, she turned her face to the side to glance at him.

"Slide the phallus into your bum as slow as you can." The muscles of his arse clenched. He couldn't wait to see her face. "Move the stone prick back and forth but don't let the cock slide out; frig yourself with your other hand."

Her smile told him she had no problem obeying the command; she nodded and moved back across the board. The devil. She could match him. He strode back to the side of the board, penis bobbling as he walked.

The next moves went swift, and none of them penetrated the fog in his brain. His mind was bumblebroth, twisted with foreign thoughts. Why did Cora stir him so?

He played to his plan; his brother would lose, and Cora

would be the one to initiate the checkmate. His cock swelled at the thought of seeing her and the rest of his pieces as they took his brother's. Yet his chest tightened.

Why was part of him not engaged? He hadn't mated with her. The idea that a piece from his brother's board would have that pleasure heretofore set his hair standing. Indeed.

Or was his distress because a piece, possibly still standing on his brother's board, upset her? He glanced at her as she stood next to his king. No worry shone in her eyes. She was aroused but well. His muscles tightened and his teeth clenched.

He behaved irrationally. His fists clenched. He never acted such.

He couldn't back out without ridicule. He ran a shaking hand through his hair. He had played the game too well and was now required to play to the end. Cora would be the piece to initiate checkmate, and he had no choice but to stand and watch her fuck another.

Rupert didn't see his brother take the queen he sacrificed. He strode halfway across the board to Cora before they began to futter. He wanted this game to end with haste. Sweat pierced his brow, and his stomach twisted in knots. Would he be able to watch this? Her eyes, blue smoke, flashed as she saw him approach.

His teeth clenched as he inhaled her spicy sweet scent. Stepping behind her, he slid an arm possessively about her stomach. Her body quivered and her head tipped back to him. Why did she have to respond as a wanton to his touch? Damn it. He couldn't resist her. His fingers trailed the silk flesh of her thigh and around the curve of her bum. Her skin dewed with arousal, tightening his chest.

He clasped her hand that held the dildo in her bum and eased the prick into her. She pressed her body down against the phallus and moaned. The devil . . . his heart raced. Slowly, he pulled the stone cock out, watching her body quiver with each bit that slipped from her. His sex could enter in the stone prick's wake. *Stop!* His fingers released and the phallus dropped to the floor.

Taking a damp cloth from the servant behind him, he rubbed the soothing coolness down the crack of her bum, then dropped the used rag to the tiles. *Take a big breath, chap, and start. The sooner you end the game the better.*

"You have done well, Cora." His fingers found the slick entrance to her cunt and slid in. She tightened the spongy walls about him. His staff strained, imagining those strong muscles doing thus to his cock. Fire raced through his core and burned his lungs. Bit by bit he slid his thumb into her arse and pinched the flesh between. Her bottom arched back and she whimpered.

"You will be the piece to force checkmate." His fingers slid in and out of her. Peering over her shoulder, he watched her nipples strain and stomach muscles quiver. He squeezed his eyes shut. *Get this done.* "Do you know what that is?"

"I know what checkmate is." She squirmed.

His eyes snapped open. "In sexual chess, the remaining pieces on the winning team pick pieces on the losing team to futter. A mass fuck of sorts." Bloody hell, he didn't want to do this.

She nodded her head.

"Once you make the checkmate, you will futter the king as my pieces make selection. I will come for you once the game is done." His muscles shook with the force of this strange emotion.

Cora stood motionless, but her inner muscles clenched about his fingers.

"Cora?"

Blue eyes, wild and passion-filled, stared back at him. "I will think of none but you."

I will think of none but you. The words slammed into his chest, locking his lungs. He couldn't breathe. No one had ever said that to him, and he had never expected such. His throat constricted and he coughed to clear it. Leaning in, he pressed his lips to the balmy skin of her shoulder and closed his eyes. "Thank you," he breathed in a whisper.

He wanted to take her from here. To wash her body of the sticky arousal this game created and bring her skin to dew again as he fucked her.

A finger traced his shoulder, then down his side. His eyes shot open. Mary stood beside him, staring at him with pale green eyes and black hair flowing to her waist. At the age of two and fifty, she still brought men to their knees.

She gazed at the floor as a blush crept up her face. She knelt, trailing her hand down his and Cora's legs to grip their feet. Damn it all, what was she about?

"Mary?"

"Master Rupert." She stayed in her position on the floor and lightly stroked their legs and feet. "I have been watching Timothy this night, the king on your brother's board. A woman as old as I would never pique his interest off this board. I desire to fuck him."

A swap. Oh sweet devil. Mary was his savior. She would swap with Cora. He fought his lip's making them twitch so not to grin like a buffoon. All tension left his body, and he stared at her, unsure whether to cry or laugh.

Mary's eyes lit, a wicked smile on her lips; then she winked up at him. She knew. Any man, including Timothy, would bed her. Of course she knew . . . he wanted Cora.

"Stand, Mary."

She unfolded herself.

"Cora, Mary is to take your place for the rest of the game. Step from the board." Sweet devil. A smile that he just couldn't suppress tugged his lips. His heart raced. He would have Cora for himself. *Now end this quickly so you can leave.*

"Cross the board and stand next to the black king. Suck him until he shudders, then push him to the floor and mount him."

Mary nodded and strode off.

He turned, his gaze darting around the room. Where was Cora? He sighted her as she stepped into the retiring room.

Cheers rang out all around him. His pieces strode forth for selection, and he inclined his head to his brother.

His brother inclined his head back and mouthed, "Well done," from across the mass unfolding orgy. He could leave now.

He gazed at Mary once more, her head tossed back as she rode Timothy, clutching at his chest. She enjoyed her act. And Timothy, well . . . judging by the strain of his muscles, he was about to spend. Rupert made a mental note to send her a big arrangement of flowers and just maybe have Timothy deliver them.

Striding purposely down the wall, he stared at the large wood door to the hall and retiring room that Cora disappeared through. His blood rushed so fast through his veins he could concentrate on little else but possessing Cora. Members called after him to offer congratulations or favors he didn't want. He held up his hand and strode past to push through the door.

Cora stood leaning against the wall, grinning at him. Her strawberry-colored hair set off by the sapphire walls. Her blue eyes sultry. His siren.

"Well." Her head tilted to the side.

He grinned, his throat tightening as prickles raced across his skin. "Well indeed."

In two strides he pressed to her, their lips grabbed urgently for the intimacy they craved. Her hands wrapped up about his shoulders. The balmy touch tingling his skin as her naked body pressed to his.

Hard nipples pressed and rubbed the hair on his chest, sending molten fire pounding though him. He swept his tongue over hers, tangling, stroking, drinking in every moan and gasp she made. She tasted like good scotch, smooth with heat. His hands, wanting to know every bit of her, slid grazing the side of her silken breasts and down her curves to her hips.

By God, he'd gone mad. Mad for her. The need for her coursed through him. With each touch he needed more and more of her. He had lost control. Chills raced up his spine. Damn it. He pulled back and glanced down at her lips swollen from the force of their burning kiss. Beautiful.

"Mmmmm. Cora, Cora." His thumb pulled her lower lip, and he leaned in to trace the plump surface with his tongue. Heady. His head swam. He wanted to savor her alone.

"I want to take you home, lovely. Will you?" *And what if she says no? Control . . . take her, you half-wit.*

She tilted her head up, eyes flashing blue. "Now? No, my flesh throbs for you to fill me this instant."

Cora screeched as Rupert's fingers wrapped about her wrists. He hefted her up and onto his shoulder as if she were his right prize.

A huge grin crossed her face. He was anything but the ape she first thought. Not only were his motions smooth and graceful like a deer bounding through a field, his heart, his emotions held true and strong, though hidden. A silly thought, truly, since she had spent such a short time about him. But she would bet her toes on the emotion, and she adored her toes.

He set her down in the empty gaming room and bowed. "Go through that door." His hand motioned behind her. "Your clothing will be brought in. I will see you in the entry in a moment." He backed away from her, grinning.

Rupert Roland. Never in her maddest dreams had she envisioned taking him to bed. She shook her head. How did she have him so wrong?

Turning, she stepped with wobbling knees through the door he indicated and paced the coarse-tiled floor. Two candelabra cast a low glow in the sparsely furnished room.

She would dress and he would take her to his home and love her all night. Chills of excitement raced across her skin. Tonight had changed her life. She faced Matthew, regaining her pride, and she had taken control of her desire to be with a potent man.

A servant came forth in the dimly lit room and handed her a sack filled with her neatly folded clothes.

"Thank you."

She placed the cloth bag on a small table at the side of the room, opened the flap, and dumped the contents on the wood surface. Raising her shift, she pulled the soft garment over her head, letting the silky material tickle down her body. Did Rupert like frilly garments on his women? On her? Maybe only nudity aroused him. He didn't seem to care about her fading looks. She couldn't wait to find out. She absently clutched her petticoats.

A warm finger traced up her spine and she shivered, closing her eyes. Rupert. "Mmm, I thought you were to meet me in the entry."

"Heading out, were you?"

Damn and blast. She spun around and tilted her head back to meet Matthew's eyes.

"Come back for more, pet?"

Comprehension dawned and her eyes widened. He meant to have her. "Matthew." Her body tensed and she stepped back, sidestepping the table as he came forward and caged her against the wall. She braced herself against the barrier of human flesh and tried to slip under his arm. He was too large, too big, and he smothered her. She choked, gasping for air.

Relax, Cora. You stood your ground earlier. Use your strength again.

Sweat burned down her back, and she shook uncontrollably. Sweltering fingers wrapped about her arm, and with a quick jerk, he turned her face against the wall, pressing his body to hers. She shrieked as memories and emotions locked for years in her mind struggled to break free. She wouldn't let them.

The feel of his erection against the small of her back sent pricks of fear into her lungs. "Matthew, stop!"

"As soon as I sighted you, I knew you were ready for me again. Why else would you venture into my world?" Matthew cooed. Fluid from his erection seeped through her shift, sticking the fabric to her lower back and to him. The heat of his prick burned her skin, bonding the spot together.

Cora gritted her teeth. "Take your hands off me." Her heart closed off her throat. He would not let her be.

"Now, pet, why would I do that? You are displayed perfectly this way." His hand wrapped about her neck and pinned her to the wall.

She whimpered, struggling to breathe. If she could just kick him. Her lower leg thrust out trying to reach his knee, his leg, his ballock. Anything. *Please don't let this happen.* Tears sprang to her eyes and stilled. He would not force her to cry. She squeezed her eyes shut and fought down her fear and anger.

He chuckled. "You never could resist me." Touches slid down the curve of her waist to the swell of her bottom, and she squirmed to get away from him.

That statement rang true once. But no more. She would not have this, not with him.

She needed the right moment; then she would escape him. His fingers slid around to her stomach and pulled her shift up. The branding touch traced her scar. Ice ran across her skin, and she shuddered, unable to stop the frost that slid into her veins.

"The tear healed nicely. You were so silly then. Just wait,

you'll see, Cora. Our life will continue from this point as if that night never happened. God I missed you." He buried his face in her hair and tongued her neck.

Waves of disgust slashed up her spine and down her arms. "Don't touch me. I will not have this." Fresh tears welled in her eyes as memories of how he crushed her flooded back.

The pain in her heart and in her stomach returned as if that night happened yesterday.

The previous day her child had moved in her. She told Matthew, foolishly excited, and expected him to be happy. He was not.

"I will not take them. Matthew."

"The herbs are safe. You know I would not harm you, but you will take them if I have to force you. I will not share you, Cora. You will bring on your courses."

The scene played in fractured bits in her mind.

The air swirled as the stone-topped table flew across the room and hit the wall, shattering in his rage. His sticky hand hooked her arm, tears ran down her face, and she screamed as he hurled her naked body at that same wall.

She could feel the hard edge of the stone tabletop tearing the flesh of her slightly rounded stomach anew as the broken jagged edge dug into her flesh.

Tears gushed down her face, and she stifled a sob, choking as she lay on the floor. She clutched her stomach, and blood coated her fingers as he forced the drink down her throat.

In the end, the cut was mild; some would consider it a scratch. The drink had forced the cramps to come.

"I will not have you, Matthew." She straightened her spine and locked her jaw. "I wanted that child and you took the babe from me."

He pulled her away from the wall and slammed her back.

Her head hit hard and she whimpered, eyes fluttering as pain sparked her vision and blackness crowded in.

"There will be no more talk of something that never was."

"Say here, Dranger, get your hands off my property."

That deep animalistic rage in his voice reached through the spinning of her head. Rupert. He would stop this. Property?

Why did men assume that by sharing yourself, they owned you?

Her teeth snagged her trembling lower lip. How would anything be different? She would be just that, a piece of property. An unnamed person Rupert came to when his need arose. She let her emotions, her dreams, get involved this night. What a cake she made. Even if Rupert was different than Matthew, she wanted so much more than to be owned by him. Love. Respect. Those feelings she craved.

"Your property? I beg to differ, Roland. She has always been mine." Matthews's voice vibrated through her.

"No matter, get your hands off her. She does not want your attentions."

"You scoundrel, release me!" Cora inhaled deep and kicked back, landing a harsh kick to Matthew's shin. Abruptly he spun her from the wall and wrapped his arms about her waist.

Rupert Roland, the man who piqued her hopes, her desires, stood glaring with rage at the brute who had been her first love and major folly. She would have neither of them. Tears welled in her eyes, blurring her vision as her throat constricted. She wanted so much more than either could offer her.

"To the devil, Matthew. If you ever come near me again, you won't live to see the next light." Her whole body shook as anger and hurt poured out of her.

"And you . . . you, Mr. Roland . . ." Her lip trembled and tears rimmed her eyes. His eyes narrowed with concern, that same furrow between his beautiful green eyes. She couldn't. She still wanted him so badly. Her heart would break if she hurt him with words. The sticky hot air smothered her.

She had to leave. This night needed to end. Turning, she ripped from Matthew's grasp, clutched for the plush wool of her cloak on the side table, and ran for the entry.

7

"Cora! Cora, wait!" Rupert ran down the hall after her. She pushed out the front door before the greeter could open the heavy wood. A blast of the winter night air blew his hat from his head and burned his chest as he headed down the steps after her. Blister it, she had no shoes on. She would catch her death.

What just happened? Bugger Dranger. He would not let that bastard scare her off. He didn't know what happened between the two of them, but from what he overheard, their encounter had involved a child. A child she wanted.

That was the reason she shunned him in past years. She wanted nothing to do with men who mildly resembled Dranger. Well, he was not like him. Never would be. Dranger had always been a bit queer in the attic when it came to what he thought he was entitled to.

Cora ran down the sidewalk, her cloak billowing out behind her as her bare feet hit the ground in thuds.

He was three strides behind, heart pounding in his throat. "Where are you going? Damn it, woman, halt."

She threw him a look that screamed of pain and anger. He stopped still.

"All right, lovely. Take your anger out on me. Let out the hurt and frustration you have harbored for the last decade. But don't run from me."

She flung around, her eyes narrowed and her spine stiff.

"How dare you presume to understand me?" Her eyes flashed and her breath puffed out in visible smoke.

"Cora, I'm not like Dranger. I would never consider doing what he did to you." He stepped toward her, his arms aching to embrace her and take her home.

"What?" Her cheek twitched and she waved her hands wildly in the air. "You would never think of controlling me? Of locking me away so no one could see me? Or you wouldn't force poison down my throat to kill your child?" Tears slid down her face.

Bloody devil. His gut twisted. What had Dranger done with her? "Cora." He glanced around, and two groups of passersby stopped to gawk at them. "I won't discuss this here." He paced forward, wrapped his arms about her waist, and lifted her. She pounded on his chest, her fists hitting with loud thuds he barely felt. She stilled, then sobbed, a heart-twisting sound, and buried her face into the folds of his greatcoat.

"Shh, shh, lovely." The weight of her in his arms, the smell, he couldn't seem to get enough of it. He would be damned if he let her slip away, not when she finally gave him a chance.

His carriage stood in front of the club when he approached. He deposited her on the rust-colored seat. "Home," he called to the driver as he climbed up behind her. The door closed, extinguishing all light.

"I . . . I will not be anyone's property!"

"Shh." He leaned in and kissed her with all the desperation pulsing through him. Hard and unyielding, her lips did not return the caress. Damn it. His tongue traced the crease, and she moaned, opening her lips to his. He thrust in and his pulse soared. Her teeth caught his lips, biting hard, then softened to tangle and stroke his tongue with hers. Their lips danced across each other's, eliciting moan after moan. His head spun and he couldn't tell whose breath was whose.

The skin of his cock strained to bursting. He needed to be in her, to mark her, his. Waiting to spend in her fiery cunt all night pushed hell on him; his sack ached, wanting nothing more than her sweet cunny, but he needed to speak. He couldn't lose her. Pulling back, he stared down into her dimly lit face.

"Cora. I will never force you. Well, not unless we agree upon my domination previously. You do desire me?" He kissed his way to her ear, then pushed back and sat across from her, chest tight. If she said yes, nothing else would matter.

"Oh, Rupert. I . . . I . . ." She did. But could she trust her judgment this time to be different than the past? She stared at him across the carriage, his dark black hair and emerald eyes invisible in the dark box. Somehow, his body expressed the concern, the want and desire that went bone deep, so much more than mere lust.

"Don't answer with you mind. Feel your soul. Do you desire me?"

His voice sounded strained by emotion. She closed her eyes. She couldn't lie to him. Her soul wouldn't allow that. The want for him and him alone pulsed though her veins. Reaching out, she grabbed the lapels of his superfine coat and pulled him back to her side of the carriage. "Yes, I'm such a fool."

His breath came out in a whoosh, warming the air between them. "Now, lovely. You are no half-wit." He leaned in, inhaling her scent. The warm puffs of breath heated her skin, and she arched her neck to allow him better access above the collar of her cloak. He groaned, steamy flicks tracing the bend in her column of flesh.

She had wanted this for years. Tears swelled in her eyes and her body shuddered.

"My sweet woman." He pushed her hair behind her shoulder, and the moist touch skimmed along her jaw.

His woman. Her chest tightened. "I . . . I'm not—"

"You are. I will not own you, lovely, but you are mine. There is a vast difference."

He possessed her. She wanted this, a connection to a powerful man. Her life would never be the same. Could she do this?

His hand slid inside her cloak to cup her breast, and steaming pleasure washed through her.

"You will not work for anyone. I will give you anything you have ever wanted, Cora, including a houseful of children. Are you willing? Willing to accept my plight?"

Children. Her teeth snagged her lip. Could she bear a child? She was so old. But children. Having a babe was a dream she carefully denied with lemon halves for years. A dream she had but never thought she could make reality.

She raised her eyebrows. "Am I to understand you would not want me to pleasure others? That I don't believe. You enjoy watching."

He laughed. "Of course I will watch you. I am who I am, but in the end I alone will sleep in your bed." He pinched and twisted the rigid peak of her breast between thumb and finger. A gasp rushed up her throat as pain turned to delicious delight. Heat speared through her body, flooding her sex with moisture.

To be with one man again. Waking in his arms each morning. It was all the dreams Dranger had burnt to dust.

Deep down in her heart she wanted what Rupert said . . . and only him. There was a kind and gentle aspect to all of his moves. No one could fake that bone-deep grace, and the Hell

Knights respected him too. She was reckless to desire a commitment so monumental when they had just met. But she did.

The carriage rolled to a halt. Rupert stopped caressing her breast and opened the door in advance of his footman. Alighting from the box, he turned and scooped her off the seat in haste. She snuggled into his strong arms as he strode up the steps.

The grand house evoked a warm comforting emotion. The main hall shocked her as his butler closed the door behind them. The walls were painted a burnt orange and cream, and rich Oriental rugs covered the floors. This oasis opposed the typical bachelor home. The furnishings were chosen with care to accent the space and create a desired feel. Did he decorate this house?

"Edward, send up hot water for the bath."

"Yes, sir."

Cora snuggled into his coat and inhaled his smoky honeyed scent. She belonged here, smelling him. Where did the delicious aroma come from? She wanted to lick every part of him and find out. Her nipples hardened into tight buds.

"A bath?" Her fingers massaged into the hairs of his chest beneath his coat in a quest for his nubs.

"Yea—to wash the old memories away."

Bloody hell, he had turned into a milksop. His father had always said he possessed too many of his mother's qualities. *Painting is effeminate. You will fence or box, boy.* Quite. He rolled his eyes.

She snuggled closer into him as he strode up the stairs. Her hair, smooth against his face, tickled his hands about her body. He needed to convince her to stay. But how?

Turning the corner, he walked into his bedchamber and shut the door with a kick from his boot. He strode across the blue and gold carpet and deposited her on his large bed, wanting nothing more than to see her blushing body against the deep blue silk and linen each night. He inhaled a steadying breath.

She inspected the room lit by the candles his valet left burning for him. "This is beautiful."

"Indeed." If she only knew he referred to her presence here. He shouldered out of his coat and tossed the dark gray wool on the chair by the fire.

"And the paintings." She stood and walked to the gold frame above the fireplace. "I wish I could see them better."

His heart constricted. The painting was of a young woman sitting beneath a spring flowered fruit tree while a kitten played with the ties to her bonnet. He had painted the scene when he was twelve. "In the morning you can search the house until your desire to do so wanes."

She smiled but said nothing. She still hadn't agreed to stay the night or to stay for longer. *One step at a time, chap.*

"You will stay the night, lovely?"

"As you wish, sir."

He rolled his eyes. "Stop calling me sir. You sound like one of my bloody servants, and I would never bed one of them."

Her lips curved up into a mocking smile. "So you do have principles?"

He chuckled. "None where you are concerned. Please call me anything but sir."

"My Ape, then."

A laugh burst from his chest. "Your ape; well, ape is better than sir. And at least you used *my*." He winked.

A light knock came on the door to his dressing chamber, and his valet slid his head inside the room, staring at the floor. "The water is here, sir."

A smile tugged the corner of his lip. "See, no sir."

She laughed, a girlish sound that broadened his smile.

"You have a pretty laugh," he said as he walked to the dressing chamber door and stepped inside. She would follow without a doubt.

"You may leave, Jimmy. Have a good night's rest and don't wake me in the morning. Not for anything."

"Thank you, sir."

Cora's laughter bubbled up from behind him.

"Every time I hear your servants say sir, I will no doubt giggle."

He turned around and her lips settled on his, sucking his breath from his lungs ever so sweetly. "Mmm." His hands wrapped about her naked waist, and he kissed her back, taking his time to appreciate her. He would not rush this.

He ran the backs of his fingers along both her cheeks, then slid them into her hair. Their tongues coiled about each other. His muscles shook and his head spun. He needed her.

Scooping her up in his arms, he twisted his waist and dropped her into the steaming tub with a splash.

"Oh . . . It's hot." She scrambled to get out.

"Indeed." He wiggled his eyebrows. "Now sit back down so I can wash you."

She did so, sucking her breath in between clenched teeth. He drew his shirt out of his pants, showing her a hint of his flesh, then pulled at his cuffs. He slowly removed his arms from the sleeves and pulled the linen over his head.

She giggled. "You seem to be having difficulties. Would you like my help?"

Her voice was deep, and as he turned toward her, his breath caught. She lay stretched out in the tub, the water reaching the peaks of her nipples. A warm red flush graced her body.

"Indeed." He strode to the tub.

Her wet hands rose from the water and butted his knees, then trailed up his thighs. The touch lingered, caressing the hardness of his ridged arousal. His blood hammered through him. Her fingers grazed his stomach as she deftly undid the buttons of his flap. He tried not to jump, but his muscles sprung, awaiting the tug of her fingers across the sensitive skin of his cock.

Cinching the top band, she pulled his trousers down, popping his sex free. She leaned forward and wrapped the length in her hand. Sliding the skin forward and back, a drop of seed expended from the swollen tip. She stared at the pearl of dew, then stuck her tongue out and touched the hot tip, lapping the honey off him.

His eyes widened. "The devil."

Her tongue circled the head, and then his length disappeared, sunk into the hilt in molten heat. His hips jerked as she pulled back to the tip and swirled the ridge with her moisture.

"Mmm. You are as sweet as I imagined." Her eyes half closed, she licked her lips.

"Sweet, eh? Never heard that before. If you—"

He sucked in through clenched teeth as she swallowed him back into the sultry haven all the way into her throat. She was good. His sack pulled close to his body, spending more arousal into her mouth. If she kept larking him, he would choke her with an explosion of seed that had built up throughout this night.

He laced his fingers into her hair, and when she pulled back to the tip, he stepped back, popping his penis from her mouth. He stood, cock bobbling as he stared at her amazing red tongue as she sensuously licked her lips. She smiled like the skilled woman she was.

The devil, he was going to regret not allowing her to finish, but he needed to wash all the other touches from her body. To start anew. An ache settled in his sack. He would fuck her soon.

"I wish to wash you, Cora." He picked up the pitcher from the nearby stand. "Close your eyes." He poured a third of the warm water over her head. The water ran down her mane in streams into the tub.

He poured soap from a bottle into his hands. Starting at her scalp, he massaged the bubbly slickness into her hair and worked his way down the length to the ends. She moaned, sloshed back into the tub, and closed her eyes. The process took a while, but the time was worth it. The look of contentedness, of utter relaxation on her face, was worth delaying a fuck. He rolled his eyes. What happened to him? Milksop.

He shifted to the side of the tub and worked the lather down her neck, stopping to feel her beating pulse. The slow rhythm slid through him like a homecoming. Her muscles were fluid relaxation, and her eyes remained shut.

Small moans came from her lips as his hands washed her arms, stopping to rub each finger, her breasts. He watched as they pebbled anew under his soapy touch, and her stomach muscles jumped. Beautiful. Her body, her reactions to his touch, all perfection.

His hands dove deeper into the water and extracted her foot. The tiny toes so perfectly proportioned, the skin the softest he'd ever touched.

He rubbed every inch of her, letting his touch know her. Feel her. His fingers traveled up her thighs to her cunt and parted the folds. Her legs opened wide to him, knees braced against the edge of the tub; he thrust his finger into her opening and pushed deep. Surely she used something. A sponge or herbed cloth. No women in her profession would have attended the Hell Knights without. His fingers grazed a hard surface—a lemon half, cupped to the entrance of her womb.

His breath wavered in and out. "Cora." He wanted to remove the barrier and fuck her, damned the consequences, but he wouldn't without her permission. She needed to want to take this risk with him.

"Mmm." Her hips shimmied back and forth, riding his fingers.

"May I, Cora? May I remove the lemon?" He stared at her face, an expression of tranquility changed not one whit because of his question.

A smile tugged her lip. "Yes."

His heart beat in his throat as he pushed his fingers back into her sheath hard, pressing to the entrance of her womb. Finding the edge, he slid a finger beneath the lemon and popped the barrier from the opening.

His cock swelled. He would thoroughly coat her with his

seed. One finger pushed the crescent down through her sheath. The lemon half peaked her opening and she grimaced; then she sighed as the fruit popped out and floated to the tub bottom. He thrust his finger back into her and rubbed the walls of her cunny, washing the last of the lemon from her body.

When he finished, her eyes stayed closed and her breathing remained deep. She slept or was damn near close. He reached into the tub, wrapped one arm beneath her knees and the other around her back, and lifted her from the tub. Water fell in streams from her body and she shivered.

"I'll have you warm in a moment." He strode back to his bedchamber and deposited her on his bed.

Her eyes opened sleepily.

"Thank you, my ape. No one has ever washed me. It was heavenly."

He smiled at her endearment. Her ape. Where did she get that name from? If anyone else called him a monkey, he would have taken offense, but the way she said it—with a slight wiggle of her eyebrows, a curved lip, and a spark in her eye—heated him from the core.

He stared down at her on the bed. "Up on your hands and knees."

She instantly obeyed him. His tongue slid across his dry lips. Her beauty left him spinning. All he wanted was to sink into her from behind. The kneeling posture displayed the female form perfectly for futter. His hands could access her breasts, her clit, all while he watched his cock spread her lips and penetrate her pear-shaped swells. He wouldn't last long, not after this night.

Gripping her hips, he caressed her shape as he pulled her toward him. The bed he had custom-made for his height, for this act, so his phallus stood at the correct height to enter her. His hands ran up her back, over her shoulders, fingers trailing farther up her neck to brush her cheek.

"Rupert. Can I kiss you once before . . . before we start?"

"Indeed."

He leaned forward and she turned, flipping onto her back. His arms braced the sides of her and shook from the desire in her eyes.

"You're beyond words, Cora."

Her hands rubbed his shoulders up to his neck and framed his face as her head pressed up for a kiss. "And you, my ape, call out to me." Her warm breath mixed with his as their lips raked across each other. Nipping and gasping, they drank each other in. Cora . . . He would finally have her.

Pulling him down on top of her, she spread her legs about his hips. Her moist petals dampened the hairs of his sex, and she arched her hips as their tongues thrust in and out. Damn, she tasted heady. His body caught fire as, like a sinking ship, he lost himself in her storm.

His hands ran down her sides, needing to caress every bit of her soft form. They twisted, jerked, and urgently rubbed every bit of each other. To slow their fever, he braced his hands on the bed and pushed away from her body, but damn it, she held firm to him, drinking in every caress and wantonly demanding more.

He had no control. He didn't care. Fucking her would be nothing like all the others. They would come together as one. Not him taking his pleasure, but giving and receiving.

Muscles shook as she slid her hips up and down him, thrusting her tongue into his mouth, begging him to do the same with his cock.

His blood pounded through him, pulsating his body as he drifted in light-headed arousal. Each tug, rub, and caress of her body spent more of his essence onto her skin. The wetness between her thighs increased, and she moaned into their kiss.

Blister it; he needed to feel the balmy heat on his cock. His knees gained purchase, and he edged back, allowing his phallus to slide between her legs as his fingers found her nipples.

Good God, he needed to be in her. He struggled, shifting his hips back and forth to find her opening with the head of his cock. Scalding wetness slid along his prick and he stilled. He had found his home.

She nipped on his tongue and a contraction of her womb pulled at the head of his cock. His eyes rolled behind his lids in sweet oblivion. He pushed in. The flesh, moist and warm, gave way to sheath him.

He clenched his teeth, trying to slow his rising seed.

Her hips jerked up, and pain ripped up his back as her nails dug deep. He pulled back to the tip—forget slow; he needed her—and lunged into her slick welcoming cunt, sliding their bodies across the sheets.

She arched her hips to him. The molten pull of her cunny clasped his hardness, milking the essence from him. He bucked into her, encasing himself again and again, desperate for her to join him when he came.

The muscles of his stomach tingled. His sack pulled closer to his body. Her oiled flesh slid, pulling him to the brink. He slowed his stroke, probing deeper, harder, pressing to the entrance of her womb.

"AAAHHHHH," he cried out, the first of the relieving bursts of seed erupting from his body and coating her womb. His shout echoed as spurt upon spurt flooded her, slickening her sheath, his cock, and oozing out onto his sack.

His muscles shook, uncontrolled, and she thrashed beneath him. Grabbing him hard with her legs, her fingers scraped frantically up his back.

"Rupert!" she screamed. Her body arching in waves as her velvet warmth clasped him again and again. Her spend depleted her, and she stilled beneath him, nipping at his shoulder.

"The devil, lovely." He stared down into her blue eyes, flushed face, and wild raspberry mane, then placed a kiss on the tip of her nose. Squeezing his eyes shut, he buried his face in her hair at the crook of her neck and inhaled her scent. "I won't let you leave my life now that I have you."

Cora stretched. A smile repeatedly tugged at her lips. Rupert Roland possessed a kindness and generosity as a lover. Her lover.

They had fallen asleep, entwined on his big bed, him still inside her, and slept that way for hours. She wasn't sure when he slid from her body, but she awoke at one point her back to his stomach and a possessive male thigh about her hip. The most glorious feeling. She hoped to never lose the emotion again or him. Her eyes fluttered open.

"Hold still."

Her gaze shot to the direction of Rupert's voice. He sat in a chair by the side of the bed, sketchbook in one hand as the other one worked the paper with coal.

"What are you doing?"

"Drawing you."

Her eyes widened. He could draw.

"Hold still a moment." He reached out and tugged the sheet down a little to expose a bit of her scar.

"Cora." His fingers touched the hollow below her throat and slid down between her breasts, to her belly. "You stir me like no woman ever has."

She bit her lip. She would not leave him, and he needed to know.

"Yes, Rupert."

"I'm no longer your ape?" A smile tugged his lips. His hair stood all a mess. His harsh angled chin unshaven, but oh the spark in those green, green eyes. Her stomach flip-flopped.

"You're everything."

His eyes widened, pinning her to the bed with just his stare. "Am I?" His voice deepened.

Oh indeed, and more. Her tongue slid out and traced her lips, remembering the feel of his firm kiss. "I will stay with you, Rupert."

He dropped his sketchbook, stood, and stared down at her from the edge of the bed. His eyes held a million questions.

"Cora?" He leaned in and kissed her possessively on the lips. Her heart soared, and pinpricks raced her skin.

She wanted to stay with him no matter what. They would work though all of the questions, the uncertainty.

"My ape." She trailed her hand into the hair of his chest and down the line to his massive prick. He had filled her so thoroughly last night. The flesh between her thighs gushed with fluid she still felt. He was a potent man.

His hand trailed to her breast and pinched her nipple. "Yes, Cora. You will stay here?" He raised an eyebrow.

"I am yours, Rupert." She pushed up onto her hands and knees to show him he could have her any way he pleased, and this was how he wanted her last night.

She turned her bum to the edge of the mattress. His steamy hands rubbed the fleshy spheres, bringing them to dew. "Enter me, Rupert. Do with me what you wish."

He growled like a cat and dug his fingers into her hip. Her ruler of the jungle. She parted her knees farther for him as touches slid down her crack and two fingers entered her pussy. Arching her spine, she pushed her bottom up to him.

"You're still soaked with my seed." His fingers slid in and out, circling her clitoris after each stroke. Her muscles tightened and clenched, a slow heat building in her veins.

He pulled her back so her knees balanced on the brink of the bed. One of his hands pressed the small of her back and the other guided the head of his prick to her folds. Just parting her labia, he stopped and rubbed his hands over her bum.

"Cora. The tip of my cock is so red, so swollen as the apex parts the pink flesh of you. Can you feel your skin stretching, Cora? It is the most magnificent sight."

"Yes, oh yes." He was the widest ever to enter her.

He slid in a bit farther, stretching the tender flesh that greedily grasped for all of him. A groan shook her body.

"You're so slick. I'm going to keep you so filled with my seed." He plunged all the way in, in one fluid movement and sucked in through clenched teeth.

The head of his prick pressed to her womb. He pushed harder, grinding his hips to her bum. Slight delicious pain sparked her womb, and she cried out.

He slid back, pulling his prick to the tip of her again. "I'm so slick, so wet from you. Fuck . . ." His muscles shook and he slid back in hard, then gripped her hips and pounded in and out.

The forceful motions shook her body; her breasts jiggled, dangling from her in rigid painful peaks. She leaned down onto her elbows and buried her face into the cover of the bed to stifle her cries. Each press of his erection into her heated flesh spread waves of delight up her body. Tingling pleasure tightened the muscles of her stomach and legs, building the bliss.

She stared down between her legs and watched the motions of his thighs hitting hers, of his sack caressing her swollen clit each time he sunk in. She groaned as pressure pushed into the tight ring of her bum.

Bit by bit, Rupert pushed a finger into her. The sensation so delightful her teeth clenched tight. She screamed, trying to prolong the time before the waves caressed her body. She failed. The blissful contractions erupted, lashing her with heat. Her pussy spasmed round his prick. Her bum locked about his finger as blinding white light flashed. She screamed again as his pace increased and fisted her hands in the blanket to steady herself.

Abruptly he slowed, pulling the head to the edge of her folds as his prick pulsed. A burst of seed sprayed her lips and entrance, then ran down to coat her clit and dripped to the bed-covers below. He groaned and sunk all the way in, pressing his erection to her womb. Pulse after pulse beat the walls of her cunny as he once again filled her to gushing, tightening her muscles anew. A potent man. She squirmed as his finger touched her clit, and another flash of blissful contractions caressed her.

A steamy palm pressed to her lower back, and he pulled from her flesh, collapsing on the bed beside her.

"Cora."

She turned her head to face him. "Rupert."

They stared into each other's eyes. Their lips curved up and they broke into a fit of laughter. "Do you think we will ever leave this room?" Cora smirked.

"Not if I can help it." He pressed himself, already hard again, to her thigh.

Night of the Taking

1

1802, England's northern border.
The hills of the Black Cullen on the Isle of Skyas.

Stepping through the butcher's door, Jessica gagged as the smell of rotting meat and blood surrounded her. How vile! Her stomach clenched, revolting against the strange aroma.

The young man behind the counter hustled over. The smile, too big for his thin face, reached to the depth of his brown eyes. "Good day, miss. What ye be having?"

She looked down at the list in her hand. Oh goodness, did she really have to get these disgusting things for Cook's stew?

"Do you have pig's knuckles?" Her nose wrinkled.

"Sure do, miss. How many ye be wanting?"

"Ten, if you will."

He nodded his head and disappeared into the back of the shop. *Make haste, dear butcher.* She inhaled and her stomach rolled. Turning around, she hurried to the open door, gasping for the fresh air coming from the lane. The breeze tickled her nose. "Ahchoo!" Blinking, she inhaled again and her stomach stopped its revolt. The shopkeeper across the way closed his door and locked it. Humph. It was too early to close for the day.

"Is there something happening in the village this night?" she called to the back of the store.

"It's the Full Moon Festival of Catus, miss."

"Ah." Her lips curved up for the first time this week. A country festival would get her out of her aunt and uncle's clutches for a few hours.

"Here's ye knuckles, miss."

"Thank you." She wrapped her fingers about the string-bound cloth, and her hand grazed his blood-stained flesh. Her skin crawled and she tried not to shudder, for she did not want to offend him. "W-what is the festival celebrating?"

"The night of the taking." A sparkle lit his eyes and he winked.

Taking . . . "Taking of what?"

"The innocents, miss."

How strange. Her uncle jested about werewolves and black magic the entire trip to his cottage. Now the locals were talking of abductions and celebrating it.

Her brows drew together and she shook her head. It sounded like foolishness to her, but she would sneak out to the celebration, if for no other reason than to escape the long list of duties her aunt had for her. If she planned to attend, she needed to know more. She eagerly leaned toward the butcher, wanting to learn all she could about this strange gathering.

"So tell me the lore of this festival."

His face turned red, and he lowered his eyes. " 'Tis the festival for the menfolk to reminisce about the Catus and pay tribute to 'em. Once the sun falls, the runners come and take the ones they choose."

Her lips pursed. "Intriguing. So how do they know someone is innocent?" Jessica's cheeks grew warm. *It's not like you can tell by looking at someone.*

"By smell, I suppose." He shrugged.

Smell? Now she knew this was all for jest; no one could smell one's innocence, but the festival still sounded fascinating. Nothing could keep her away. "And what do they do with the ones they choose?"

"Don't rightly know, miss. I have never been chosen. But the lore says blood will be shed and pleasure like none ye will experience again will be 'ad," he said with longing in his voice.

"Well, maybe this year." She raised her eyebrows at the lad.

"I certainly hope so. I'm to wed in two mont's time, and then I won't be considered."

Had he realized what he just admitted to her? She found it hard to believe a man of his age, although young, was still innocent. But who was she to talk? She had reached the spinster age of eight and twenty and still held on to her virtue. And was beginning to doubt her choice. Humph. "What if someone doesn't want to go when they are chosen?"

"Don't rightly know, miss, but I have never seen them force anyone or anyone not want to go."

Her eyebrows drew together. They must do something pleasant with them. Why else would someone allow themselves to be abducted without a struggle? She tucked her package into her satchel.

"Will we see ye at the festival?"

"Indeed."

Turning, she walked from the shop.

Walking down the dirt-rutted street, she clutched the list in her hand. Her dress clung to her sweat-soaked skin, and she raised her aching arm to wipe her brow. Good gracious, this was a rustic little town. The shops were no more than five paces wide, and they looked like one strong wind could topple the structures down.

Looking across the lane, a harsh-featured red-haired man led a horse and wagon toward her. His build was that of a laborer, strong arms bunched and flexed under the fabric of his shirt, long lean legs encased in brown trousers. His dirt-smudged white shirt opened at the neck to reveal a sprinkling of what she imagined would be soft hair.

The shirt of the common man still shocked and stirred her. That glimpse of skin at the top of the chest was so tempting to touch. She bit her lip as he continued up the lane in her direction. Before her father's death, the only men she knew were those with shirts tied up so stiffly one wondered if they could swallow, let alone breathe.

Tears stung her eyes. Papa. She looked to the sky. Blast it. It had been nine years since he passed, and if he saw her now, he would turn in his grave. He had never intended her to leech off her relatives for survival, but her stepbrother and his heir had died with him, leaving the entire fortune to pass out of the family line.

Uncle Herman was nice enough but his wife . . . ugh. Her aunt had taken one look at her when she arrived this week and set off to give her the most revolting tasks. Like this—the feel of the butcher's blood-stained flesh as she grasped the pig knuckles assaulted her again. Her body shuddered and she grimaced.

If she could only find a husband, she could start her own life.

Maybe . . .

She glanced back at the redhead. His blue eyes met hers in regard and he winked. Her breath caught, her cheeks flamed, and she lowered her eyes.

No! No! Being reserved was not how a plain spinster would find a suitor.

She forced her eyes back up to see him smiling at her. Steadying herself, she drew in a breath—*you can do this*—straightened her shoulders, and winked back.

A deep laugh erupted from him as he turned and continued to lead his wagon past her down the street.

Goodness, she had actually flirted with him. Her whole body tingled with giddiness. Maybe he was unattached. She closed her eyes and imagined running her hands through his hair, the downy copper curls caressing her fingers, the salty taste of his skin as she kissed his lips and licked his cheeks. Umm, saliva flooded her mouth and she swallowed hard.

Her fingertips foraging through the curly hair on his chest, as she relished the springy coarseness, his heart would beat strong beneath her hands. She would explore every inch of him. She shivered with longing to feel the warmth of his skin.

Oh and his hands . . . He would touch her too. The labor roughened texture of his skin, dragging across her softness. The calluses on his thumbs scratching the sides of her sensitive breasts. Umm . . . gooseflesh rose on her sun-heated arms.

Those thick fingers would feel splendid squeezing her legs and tickling her bottom. Her corset dug into her armpits as she struggled to take in air. Her breasts felt squished. How strange that never happened before. She squirmed trying to find a more comfortable position, but the garment restricted her.

A humid breeze tickled her face and she imagined the tickle against her skin came from his breath as he leaned in to kiss her.

Her lips parted on a sigh and in invitation for the sweet harsh kiss she craved. How delightful to experience the touch and passion of another. Yet nothing happened. She bit her lower lip in disappointment and opened her eyes.

He was gone. What! Blast, where did he go? A frown touched her lips. Well, she couldn't expect to catch the first man she flirted with, now, could she? Sighing, she turned and continued to her uncle's with the package of rotting meat tucked within her satchel.

* * *

After finishing her chores and pretending to retire for the night, Jessica slipped out without even the tiniest of difficulty. She now had hours at her disposal. Her heart pounded and her cheeks hurt from the grin fixed to her face. It had been ages since she smiled like this.

The joyous murmur that filled the air lifted her heart. Someone was humming a familiar tune. "Ta ta tata ta ta tata." She started to hum along as she strolled through the stalls of the celebration.

Inhaling deeply, the smell of rich mutton stew and sweet wine filled the air and her stomach growled. Oh my! She placed her hand over her middle to try to curb the grumbling. She should have eaten before leaving for the festival.

The townsfolk had set up stalls to peddle their wares. The seller to the right of her sold paintings of all sorts of cats. Her eyes dwelled on a drawing of a woman with catlike features; the eyes were drawn as those of a cat and the ears came to a point at the top. Though the artist's skill was quite amateurish, in an eerie way it looked remarkably real. What an imagination.

Meandering farther down the street, the next stall peddled magic herbs of bat dung, fairy wing, and cat whiskers. She laughed out loud. What an odd theme of cat worship and magic there was in stall after stall.

She approached one of the tables and saw that the woman sold necklaces with glass beads that looked like cat eyes. How beautiful. Her gaze settled on one set that possessed the most intriguing shade of green. Running her fingers over the smooth surface, her stomach fluttered in a peculiar way.

The urge to purchase them, to remind her of this place and this strange festival, overwhelmed her. But she had only one coin and planned to buy something sweet. Her stomach growled as if a reminder. Placing her hand over her rumbling middle, she looked at the beads and bit her lip. The color was so unique. It reminded her of the first fresh leaves of spring, and she knew she would never forget them. But no, they weren't practical.

As she turned from the stall with reluctance, a man peddling glasses of blood stood before her. Her shoulders tensed and her stomach rolled.

"Take a smell, my dear," he said as he held out one of the wooden cups.

She recoiled, expecting the horrid smell of the butcher's shop to fill her nose, but instead warm spiced wine filtered through the air.

The man winked.

A laugh escaped her. How foolish. Her stomach gurgled. Handing the man her only coin, she grasped the cup and wandered to the green, settling herself to watch the sun dip below the hills.

As the townsfolk passed her in celebration, she heard accounts of giving blood to cats, making them bleed, and there was one sick account by an elderly man about losing his innocence to one. She had no idea how that would work, but he'd been truly in his cups and followed the comment up by vomiting in the street.

The sun settled below the mountain, casting the little village into darkness. Whoops and hollers came from all around her, and her heart began to race. This was the part of the festival the man in the butcher shop had talked about. Her mind floated in a wine-induced haze, and she shook her head; there would be no abductions this night.

Hearing flutes on the breeze, she trembled. The torches on the green sputtered to life as a scream pierced the air. She froze. My stars, was that a real scream? It sounded like one. Now would be the time to return to her uncle. It was past dark and soon some strange cat-killing ritual might start. She smiled. But would her uncle care if he found her gone? No. He would in all probability assume she had run off, and being tight on funds, he wouldn't even look for her. Tears stung at her eyes.

From across the green, a tall man strode toward her. Gooseflesh pricked her skin, and her insides tingled with anticipation.

Maybe it was the redhead come to persuade her for a kiss. Her lashes fell as she remembered the sparkle of his blue eyes as he winked at her. She smiled and her chest tightened. If he tried to kiss her this night, she would not stop him. She wanted to be touched, to feel warm breath against her skin as she did now. Wait . . .

Startled, her eyes snapped opened to see intense green eyes staring at her. Eyes exactly like the beads she had run her fingers over not an hour before. But this was a man, a man whose shoulders were a good foot broader than hers and stood before her now. Her stomach fluttered and darkness slid over her as a hood quickly cinched around her neck. The breath she tried to inhale was quickly expelled from her body as muscular arms wrapped about her and lifted her as if she weighed but a feather. The man groaned.

"Put . . . me . . . down!" she screeched.

She struggled and kicked but did not find purchase. He tightened his hold on her and growled.

The taking of innocents. Sweat slid down her back.

The hood reeked of herbs and mold. The aroma so potent her eyes watered. She balled her hands into a fist and pounded on the sinews of his back, to no avail. The stench of the cloth fogged her mind and the world spun. She reached up to grasp the hood, but numbness seeped through her limbs, and her flailing became uncontrolled and then stopped.

Her mind slipped further into the fog. Was this all a dream?

Her body started to shake, and he shifted her so that he cradled her in his arms. Would he harm her?

"Please," she cried out as tears leaked down her face. "Don't hurt me."

The man grunted and howled lightly, then slowly ran his hand up and down her arm. The gentle caress massaged as it traveled her body.

Her head floated in the sensation. How strange. She truly must have drunk too much wine because she could have sworn he was trying to soothe her.

2

Jessica strained her eyes but could see nothing except the black fabric of the hood over her face. She wanted to reach up, to tear the hood from her so she could see what was happening. But she could just barely move her fingertips.

Her limbs tingled and ached, and her mind still hung on to the fringes of fuzziness. But the familiar sensation of the swaying carriage was instantly recognizable. From the grunts and breaths in the box, she could tell at least three other people traveled in it with her. One was another female, another virgin, taken by the Catus.

She held back a fearful laugh as she recalled her uncle's warnings of the magic and werewolves that lived in the area.

The swaying of the carriage stopped, and a gush of air filled the coach. The smell of something like ammonia and blood penetrated the cloth of the hood and she gagged. Her stomach clenched. Ugh, disgusting. What was that horrendous smell? It smelled worse than stagnant water. Her eyes started to tear anew and she swallowed hard. She wanted to bury her nose in her hands to stifle the smell but still could not lift them.

The man sitting next to her wrapped his warm fingers about her arm and pulled her from the carriage, making her screech. He placed her feet on the ground, and she swayed, leaning into the firm grasp. She could actually stand. It required all her concentration but she could do it.

Needles pricked at her flesh as the blood rushed to her feet, and she knew it would only be a bit longer before she had the use of her limbs. Their destination must be near.

Grunts and growls mixed with crying and trembling breaths wafted about. The hair on her neck stood, and her body began to tremble with uncertainty.

Where were they? If only she could see.

The carriage ride had been too short to travel any great distance. The hand about her arm was firm and warm yet not demanding. The touch sent an odd sort of anticipation through her. He did not want to hurt her. It was as though he was escorting her to any normal event. Courting her.

He placed his free hand on the small of her back, propelling her quickly forward. Warmth spread from that spot straight down her legs. Oh what a feeling. She stumbled, but regained her footing.

He grunted three times, then growled. Strangely pleasant quivers coursed up her spine and tickled the hairs on the back of her neck. She knew she should struggle, but she couldn't. She was curious and wanted to know where they were headed and why her fear slid away.

A deep gruff growl came from directly in front, startling her. The voice did not come from the man holding her arm. Man? No man she knew had eyes like a cat. Maybe the wine had played tricks on her, but she didn't think so; they still communicated with grunts and growls very much like a cat. What were they saying?

The fabric of her skirt and petticoat lifted, and the cool night air pierced her stockings. She couldn't let them see that part of her. She screeched, her face flaming with heat as she struggled to push her skirt back down. Her arms flailed clumsily, still tingling with the flow of new blood.

Warmth brushed her thigh, and her eyes widened as the sensation dragged higher up her prickling leg. The man grasped her jerking arms from behind, restraining her, and laughed.

She stilled. His laugh could be none other than human. What were these things? Was this all a jest put on by bored or mad gentlemen? The touch brushed the curls at the top of her thighs. Her eyes widened in horror.

"Don't touch me!" She squirmed in his hold.

The warm breath of the man who held her curled the hair on her neck as his chest labored in and out against her back. She wanted to lean back into his warmth, to turn her body into him, and remove herself from this other caress. A tickle of moisture ran down from between her legs. How embarrassing. She twisted, not wanting him to see her leak, and tried to worm from his inspection.

The touch on her curls slid between her legs and into her lower parts. She turned her torso into the man who firmly held her, burying her head on his chest and biting her lip as a finger poked at her delicate flesh.

The man behind her growled in a warning tone, and the finger stilled, then left her body. She let out a breath and gasped for air. Thank goodness.

The man behind her loosened his hold on her and pushed her forward, her skirts falling in warmth about her ankles. In three steps, his arm wrapped around her middle and he draped her over his arm, lifting her away from his body and down. She dangled like clothes on the line.

Her body tensed. Would she fall to her death? The sound of water lapping against something solid rang loud in her ears. Her muscles trembled. Would she drown?

His arm released from her middle and she fell, screeching as her feet instantly gained purchase on rocking ground. She sucked in her breath and stumbled, reaching out for the arms that lowered her.

Instead of arms, her fingers clutched at a firm lean waist as it lowered into . . . a boat? Unfamiliar yet pleasant sensations wrapped about her arms, peaking her nipples, and she moaned. Her eyes widened in shock. How could touching someone's stomach create such intense sensation?

The man growled, and with muscles tense beneath her touch, backed her until a board hit her knees, forcing her to sit.

One second she trembled with fear; then the sensation turned to longing and curiosity. She shook herself. Madness.

The young woman to her left wouldn't stop sobbing. Instinctively, Jessica reached out in search for her hand until she touched the woman's rough tweed skirt. The girl jumped and screeched.

"Shh. I'm chosen too. Give me your hand."

The girl sprung to Jessica's side and clutched her arm to the point of pain.

"Can you see anything? I hate the dark," said the girl in a trembling voice.

"No. But they don't seem to want to hurt us. The man who chose me has been nothing but gentle." Yes, there was truth to her words and it puzzled her.

"Oh," came the girl's uncertain voice.

The boat moved and cool air fluttered about them. The hideous smell intensified; surely the aroma came from the water the boat traveled on.

Gooseflesh pricked Jessica's skin and she trembled. She was cold and wished now she'd grabbed her cape when she headed to the festival. Her summer muslin wasn't enough in the cool night air. She slid closer to the girl whose hand she now held and was startled as a warm blanket settled over her shoulders from behind.

"Thank you." The warmth wrapped about her. She inhaled and smelled spices and sandalwood. It smelled like a man. Like the scent she smelled in the assembly rooms when wrapped in a man's arms during the dance, but that was long ago when Father was still alive. She sighed.

The strong scent overpowered the horrid smell of the water, and she turned her face to hide her nose in the intoxicating scent.

A growl came by her ear and her stomach fluttered. Arms wrapped about her and the blanket, sliding her down the bench, forcing her to drop the girl's hand. Hard masculine thighs slid to either side of her from behind, their heat warming her legs through the thin, summer-weight dress.

She shook despite the warmth now coursing through her. Who was this man? His hands slid beneath the blanket, connecting with her ribs; he traced down the curve of her waist. Her muscles stiffened and heated, pulling away from the intensely intimate caress. My stars! She wanted his touch to continue. Her lungs tightened and worked with difficulty to draw air into the confines of her tightly laced corset.

His hands touched the crease at the top of her legs, then settled with firm weight on her thigh. The touch burned through the layers of her dress, and her heart jumped in her chest. Moisture tingled the flesh between her legs. What a strange response. She squeezed her thighs together to ease the sensitivity to his touch.

Fingers pushed to the crease and pulled her thighs apart. She crushed her legs together and his hand massaged. A bubbling sensation pricked through her muscles. Goodness. Her eyelids fluttered shut, and she relaxed her legs as the intense touch, the heavenly touch, continued.

A sudden jolt brought the boat to a halt. His hand brushed the curls at the top of her thighs; the flesh throbbed and she gasped. The pleasure of his caress on her body and skin overwhelmed her. She had missed being touched. The arms dropped from about her and he stood, leaving her cold and trembling, even with the blanket about her shoulders.

It had only been a few moments but her body wanted his caress to return. How could that be? She didn't even know him.

The short boat ride indicated they must have crossed either a river or a moat. Which? It was impossible to tell. She heard a scream, then a moan from somewhere far behind her. Her shoulders tensed. They did not sound like screams of pain. But why else would someone cry out in such a way?

The young girl next to her screeched again.

A muscular arm wrapped about her back and one slid beneath her legs and she rose into the air. The distinctively masculine smell wafted about her again. The man, or cat-man, who carried her was very strong. Through the blanket wrapped about her shoulders, the man's muscles flexed and locked about her.

"Umm." He cradled her like she was precious, as if he cherished her. Her body relaxed on its own into his embrace and the fear disappeared. This strange man who carried her soothed her. She felt safe. But why? None of her reaction to this man made sense to her.

His chest rose and fell as he breathed and her stomach fluttered. She slid her hand out from the covers. Reaching toward his chest, smooth silk met her fingers and she trailed her hand upward to his neck, where intricately tied stiff crisp linen lay. A cravat. A gentleman's clothes. Had she been right? Was this all some jest?

Sliding her hand around his neck to the back, her fingers met long hair wrapped in a leather tie, hanging down his back. Her brows drew together as the strands slid through her fingers like finely spun embroidery silk.

A growl rumbled deep in his chest and spiraled through her. Her heart sped. She wanted to know what this man looked like.

Was he the same green-eyed cat-man who dragged her from the green? How peculiar; she wanted this man to be him.

People rustled about them, and he nuzzled between the blanket and her head, reaching for the bare skin at the crook of her neck. The puffs of his breath scorched her shoulder and clouded her mind. The delightful sensation of being carried by this strong powerful man pulsed through her with every thought.

Something bumped into her leg and she winced. The cat-man hissed. Shifting his hold on her, his stomach rubbed against her hip as he jostled her. The friction tightened her thigh muscles and curled her toes in anticipation of more. Anticipation for more what? She shook her head. She had no idea.

After a few paces, a door closed and he lowered her to sit on a plush surface. The blanket fell from her shoulders, but the air was warm. A hot touch traced the edge of her bodice down around the top of her breast. Startled, her breath hitched, becoming shallow. Tingles shot through her breasts and her nipples hardened to a point. Oh what heaven! She knew she should push the hand away but didn't want to. A man had never touched her bare skin so intimately, and it had been ages since anyone showed her any affection.

Each of her senses strained toward this man. She could hear labored breathing as he stood before her. The warmth of the room now seemed almost stifling. Who was the man who caressed her? The smell of strong spices and male came from his skin. His hand delved into the hollow between her breasts, and with a soft touch, he stroked first one aching swell, then the other. A moan bubbled up her throat and he growled.

The urge to feel him overwhelmed her. She reached out and her hands met his legs. Below the thin fabric lay a large ridge along one of his thighs. Her fingers traced the thick projection as exquisite sensations shot through her breasts. Her hands shook. She wanted to feel the warmth of his skin beneath her fingers. Not fabric. His hand stilled and he made a purring sound as her touch firmed. When she reached the end of the ridge, it flared then narrowed to a point and wetness seeped through the fabric.

She squeezed her eyes shut. If she was ever going to be bold, this was the time. She needed to feel his skin, to know what it was like to feel a man beneath her fingers. She knew it was wrong but the desire pulsed through her at a maddening pace.

She moved her hands up to his waistband in search of his buttons. The muscles beneath his shirt jumped as she found the first button and slipped it from the hole. Trailing her fingers across the band to the opposite side, she undid the top button there as well.

Her hands shook with excitement and fear as she found the next lower button.

His warm fingers slid over hers. The heat and soft rub of his flesh against hers steadied the tremble so she could complete her task. Once she undid the last button, the flap at his crotch fell open.

Could she do it? Her breath jittered. She traced the edge of the fabric where the flap had been. Crisp curls of hair met her fingers and curled around the tip. His legs shifted apart, and she leaned in, placing her ear on his stomach to listen to his labored breath. He pushed his hips toward her, embedding her finger in the springy curls. The heat of his skin blazed with need beneath her touch.

The sound of the door opening caused a growl to vibrate through her, and his body disappeared from her touch. *No!* She dropped her hands to her lap with a muffled thud and fought with her conscience not to call him back.

"Pardon, sire," a woman's pert voice said. "I'm here to ready her for the rites."

Sire?

He grunted, then footsteps fell on the wood floor and the door opened and shut. Her breath came out in a whoosh. Why did he leave? She wanted to know him, to see him with her eyes, to continue the intimacy that they had created.

A pull came at the cord securing the hood over her head and then it lifted. She blinked as her eyes adjusted to the light. The young girl wore a maid's uniform of dark gray and white.

She curtsied and smiled. "Mum, I'm here to prepare you for the rites."

"What are the rites?" Jessica stared at her.

"I'm sorry, mum, I'm not allowed to say."

Humph. Jessica looked around the room as the maid unbuttoned her dress. The fabric lifted from her body, and the maid's fingers tugged and pulled to unlace her stays. Burning candles lined the room, casting a warm glow on stone walls hung with tapestries.

Her eyes widened as the scenes of naked men and women, doing shocking things to each other, filtered in through her mind. She shivered as the sensation of the man touching her breasts returned to her.

The stays pulled from her body, and she stood in nothing but her chemise and stockings. The images intrigued her; she had always wanted to know about the mating act, and being a spinster, she had given up hope.

The man's sex stood straight out from his body, and in some of the scenes it pushed between the woman's legs, sometimes from behind, sometimes from the front.

A tingling pricked the flesh between her thighs, and she shifted her stance. Over thirty scenes in total graced the walls, and in each one, the man and the woman mated in different positions.

Her breath caught as her gaze settled on a scene vividly depicting what the man's sex intended. The woman lay on her back with her knees bent and legs spread wide to reveal a hollow between her thighs. The man stood between her legs, and his sex pressed into the opening.

Jessica's heart sped and her nipples tightened. That ridge she caressed on his thigh was his sex, and the curls she felt with her fingers was the hair his phallus sprang from. She was a mere touch away from discovering what his sex felt like. The heat of the skin beneath the curls of his sex had scorched under her touch. What would it feel like to have that thick heated ridge pressed into her like the women in the tapestries?

"Raise your arms, mum."

She raised her arms and her chemise lifted from her body. Oh my! She knew it would feel good. How could being so intimately joined bring anything but pleasure? Her skin burned with excitement and fear. She looked down at a light shade of pink gracing her skin. Did she want to experience loving here in this strange place? She bit her lip, the question swirling in her mind.

The maid pulled out Jessica's hairpins and ran her fingers through the long tresses, spilling it over her shoulders.

"Please stand over the basin so that I may wash you for the ceremony."

Jessica hesitated; the maid was going to wash her. She eyed the small shallow tub. Had she a choice? Not if she wanted to learn what the rites were.

With her legs straddled over the basin, the maid lathered the soap and washed Jessica's legs. The higher the slippery cloth wandered, the more her muscles jumped and tightened. She stared at the couple mating in the scene on the wall. "What is this ceremony?" she asked again.

The maid remained silent.

The cloth skimmed up to the top of her thigh and a prickling sensation bubbled through her body. The rag grazed over her private place, and her flesh throbbed as intense pleasure flooded that part of her body. She gasped.

Without a doubt the pictures on the walls somehow made her sex more sensitive.

The maid smiled. "They will be pleased with you, mum."

She gazed down at the top of the girl's head. What a strange thing to say. "Why?"

"Your reaction to the tapestries. You are aroused."

What? "I don't understand."

The cloth parted the folds between her legs and brushed between. Her eyes snapped shut and she trembled with heated pleasure that weakened her knees. She sighed and savored the new experience. It was a bit embarrassing to have someone wash her so, but at the same time, the sensation was splendid.

The maid stood and reached for a bottle filled with what looked like oil. Pouring it into her palm, she knelt, rubbed her hands together, and ran her fingers through the curls and folds of Jessica's sex. Waves of intense need pulsed through Jessica, and the muscles between her legs clenched in a blissful, rolling flash of light. Her vision hazed. *My stars, what was that?*

The maid stood and smiled. Grasping the folded white robe from the stool, she wrapped it about her.

Jessica stumbled to the only chair and sat. Goodness. This entire night was just beyond her imagination.

A knock came on the door.

Would it be her captor back to claim her for this ceremony? She wanted it to be. Her curiosity over the feelings he provoked in her was too tempting to let go. The door opened, and to her disappointment, a boy entered with a tray of fruit, cheese, and wine. He placed it on the now-empty stool and left. She sat and ate while the little maid gathered up her clothing.

A faint screech reached her and then the sound of a cracking whip. The hairs on her arms stood and she closed her eyes. Was that part of the ceremony? Would she be whipped? Icy sweat lifted the hairs on her neck, and she jerked to her feet in fear.

A loud gong sounded and the little maid stood.

"It's time, mum. Please come with me."

Jessica hesitated, the sound of the whip ringing though her mind. She glanced at the door; if she wanted to see her captor, she needed to go. Anticipation of his touch drowned out all her fear, and she left the room with the little maid.

3

They entered the hallway, as others did from rooms scattered along the long corridor. The stone floor chilled her bare feet and she trembled, her nipples pebbling beneath the thin covering of her cotton robe. Jessica stood on her tiptoes trying get a glimpse of the hall ahead of her.

Torches lined the hall and at the end, the corridor opened into a large chamber filled with golden light. Ten women and maids stood in a line stretching the length of the hall. She stood in the middle.

"Let go of me!" The curly brown-haired petite woman in front of Jessica struggled with her rather large maid in an attempt to flee.

She recognized the woman's voice as the girl from the boat. Odd as it was, she never even considered escape. Where would she go? They were in some sort of castle, and there were too many people about. Moreover, her curiosity about the rites and her captor made her stay.

A large man in shirt and waistcoat approached with a length of silk rope stretched between his hands. He grabbed the woman's wrists in one of his hands. "'Tis all right, miss." His voice gentled as, with quick jerks, he bound her hands as she sobbed and struggled.

Jessica's maid glanced at her. "Don't worry, mum, she will be excused from the rites. They will not force anyone to participate. There truly is nothing to fear."

Jessica bit her lip and watched as the small woman quivered with fear, fear she didn't feel herself. She believed her maid; this place did not scare her.

Staring at the man as he led the woman back to one of the rooms, she searched his face, looking for cat eyes. His gaze settled on her briefly before passing. No, his eyes were normal, plain brown human eyes. Hmm. Maybe the wine she drank played tricks on her. She had just admired those same green eyes in the glass beads at the fair.

The gong sounded again and her shoulders trembled. She wanted to see what lay at the end of the hall. The line of women slowly paced forward. Following one after the other, they traversed a long hall; white robes billowing out in the pathway as a slight breeze pushed against them.

Jessica's heart pounded in her ears. What lay ahead? She wanted her captor to appear, to take her and touch her breasts the way he had in the room before the maid entered. The air turned warm and sweet as lilacs as they neared the light at the end of the hall.

Reaching the main room, the remaining women were ushered down a series of curved stone stairs to a center circle. In the middle stood a single wooden ladder-backed chair with no arms and a stone table like altar. She imagined some sort of offering happening here.

Her skin tingled with anticipation as her imagination went wild. What would happen in this room? Would she witness the scenes from the tapestries? Or was this ceremony for something more sinister? No, nothing had happened thus far to indicate anything harmful would occur. Just the contrary, she had only experienced bliss from a man she never laid her sight on.

Two large black-painted doors opened to the right of them, and a line of naked men and women of varying ages entered. Jessica's gaze locked on the first woman's eyes and her breath caught. Deep blue cat eyes. She studied the next person who entered and the next one. Each of the naked beings possessed cat eyes, and their hair hung in long tails down their backs. She hadn't imagined it. Where was her captor?

Her gaze darted through the crowd, searching for the intense green eyes of the man who possessed her in town, but he was not among them. Dash it. She inhaled deeply to squelch her disappointment. Had she imagined those green eyes?

One naked woman strode to the center of the circle, and the rest of the cat-people filled the tiers lining the room. A bang came from above and Jessica looked up.

Above the center of the room hung a circular balcony filled with older cat beings. A reddish-haired man with thick gray streaks in his hair slammed his cane on the rail once more. Everyone looked up and the room hummed with concealed excitement. Every nerve in her body tingled as if a feather caressed her skin. She could do nothing but await the upcoming rites.

The woman in the center was beautiful, with long multi-colored hair that hung in a straight line to her waist, like a tail on a calico cat. Dark peach nipples stood at a point on her breasts and red hair flamed between her legs. Jessica wet her lips. What was to happen with this beautiful woman?

The calico growled and grunted to the crowd, and when she turned fully to Jessica, her eyes flashed a crystal-clear blue with an oblong center that grew. Just like the eyes of the man who had carried her from the green.

Her facial features were human but with subtle differences—the nose had a thick bridge, a deep ridge below her nose possessed the same hue as her lips, the top of her ears came to a point and she possessed no earlobes. The painting she saw in the village had not been one of fantastic imagination. The artist had seen these beings. It was almost too fantastic to be real.

A gong rang three times, and the woman motioned to the other side of the room. The young virgin men stepped forward into the circle. They were dressed in black robes and lined up facing the calico.

She motioned to the virgins' companions, and each robe opened up the front, revealing the young man's sex standing straight from his body, like on the tapestries. Jessica's eyes widened and she worked to force her jaw not to drop open. Goodness.

She shamelessly studied each man's manhood. They possessed different lengths and widths, one of them even curved to the side. Her chest tightened and her skin dewed. She had never considered that they might be different. Fascinating. How many women ever knew this fact? Most women would only ever see their husbands.

The calico walked down the line sniffing the air, then pointed to one man with red hair and to the one with the curved sex. Both came forward with easy smiles on their faces. They did not appear frightened; in fact, they seemed fascinated by her. Their chests rose and fell and the one with the red hair kept fisting his hands as if to keep from reaching out to touch her.

She circled them, then reached out and grasped their manhood, one in each hand.

"Oh God," the redhead said, and he closed his eyes.

The other groaned, his buttocks clenching as he spilled his seed onto the floor.

My goodness. Jessica could not tear her gaze from them. Her heart pounded so fast in her chest she could see it in her breasts, and she could barely catch her breath. Did that happen often? How amazing that a man could spend his seed just from the touch of a woman's hand.

Smiling, the woman released the one with the curved sex and pulled the redhead to the chair, pushing him to sit. He did so, staring at the calico with heavy-lidded eyes. The one with the curved sex returned to the line, his face the color of a cherry.

Jessica's breath hitched as the woman clutched the man's erect shaft and stroked from base to tip. Her hand rotated about the top and the redhead groaned. He reached up and cupped the woman's breasts and the calico growled.

This was the rites and Jessica's desire to view this act as she'd viewed the scene on the tapestries shocked her. She wanted to see the mating of a human with her own eyes. The image of the man's phallus pressing into the hollow between the woman's legs from the tapestries flashed before her.

Blast it; she was not quite close enough to see if his staff slid into her body, if she could only move a little closer. Shifting her stance and inching a bit, she found a better view.

The young man's phallus swelled and the tip turned a more intense red. The calico straddled the chair, trailed her hands up the man's chest, and kissed him with an open mouth. He returned the kiss with equal ardor. Rocking her hips with each move of her mouth over his, the flesh between the calico's legs shimmered with moisture . . . Or was it the oil? Her fingers circled the man's nipples, then pinched.

Ouch! Didn't that hurt? Jessica rubbed her hand over her pebble-hard nipples, trying to imagine that kind of caress.

The redhead groaned as if the touch pleased him, then reached out with shaking hands and grasped the woman's waist. He obviously enjoyed the pinch. Did women as well? Her fingers lightly plucked the buds beneath her cotton robe and she gasped. A stingy pressure radiated the nipple, yet her body trembled. How odd.

The redhead's fingers clutched at the calico's flesh, grinding each press of her hips against his stomach. A low rumble of a purr came from the calico, and her hand traveled down his stomach to his penis. She clutched the stiffness and squeezed. The redhead's head jerked, hitting the back of the chair, and his body arched toward her.

That touch seemed to startle him, but he didn't push her away. The calico slid her hand up and down the skin, slipping back and forth. Jessica wanted to know what a man's sex felt like. It looked hard and stiff, just like her finger, but a penis didn't possess bone. After the curved-sex man had spent his seed, it had collapsed. Hmmm.

His hands slid to the calico's bottom and massaged as he pulled her toward him. The tip of his sex pressed to the woman's glimmering lips, and with a small thrust, the deep red point disappeared inside her body. He inhaled through clenched teeth and the calico cried out, sinking down fully into his lap as she tossed her head from side to side.

Amazing. His sex thrust right in. Wetness slid down Jessica's leg from between her thighs. Oh, that strange delightful sensation. The dew coated her sex and the flesh tingled. She wanted to reach down and touch herself, to feel that hollow and find out why it now grew moist when viewing such an event.

Growls resounded throughout the room, pulling her attention to the fact she was not the only one watching them.

Oh goodness, what are you doing? Glancing around at the others in the chamber, a good two feet lay between her and the rest of the virgins. Her cheeks blazed with warmth. This should be a private act and she ogled them.

Tilting her head down, she inched her way backward toward the line. Only a couple more steps and she would stop making a spectacle of herself.

Sliding one more foot backward, she collided with a large male. A long ridge pressed to her buttocks; recognizing it as his sex, she gasped. Spices and sandalwood enveloped her. He was the man who had carried her. Her captor. Chills raced her skin. She wanted him to touch her.

A gentle finger slid beneath her chin and raised her head to watch the calico and redhead. Her eyes fluttered as heat spread through her so hot she couldn't hold back the groan that came from deep inside her.

The couple in the center panted and growled, clutching each other as the calico raised herself up to the tip of the man's stiff rod and sank back down.

Jessica shamelessly watched as the gentle finger beneath her chin stroked her in the same rhythm as the mating taking place in the ring. The need his touch created in her was exhilarating. Her nipples ached and her knees weakened, swaying her body back into his.

His naked length pressed to hers and bubbles of delight coursed straight through her body. Everything about him was different than her. His strong hard muscles pressed to her soft flesh; his coarse hairs tickled her smooth skin.

Trailing his hand to her throat, he found her pulse, then with a feather-light touch stroked it. She bit her lip and trembled. Why did his touch affect her so?

"Oh . . . my . . . God!" the redhead cried out as his body clenched, and he held the calico seated in his lap.

The calico purred.

Jessica held her breath, wanting the eyes of this man who touched her to be the green she saw in the village. She turned her head toward the man. Intense green cat eyes observed her. He was her captor. She hadn't imagined those eyes.

He had wanted her to watch this event, the rites. Her chest rose and fell and her heart raced. Did he intend to do this act with her? Her head spun at the scandalous thought.

Goodness, he was handsome, with reddish-brown hair and a narrow nose.

He grunted, stepped beside her. With his head he indicated the couple in the center.

Masculinity hung in an aura about him; he stood naked, his chest sculpted like lean marble and his shoulders held broad. Her hand rose as if to touch his chest, but with so many people around, she didn't dare.

The distinct sensation of him carrying her returned. She swallowed hard, then licked her lips to moisten them. Letting her gaze travel lower to his abdomen, she viewed a sprinkling of curled ruddy hairs.

His stomach muscles clenched and he growled. Before she could look lower, he turned and descended through the crowd. The people standing in the great room parted to let him pass.

No! Don't leave again. Her eyes focused on the muscles of his well-shaped buttocks as he disappeared into the crowd.

The tingling sensations of his touch lingered as well as the dampness between her thighs. Closing her eyes, she imagined him fondling her breasts the way the redhead in the center had cupped the calico's. His green eyes watching her every expression as he weighed the round swell of her bounty. She trembled. Oh how she wanted that actual caress.

Turning her gaze back to the ring, she gasped. Every cat eye in the room stared at her; even the woman in the center of the ring turned her way. The man she still straddled looked up at her too.

Her face flamed with heat. Oh God! She wanted to hide at her shameless desire to learn this act and to take in the naked form of their bodies.

The redhead smiled at her, then winked. Blast it. He was the redhead from town. Her face grew hotter still. How embarrassing. She looked down, trying to hide her discomfort. What a bizarre evening.

She searched the crowd again for the green-eyed man. After years of preserving her virtue, why was it she now didn't care if she gave her innocence to one of these cat-men? Well, at least she didn't think she would mind giving it to the green-eyed gentle one.

Abysis strode through the crowd. Damn it, now that he'd found his queen he did not want to wait until the female Felis finished with their rites. He clenched his teeth. It was for the best; he knew that. Watching the eager human male spend his seed deep within the Felis womb relaxed and readied the female humans for the male Felis vigors. He'd waited so long.

Abysis could sense all eyes on him. They knew his queen was present. How could they not? He'd entered the common room with his cock erect, something only the queen could do to him. All other male Felis could mate with any human female. Many of his years already knew the delights of spending their seed in the warmth of the human womb.

He had never experienced that thrill.

His curse as the heir to the Catus was that only the one woman the goddess chose for his queen could arouse him, and she was here. He rolled his shoulders and everyone gave him space. His body ached for release, craved the caress she began in the preparation room.

His cock strained, remembering her shaking hands as she undid the flap of his trousers. He'd wanted to shed her innocence there and then and start his life. Damn the rites. No! It was good Sophie entered to prepare her. The rites were important. Without them their kind would have died off years ago.

He needed to wait, but he'd searched for years for her, participating in every corral, and never had his flesh stiffened and grown. Tonight it did. He glanced down at his swollen flesh—it was agony to stand here watching the rites, while his queen stood among the offering.

He turned and glanced at the line of virgin women, his gaze

instantly locking onto his queen. Even being heir did not guarantee him the innocence of her. His fists clenched.

Any one of the older males who went before him could select her. That was why he made the spectacle of touching her during the rites. Now they all knew their queen. He ground his teeth together. And curse the Felis who would dare cross him by choosing her from the line. His fingernails dug into the flesh of his palm, and he glanced at the elders.

Unless the elders took pity on him and allowed him to claim her first, he would have to wait through three male selections before he could claim his fair-haired queen. Though, he thought the elders enjoyed seeing him acutely hard, his cock bright purple, slapping against his thighs as he walked. He doubted they would yield. This was, after all, tradition.

He wandered to the back of the crowd. Watching the rites only heightened his arousal, and he needed none of it.

He inhaled a tense breath, and the smell of her desire filled his senses from the other side of the room. The tangy aroma hung in the air so heavy he could taste her. His tongue traced his lips, gathering her scent. She was delicious. He couldn't wait to lick her slick flesh and taste the thick cream that coated her.

Desire for her touch, to make her his, pushed through him. He spun on heel and stepped toward her. He needed her.

No, damn it! He turned back around and growled through clenched teeth, causing two Catus standing nearby to flinch. His muscles shook as he forced himself to remain on course and head for the back of the room.

He could not break all the rituals, and it required all his strength not to bury his cock in her out of the circle.

4

The rites continued for several more female cat-eyes. What else should Jessica call them?

Throughout the selections, the procedure remained the same. A cat-eye would select one or two humans from the line and commit the mating act with one of them for the audience, spilling the evidence of their innocence on the floor of the circle. The cat-eye in the center and the human they chose would then leave the room. What they did after that? She had no idea.

She shifted her stance and delightful twinges filled her womb. Her mind and body hummed to the sensations coursing through her. Her nipples stood erect and a pulse beat between her legs. She never dreamed watching people in the act would cause her body to respond in such a way.

She was not the only one affected by the rites, and each labored breath that hung in the air caressed her nerves, increasing her excitement. All the male cat-eyes' sex stood erect. One of them even stroked himself until he spent his seed as one couple mated in the ring. He had truly enjoyed himself, growling as he discharged, then purring after. It was strange to hear that purr, a genuine cat sound, come from someone who at first glance anyone would take for human.

The aching flesh between her thighs pounded, wanting the caress the maid had provided with the cloth while preparing her. Could she achieve the same delight by touching herself on her own? She glanced around the room. No, she couldn't touch herself intimately here. In the privacy of her own room she would experiment with touching herself, but not now. She rubbed her thighs together again and trembled.

A male stepped into the circle, and the remaining two male virgins walked from the room. Her eyes settled on this first gruff male cat-eye. He possessed long multishaded black hair and golden eyes; the same black hair covered most of his body in small tight curls. His shoulders, as broad as the green-eyed man's, seemed to have a roughness to them.

Nothing about this man excited her. She hoped he wouldn't pick her. She scanned the crowd. Would the green-eyed man participate? She hoped he was not merely viewing the rites, as so many of the cat-eyes were.

Her maid placed her hand on Jessica's arm. "It is time, mum." Then she pointed to the front of the circle.

Jessica's eyes widened. She would now participate. Her hands shook as she stared at the cat-eye in the center. She did want to see her captor again and to experience his touch, but what if this man chose her? If she did this, she would have no choice of who she gave her innocence to.

The maids led the nine women to the front of the circle and one by one opened the women's robes. The cool air caressed Jessica's heated naked flesh and goosebumps raced across her skin. Her hands fisted and her cheeks washed with heat. She wanted to close the robe. Never had she stood naked in front of this many people. What was happening to her? She was still willing to stand here. To allow these people to see her like . . . like this. To risk everything she knew for the possible touch of her captor. Was she being foolish?

The gruff one paced in the center as he surveyed each virgin in the line. The gong rang and a vice locked about Jessica's lungs. There was no going back. She nodded her head to herself. Indeed, she would stay in hopes that the green-eyed one would be the man she yielded her favors to.

The gruff one strode to the beginning of the line and slowly raked his gaze over each woman. Growling, he smelled the air and touched the first woman's black hair. He did not touch any other part of her, but the woman's hands trembled, and when he touched her, she gasped.

Jessica stood in the middle of the line and tensed as he grew nearer. He kept glancing at her from the corner of his eye, and the hairs on her neck stood. He did not look at her like he desired her. There was something else in his eyes, but just what emotion she didn't know.

To her right, the whole body of a plump woman quivered as he inhaled the scent of her. Growling, he ran his hand through her red hair as his head jiggled and he kept sniffing her. He appeared to like her scent.

His touch trailed down her arm and she gasped. Wrapping his fingers about her wrist, he pulled her into the center of the circle.

Jessica let out a tense breath. Maybe he leered at the plump woman and not her. He may only pick one woman; two of the cat women did that. *Please let him only pick one.*

He returned to the line and she cringed. His eyes narrowed as he approached her. He puffed out his chest and inhaled her scent. His breath wafted against her skin, and gooseflesh rose in a wave of unease.

Please don't let him pick me.

Jessica closed her eyes and held herself still. Her body

pulsed to the rapid beat of her heart. He ran his hand through her blond hair, and a rumble came from deep in his chest. The hair on the back of her neck lifted.

Please, please, please . . .

She opened her eyes as he hesitated and then turned and went on to the next girl in the line. Her breath came out in a whoosh.

Thank goodness.

He did the same thing until he reached the last girl. Turning, he gazed at all of the women standing before him. His shoulders straightened and he rolled his neck. Striding back up the line, his eyes fixed on her.

He was coming for her.

Her stomach knotted and she couldn't breathe. Shivers cascaded up her spine. Stopping before her, he reached out and grabbed her hand, pulling her with such a force she shrieked and stumbled into the plump woman in the center of the ring.

"Pardon." She glanced at the woman's startled face, then turned to face the gruff one.

Jessica's hands began to shake with nerves. She tried to swallow, but her throat closed and she gagged.

This can't be happening.

The gruff one strode around them, circling. Jessica's heart thundered in her ears, her eyes riveted on the large red phallus protruding from between the gruff one's legs. It looked smooth with a large ridge down the center and around the tip, in a fashion like an arrow. Her gaze scanned the crowed but the green-eyed one was nowhere. The gruff one stopped before her and made a noise low in his throat.

The cat women had acted bold toward the human men. Was she supposed to do the same? Should she step forward and grasp this man's sex in her hands? She looked at the large red sex with black hair all around it and shuddered. No, she couldn't do it. She didn't want this man. She closed her eyes.

Lord, let him pick the plump woman.

A loud howl rose from the back of the room. Jessica's eyes shot open. Everyone turned in the direction of the sound, and the crowd parted to reveal the green-eyed one as he entered the circle. His eyes flashed as he looked at her standing with her robe open. Heat bloomed through her body with excitement. Was he here to claim her?

This man intrigued her; she would gladly give her innocence to him. He placed himself between her and the gruff one, then turned his back to her and blocked her sight of the other man.

A deep growl wracked his body. The gruff one growled back. She saw every fine fawn-colored hair on her protector's back stand on end as he inhaled a breath that sounded just like a hiss. Oh my! The gruff one growled low in his throat twice, then laughed. Laughed! How odd.

The green-eyed one spun around to reveal the gruff one on his knees with his head bowed. With eyes wild, his gaze swept her. Leaning forward with a growl, he sunk his teeth into her neck. Pain shot through her and she cried out.

His arms came around her and he nuzzled her neck and licked the blood dripping from her wound. Every muscle in her body quivered, and wetness leaked from between her thighs.

How could he have bitten her? Yet her whole body seemed to crave him with an overwhelming desire. All she wanted was him to hold her and to feel his caress. Her stance opened, parting her legs to him. He pushed a thigh between her legs and clasped her to him. Leaning her head into his, he licked her neck with his tongue, each flick in unison with the quick shallow puffs of her breath.

His thigh rubbed against the flooded flesh between her legs, and light flashed before her. Her hips sliding against him as pleasure sparked from her every pore. Oh, that same sensation the maid had created. Her head swam and her vision clouded.

He raised his head and stared her in the eyes. *"You're mine, no one else will touch you."* Then he turned and disappeared into the crowd.

She blinked. Had he actually spoken those words to her? No, his lips had not moved.

The gruff one stood, grasped the plump woman by the hand, and pulled her to the table in the middle of the room. Jessica returned, legs wobbling, to the line alone to watch as they mated.

The gruff one leaned the woman over the end of the table and parted her legs from behind. Jessica wanted the green-eyed one to mimic this act with her. She wanted him to fondle her breasts and touch her between her legs.

The bite on her neck began to throb and with each thought of the green-eyed one the pain increased until a trickle of warmth ran down her shoulder.

She looked down as a line of blood ran off the tip of her nipple. The feelings of his arms about her and him biting her assaulted her again. Her knees weakened and swayed, catching herself just before she fell.

"Yes. You know you're mine. If only my turn will come."

He would be participating. She shook her head and placed her hand on her temple. Was he speaking to her? That wasn't possible. He was nowhere near her.

A growl came from across the circle, and her eyes snapped to the green-eyed one as he paced. She watched fascinated as his hard, inflated condition hit his legs, bobbling back and forth as he strode. Did that hurt?

"No. What is agony is having to wait once I have found you."

Found me? What does that mean? A cry pulled her mind back to the mating taking place in the ring. The gruff one grasped the plump woman by the neck and pumped into her from behind. The woman's face strained with pain.

Jessica sucked in her breath. Was there pain for human women with them? The human men seemed to have nothing but pleasure from the cat-women. She closed her eyes.

"I'm not doing this," said a young woman in the line to the left of her.

Jessica watched the maid lead her from the room. She would not be participating. Jessica gazed back at the couple in the center, bit her lip, then looked at the door. She could leave.

"No, don't pull away," came the voice. *"Coon is rough. It's the way he finds his pleasure. I will not be aggressive. You will find pleasure with me. There can be no other outcome. You are my match. Coon is not with his."*

She shook her head and closed her eyes. She was going mad, hearing voices in her head.

Abysis paced, watching Coon sate his vigor with the human he chose. How dare he try to take her after he pointed her out to the Catus? He fisted his hands. Coon wanted to provoke him. As would Haven, the next male before him, but Haven would push him further; he always did. Damn it!

That was why he marked her. She could now hear his thoughts, so if things got aggressive with Haven, she would know why and would not fear him.

All the males in this year's rites had mated before. He had only watched the rites. His lessons consisted of how to pleasure and how to mate. In years past, he even helped ready the female Felis for the rites by stroking them, but he had never sunk his stiff cock into the warmth of a woman.

He clenched his teeth and glanced around the room. All eyes were on him. The male Felis enjoyed watching him react to her presence and would do nothing but provoke him until he claimed her.

He growled. Her pleasure that had coursed through him as he rocked her against his thigh amazed him. She enjoyed the touch. The goddess had been kind to him. Three of the past queens had not found bliss in the act. He had always worried about making things pleasurable for his queen. The intensity of the pleasure he felt only meant he would be able to do as he wished with her.

He'd almost given up hope he would find her. The Catus had been waiting for him to claim his life mate. To start the new line. Finally. He didn't even care all eyes were on him and not on the entertainments in the sacred circle. If only the elders would yield and let him in. His teeth clenched.

He looked back at his queen with her golden hair and her blue eyes. Their whelp would be fair. It had been generations since the queen possessed light coloring.

He turned again and looked up at the elders watching the rites from above; his uncle shook his head at him as Coon left the circle. Abysis growled. Damn it.

Haven would go next. Abysis stood across the circle from his queen and scrutinized Haven. Haven watched him closely, then grinned. Haven would pick his queen.

His chest tightened, possessiveness raging through him. He wanted to spring across the circle and claim her before Haven had his chance. If he did, the entire Catus would see him as weak and not willing to respect the traditions. He did respect them. He would have to find another way.

His friend licked his lips and flexed his hands as he stood at the entrance to the circle.

Abysis pushed out his chest and bared his teeth. Haven's smile grew even bigger. Shit! What was Haven about to do?

5

The man who entered the circle next had his green eyes fixed on Jessica. His mahogany hair shone in a brilliant gleam down his back. He smiled at her in a devious kind of way. What was he up to? His look and way of holding himself reminded her of her youngest male cousin, the one who always liked to play games.

He turned about and stared at her captor. He rolled his shoulders, then turned back to the line of women.

He possessed strikingly handsome features, yet he was almost too pretty. His long legs were sculpted with muscles, and his fingers and toes were the longest she had ever seen.

Starting at the head of the line, he sniffed the black-haired woman. He reached out and instead of touching the woman's hair, he trailed his finger along the woman's jaw bone to her ear; then his long fingers slid into her locks. The woman groaned and his smile grew broader.

His hand stayed in her hair, and he fisted the strands. Moving his hand back and forth, he tickled the flesh of her lower back with the ends. The woman's bottom jiggled and her eyes snapped.

He stared at her with such intensity. Jessica's heart sped. He wanted her. The woman licked her lips and his hand released. His touch trailed her shoulder blades to her side; then he moved to the next in the line.

It became apparent after the second woman he touched that this man loved women and they fancied him. Each woman in the line before her would have gladly given her innocence to him if he had only trailed his fingers to the hair above her thighs instead of the locks on her head. Jessica gasped. What a forward thought.

Never in her life would she have had a thought like that before this night. Maybe viewing such an event was bad for her. Well, maybe not physically harmful but watching this had shifted her view on propriety.

She glanced at her captor standing at the side of the circle, his eyes on this man, a deep scowl on his face. Why did this man bother him so?

"Haven knows you are mine. Yet he will in all probability choose you from the line to provoke me."

Her hand rose and she stuck her finger in her ear wiggling it. Was he really speaking to her?

"Yes. I cannot speak to you with my mouth. I don't have that capacity. My mark on your neck connected us, and I now speak to you with my mind."

Haven stepped next to her, and her captor's eyes darkened as he stared at her from across the room. His expression was one of fear and desire. Her captor truly wanted her, and she wanted him, wanted his touch on her body, easing the ache that was building again between her thighs. She would allow him to take her innocence. If only it was he who stood before her now.

Jessica tore her gaze to the striking man before her. Haven's smile widened. He leaned in, his head just above the lobe of her ear, and inhaled. The breath puffed in a steady stream that lowered in a trail down her neck. He stopped and the humid air caressed the mark her captor made. Chills raced her skin and her body trembled. The sensation was exquisite.

He raised his hand, and she prepared herself to be touched, but instead of running his fingers through her hair, the tip of his finger landed on the mark. She flinched as pain prickled up her neck. With a light touch, he stroked the tender skin and wetness dripped from her sex. Wanting her captor to be the one touching her, she squirmed, pulling her neck away from the touch.

He inhaled again, and his black tongue slid out, the prominent tip tracing his lips. Jessica's eyes widened. A black tongue?

Haven's eyes sparkled and he leaned in again, tracing the puncture with that black tongue. The persistent flick against her neck weakened her knees, and she swayed into him, arms coming up to his as he continued to lick her. The skin of his arms blazed beneath her touch, and she almost released her hands at the intensity.

A growl came from behind him followed by a deep throaty hiss.

Jessica tensed. Haven did not move. Instead his hand reached up and grasped a fistful of her hair. He tugged on the strands, arching her head away from his. His tongue continued to flick the red mark, swirling and tapping to the beat of her heart. Her sex contracted, the ache in her womb almost unbearable. Her arms and legs trembled, thighs opening against his legs, searching for release. Good gracious. What was he doing to her?

A series of curses rang through her head from her captor. The air swirled behind her, and Haven pushed his penis into her stomach. He was long and thick, thicker than any of the men she had seen thus far. The skin of her abdomen tickled at the contact, and she pulled backward only to push up against more hot skin. She jumped. The smell of sandalwood and spice enveloped her, and she trembled all the more. Her captor.

Haven continued as if nothing was amiss. Her body pulsed to the rhythm he created, and she relaxed in the presence of her captor. Her captor would watch out for her.

His warm fingers wrapped about her arms and pulled her clutch from Haven's body. Haven pulled his head from her neck but did not back away from her. His hand remained in her hair. She panted, looking up at him from beneath her lashes.

"Don't be frightened. I cannot allow him to touch you more. I will go mad if he chooses you."

Her captor grunted, then growled. Haven stood unmoving with a smile on his face. He rocked his hips, rubbing his penis against her abdomen. She trembled. Her captor placed his hands on her hips and pulled her back, holding her against him, his sex pushing against her bum.

They both growled and her body ignited in heat, melting her joints and creating an intense need between her legs. If both of them had not been holding her, she would have toppled to the floor. She wanted her captor to take her innocence now, pushing his sex between her legs instead of against her bum. She shifted, pushing her body back against him.

Haven opened his mouth and hissed. The hand in her hair jerked and pulled her to the side, out of the sandwich between them. Her captor's hands fell from her hips and she stumbled, her scalp pricking in pain. Haven released her hair and grasped her hand, twirling her into the center of the circle.

He had chosen her from the line.

"Damn him!" Her captor stepped forward into the circle, and a loud bang came from above.

Everyone in the room started and looked up at the balcony. The red-haired elder stood, a cane in his hand. He had used the cane to get everyone's attention. He grunted and his head shook toward her captor.

"Yes, sir. I know the rules of the ritual."

The man up in the balcony growled, and his gaze slid down her body.

"I cannot let Haven take her. My will won't allow it."

The elder's gaze then slid to Haven, who stood by the line of women, a wicked smile on his face.

Oh he was devious, just like her younger cousin. In her experience the only way to get around this was to play along to a point, then flip the game back on him.

What could she do?

Would he choose another woman from the line when he continued the rites? If he did, she could surely devise something. But if he didn't . . . No, she wouldn't think about that. She should easily be able to transfer his affections to the other woman he chose.

If she could be bold enough.

Her cheeks grew warm. It would require touching him and the other woman boldly. What was she considering?

Her gaze fixed on her green-eyed one, and her body trembled in desire. She just couldn't bear the need for him to touch her, possess her, ease her ache deep within. Indeed, she could do this. She would be bold and try to trick this man into choosing another.

6

Abysis stood at the side of the circle and watched Haven carefully. What woman did Haven truly want from the line?

Haven circled his queen, his gaze traveling to the elders, then to the line of women. He assessed each woman, and as his gaze settled on the woman at the front of the line, his eyes flashed with arousal.

The first woman he'd touched. Of course, the woman with black hair. Haven always had a weakness for women with her coloring.

Abysis skirted the circle's edge and came up behind the dark-haired woman. He glanced at his fair-haired queen. She studied Haven. Touching this woman was not forbidden in the traditions because he was king. However, it did push at some of the rituals. He didn't care; as long as it was not forbidden, he would do what he needed to in order to take her. Her eyes locked onto him.

"I will not let him touch you. I will provoke him the same way he has me. I will be the one to claim you."

She smiled tentatively. His body warmed and his cock jumped, bursting to sink into her.

Haven walked back to the line. There were three more women for him to appraise before Haven's rites would begin. Abysis reached out his hand and lightly dragged the woman's black hair over her ear.

She was pretty. However, in a way, he felt sorry for her. Haven would use her as he had all his previous rite mates. She would bear his child, and he would send her back to the human world never to see that babe again. Why he did such, Abysis didn't know. She had every right to stay, and most of the human women did. The males, however, usually returned to the village.

Haven had yet to find his true mate, yet he had three whelp all from black-haired women. Could this woman be his true mate? It was possible, but somehow he didn't think so.

She trembled as his finger trailed the edge of her hair and down her dew-aroused back. He glanced down at his cock. His phallus still stood stiff. In past experience, touching a woman never achieved this state. He knew his prick stiffened because his queen stood in the center, that he was primed and waiting for her. He wished he could have her now, but he would use his condition to get Haven's attention.

He glanced down the line at Haven, whose eyes kept glancing back to him. It was now or never. His finger traced the swell of her bottom and delved into the humid flesh of her sex. Haven's eyes widened. *That's right, Haven, I have an erection this time. You can't assume I won't use it.*

Jessica watched as her captor caressed the black-haired woman at the front of the line. His hands traced her spine, the swell of her bottom, then the line at the top of her legs, only to backtrack the caress and start over again. The dark-haired woman's head tilted back and she groaned, her body shaking.

She glanced at Haven, who now stood staring at her green-eyed one.

He strode down the line and stopped directly next to the black-haired woman. His eyes traveled down her captor's body and focused on his sex. How strange. Her captor, seeing Haven's gaze, stepped closer to the black-haired woman and pulled her back against him. He bent his knees and pushed his hips forward. The woman groaned and widened her stance.

Jessica gaped as his penis pushed through the woman's legs and the head emerged by her front curls.

"I am not doing this out of pleasure. I am doing this to get you. To force Haven to pick the woman he truly wants."

She understood that. However, her heart sped and the flesh between her legs tingled. Watching him arouse and touch this other woman for her had a tremendous effect on her. How could she enjoy watching a man she wanted pleasure another woman? Wasn't that wrong? Scandalous? She didn't know. All she knew was that he was doing this act so he could claim her as his. Her heart swelled.

She began to think that none of what she believed held true in this place. Here she didn't seem to be the plain spinster the outside world saw. Why was that?

Haven grasped the woman's hands and jerked her away from her captor. Her captor's lips turned up into a smile. Haven pulled his fingers in close to his palm and boxed her captor in the ear with his hand. Her captor hissed.

"How dare you." He lunged at Haven, toppling him to the ground. Pinning Haven beneath his weight, he leaned back and hissed. Haven turned his head to the side and pushed away from him. He stood, as did her captor. Their green eyes flashed in defiance at each other, and slowly Haven lowered his eyes.

His head bowed, he grunted. Her captor strode forward and wrapped his arms about Haven, giving him a squeeze.

He cared for this man. She shook her head. Boys.

Haven turned and stared at the black-haired woman. She smiled coyly at him. He strode to her and pulled her to the chair in the middle of the room.

The elder from above slammed his cane on the rail and pointed to her green-eyed one, then to the edge of the circle. Her captor nodded and strode to the edge. Jessica stumbled back to the side of the ring and turned to watch Haven.

Haven's hands caressed the swell of the black-haired woman's breasts. His fingers cupped the underside while his thumbs flicked her nipples. The woman tossed her head back, and Haven pushed her to sit. He knelt before her, worshipping her body; never once did his hands leave her skin.

Closing his eyes, he sighed as his hands pushed back her robe and traveled the sides of her waist to her hips, then back up again. He leaned in and suckled a nipple into his mouth. The woman arched into him. His hands slid around to her back and anchored her as he continued to play with her nipples.

Jessica wished she could see the expression on Haven's face. The woman seemed to be enjoying his touch. Her eyes were closed and her lips slightly parted as if with a sigh. His actions from behind seemed slow as if he relished the feel of her skin beneath his fingers.

The black-haired woman's hands slid over his shoulders and down his back, her fingers entwining with his gleaming mahogany hair. That hair looked so soft and silky. Jessica wondered what the fine strands felt like. Were they softer than the finest silk or coarse to the touch?

Haven's fingers rubbed down her arms and pulled her touch from his body. Grasping her wrists, he pushed them behind her back.

The black-haired woman's head tilted, exposing the underside of her neck as his black tongue slid out, circling one of her erect nipples; then his mouth closed over the peaked bud. The woman groaned in pleasure.

Jessica had yet to experience the pleasure of having her nipples caressed. Did having a man suckle your breast feel the same or different from a child? Not that she knew what a child felt like either. Goodness, the thoughts she had this night would put any respectable woman into a fit of vapors or titters.

The black-haired woman's head jerked backward as if Haven tugged on her hair. The muscles of her neck strained, but her head appeared unable to move. His hands reappeared at her hips.

Had he secured her hair somehow? And her arms, too, did not move from behind her. Had he tied her hands with her hair? No, that wouldn't work. He must have used something else . . . the belt from the robe maybe.

Why would he bind her hands and not experience the touch of the woman he chose? The human touch evoked the most powerful emotions. She had lived without it for too long, and she would not do so again. She glanced at her captor. She needed his touch. The mark on her neck began to throb anew.

"Indeed . . . My rites are next. You will be mine."

She would be his. Her skin tingled with the thought of his caress. Of his lips traveling her body as Haven's lips did the woman he chose. The strength of his conviction made her mind spin.

Haven parted the woman's thighs and sniffed the air. He purred, then thrust his finger into her shimmering cunny. The woman tensed as he withdrew his finger. A gush of cream-colored fluid slid from her sex and clung to him. Jessica felt that same gush sliding down her leg.

His eyelids hung heavy as he rubbed the fluid between his thumb and fingers. He grasped her hips and pulled her to the edge of the chair. Unable to move her hands or neck, she rested her head on the curve of the chair as if sleeping. Her eye fixed on the man who caressed her, she moaned. She truly wanted Haven's touch.

Haven's sex stood at the entrance to the woman's womb. His hands massaged her stomach, fanning out in a starlike pattern from her button to her hips. The woman arched into his caress.

Jessica's hips pressed forward in unison, and she felt to her bones that she would do the same. To feel that intimate caress on her bare skin, possessing the core of her. She trembled. There would be nothing like it in the world.

Haven stared at the arch of the woman's neck. He flexed his hips, and the tip of his phallus disappeared into her hollow. The woman cried out. His hands shifted to her thighs; wrapping his fingers about her fleshy legs, he lifted them and placed her feet on his shoulders.

One of his hands settled between her legs while the other rubbed up the arch of her neck. He slowly pushed his penis into her. She whimpered and he pulled his prick back out. Jessica saw the blood from the woman's innocence drip to the floor. The members of the audience meowed deep and low in their throats.

Haven continued to rock his hips in a steady and harsh rhythm, pushing his stiffened flesh into the woman. His never-settling hands rubbed every inch of her skin. His head tilted back, and with a groan he shuddered, sinking his phallus into the woman fully and holding himself there.

Murmurs and grunts resounded in the room. Haven slipped his sex from the woman and stood. He wrapped his arm around the woman's waist and hefted her up and over his shoulder, her head falling down his back. Strands of black hair trailed to his knees, but the majority of it remained tied with her hands in the belt of her robe.

"Now, you will be mine."

Jessica's eyes snapped to her captor as he strode into the circle. His green eyes alive with passion, with possession. Her body trembled. They would now do the act in the circle, in front of all these people. Her heart sped. She would experience the touch of another . . . Her chest tightened. No, she would experience his touch.

7

Damn the formality of the rites. He would not smell every woman and feel their hair. He knew who he wanted and he was through waiting. He strode to his queen, and the Catus grunted and howled.

She tilted her face up to his, and he captured her lips in a singeing kiss. He tasted her essence, and she flooded his senses with each movement of his mouth over hers. Her body pressed against his, hands clinging to his shoulders. Her touch fluttered over his skin, pushing his heartbeat through every muscle, driving the rhythm of his tongue, of his fingers, of his hips against her stomach. He had waited too long for this.

He tasted the warmth of her lips, the soft pliant plumpness, and knew without a doubt this was what he was made for. Pulling on her belt, he propelled her to the center of the circle.

One quick display of the loss of her innocence and she was his to do with as he wished for the rest of his life. His throat tightened on tangled emotions of need and relief that he had finally found her.

He pulled her to the table and wrapped his arms about her slender waist. Her skin blazed with the call of her need. A need that echoed his. It seeped through his hands, rousing the animal in him.

Without losing touch of her lips, he lifted her until she sat on the table ledge. Pressing his body between her thighs, she spread herself wide. Her tart scent filtered up to him, and he roared into their kiss. He needed to be inside her, to feel her clasp hot and tight around his cock. To feel the delicious sensation of spending in a warm body for the first time. His muscles shook with an overload of impending pleasure.

Everyone would be expecting him to perform for them, but, damn it, he did not want to draw this out. His hands shook as they slid between her thighs and into her engorged lips. He lightly traced the slick flesh with his thumbs, parting her opening, rubbing her wetness into the skin. To his delight she trembled against him.

The thought of her undulating beneath him propelled his need, and he pressed his hips against her. She parted her legs farther for his exploration.

"I shouldn't want this but . . . oh please, touch me there," said her thoughts.

Ah, she was almost in as frantic a state of arousal as he was. His marking had made her juices flow heavy, and with every touch of his fingers he heard that slickness louder than any sound in the room. The sound was the sweetest thing he could imagine. His queen's body begged him to mount her.

He parted her folds with the tips of his fingers, and she arched into his hand. Wanting to satisfy her need, he pushed the tip of his finger inside her.

"Oh!" She squirmed.

Oh sweet goddess. The warmth of her tight muscles about his fingers made his sack contract and his seed rise. His need matched his pulse in a thundering that blocked out her thoughts. All his instincts focused on claiming her. He positioned himself so he could enter and she tensed.

"No. Relax. I will not harm you."

She pulled her lips from his and looked him in the eyes. "C-can I explore you too?"

Lightning streaked through him at her words. *"Indeed."* He grunted.

Her lips curled up as her tentative shaking hand traveled down his chest. Heat engulfed him. Her fingers shyly stroked through the curls of his rod and his muscles jumped.

Damn! Each finger slowly wrapped around his staff, and she squeezed his hardness with blissful pressure. *"Ah, my goddess."* His head fell back as his ballocks prickled, spending wetness from the tip.

Her thumb ran over the head, spreading the drop about his scorching skin. The slippery slide of her touch was more pleasurable than anything he had experienced.

He looked into her eyes; the round centers were large in arousal. Her hand slid and her finger exquisitely traced the ridge of his prick head. Goddess! All his muscles tightened and air rushed in through his clenched teeth. He was stunned; he never imagined his queen's touch on his aroused cock would feel this amazing.

Leaning in, he licked the bite wound he inflicted, and she trembled in his arms. *"You are mine. This is our way; your blood shed here in the circle will allow the other female Felis, who have shed their innocence in the past, to mate."*

He continued to lick at her neck and with his fingers drew slow circles between her folds until her muscles jumped and quivered, delighting in his touch, spending more of her sweet juices into his hand.

Her hands reached up and wrapped about his shoulders, leaving his cock straining for any touch from her.

"Touch me again," he demanded.

She wrapped her hand around the bind of his hair and pulled his mouth from her neck. Her lips parted on a sigh, and he captured her lips, pushing his tongue into her honeyed slickness. He slid two fingers into the steaming heat of her sex, withdrew them, and plunged them back in, fucking her with his fingers. *"You are ready for me."*

"Yes." Her voice shook in heavy arousal.

Her hands wandered down his back to his buttocks. Her touch on his bare arse burned his aroused skin. He kissed her harsher as his muscles clenched in anticipation.

She moaned, the inside of her womb tightening in waves about his fingers.

Pleasurable sensation shot through him. She stiffened, the entire room fading away as a bright light flashed before him. Her muscles convulsed about his fingers as he moved them to the same rhythm, prolonging her spend. He closed his eyes, feeling to his bones the pulse of her pleasure. Her slick folds continued to release, and she fell into beautiful contentedness. He could wait no more.

Her body sated, he slid his fingers from her swollen flesh and dragged her hip forward. *"You are a sensuous one."* He pressed his cock to her swollen folds, painfully needing release. He hesitated, knowing he would cause her to bleed and he would experience her discomfort.

Her nether lips scalded, and the need to claim her, to feel the rest of her about him, overrode any hesitation.

He growled. Her eyes opened and met his. *"It will be quick."* He thrust into her in one motion. Her slick oiled flesh gave way to encase him.

She cried out as he filled her, and he felt her opening burn. Sweet goddess, she was an inferno. He struggled to find his mind in the heat of her. He did not want to complete the act in the circle. His body shuddered as he willed himself not to spend, and her pain spiraled through him. He concentrated on the pain she felt, and he was able to pull back.

Their eyes still locked, he withdrew and the precious virgin blood dripped from his staff onto the floor.

The Catus howled and without sparing one glance to any of them, he picked her up, cradled her in his arms, and ushered her from the room.

He nuzzled her neck. *"Sorry, it is our way. Innocence must be shed for the Felis to see. I would do no more with you there. My pleasure will come in private."*

A sob escaped Jessica and the entrance to her womb burned. *"Shh, shh, I will make it better. Give me a moment."*

He carried her upstairs, entered a room, closed the door, and deposited her on a bed. She watched as he turned and walked to a washbasin. Emotions overtook her and tears ran down her face. He was an amazing creature. Beautiful. His body, lean and hard. She watched in wonder as each muscle flexed with power and grace as he wrung out a cloth.

How could this handsome creature desire her with such passion? He strode toward her with the damp cloth in hand. She studied his face—his brows were lowered and a tight frown formed on his face as if something pained him.

"Please spread your legs." He spoke but his mouth did not move. How strange to hear someone's voice yet not have them move their lips.

She did as he asked, and he placed the cold cloth to her throbbing flesh. Desire flared in her and another spasm built. What a wanton she was; even with the pain all she wanted was his touch.

"Ah, my sweet. The goddess has picked a prime one for the new queen."

Their new queen? What does that mean? Her mind couldn't

focus on the words as he continued to stroke her with the cool dampness.

A dull ache replaced the burning in her sex, and she laid her head back on the bed, closing her eyes. The muscles in her legs tensed and jumped as his arms lightly brushed her skin. The coolness of the cloth left her and a soothing warmth inserted up to her womb. Her hips arched against the blissful sensation.

What was that? She leaned up and watched as he licked her beneath her curls. His tongue. Good gracious.

The warmth flicked in tiny flutters all along the crease of her sex. Reaching the top, his tongue touched something and her cunny clenched in delight.

He laved down the crease of her leg, and her entire body jumped, her hips arching into his head. His tongue swirled her anus and she squirmed. Then in one long, exquisitely slow lick, it traveled up her sex, pressing into her opening.

She whimpered and the pleasure blazed on her so fast, her body pulsated, bucking with waves of delight, and the burning light met her again.

He purred, a contented happy sound, and hooked his arms beneath her, pushing her up to the pillows on the bed. He spread himself over her. Feeling his hard length pressed against her softness, quakes of satisfaction washed through her. She had never been held so, possessed so by another, and he obviously wanted nothing but her. Her heart swelled.

"*Dear sweet one.*" He brushed a hair from her face. "*I need to be inside you.*"

His phallus probed her opening and with a roll of his hips filled her. "Oh!" Her body arched against his, and she squeezed her muscles about his hard invasion.

The ache remained, but when he slid out, she only wanted him to return to fill her. All she wanted was to be one with this man. She clutched at his hips, pulling him back. He groaned, reentered, and repeated the rhythm, increasing the pace as her hips kept arching and pressing against him. Her body seemed to know what to do and matched his rhythm.

With each thrust, passion seeped into her. Every inch of his body possessed her as his pleasure coursed through her. It spiraled up and up, then intensified.

His hard sculpted body flexed with each movement, and sweat trickled from his brow, a serious passion-filled expression on his face. His hip motions grew harsher, their bodies slapping against each other as his sex plundered her. Her hands reached up and grasped his shoulders.

With a roar, he leaned down and bit her neck. She exploded in sensation, her muscles convulsing about his inflated flesh as a gush of warmth filled her womb.

Abysis lay atop her. What an incredible experience. He now understood why the males of the Catus fought over the lottery. He rolled off her and lay on his back, breathing wildly. His queen. He intended to do this every day for the rest of his life.

"Sweet one." He looked at her golden beauty from the corner of his eye. *"Are you well?"*

"Yes," she said between passion-spent pants.

"I am Abysis, now king to the Catus. You are?"

"Jessica, Jessica Wellomb."

"Jessica, queen of the Catus."

"Queen of the Catus? What do you mean?"

"You are my queen. Queen of our kind."

"I don't understand. Why me?" She rolled onto her side and looked at him, her fair hair falling in front of her face. "I'm not the youngest, nor am I that pretty."

He studied her face, the passion blush that tinged her cheeks and her lips swollen from his kiss. She blew him away.

"You have been destined to me from birth. The goddess chose you for me, and you are beautiful, my fair one." He loved

that hair. Reaching up, he ran a hand though the light locks, letting the silken strands caress his hand.

He could still hardly believe she was here. Part of him expected to wake up any moment and realize it was just another one of his vivid dreams.

He looked at her creamy white skin and the rose-colored nipples that peaked her breasts. She was perfect, and the way she looked at him caused possessiveness to swirl in him. Now that he found her, he would not allow anyone else to touch her.

8

Jessica ran her finger down Abysis's stomach, taking pleasure in the way his muscles jumped and quivered. She had never touched a man so boldly before. It felt wonderful.

A purr came from his throat, and her cheeks washed with heat. She brought him pleasure.

How strange it felt to be welcomed in this odd place. She had spent years wandering from relative to relative, living off their kindness, and all along, she was destined to be here with these cat-beings. The idea was difficult to wrap her thoughts around. Where was here anyway?

"Abysis, where are we?"

"*At the Felis castle at the foot of the Cgurr Aybasair Mountain.*"

He jumped off the bed and placed his hands on his masculine hips and scowled at her. "*You have to stay. You are the queen. You are carrying the next in the line. The next Abysis. The next king.*"

A smile quirked her lips at his insecurity; to think this man wanted her that much warmed her soul. "I think you misunderstood. I don't want to leave. I just wanted to know where my new home was. You do intend for me to stay, then?"

"Goddess, yes, you are my mate for life. I will not let you out of my sight. I will not live without the pleasure of what we just shared." He leaned forward and grasped her face in his hands.

The moment his skin touched hers, she could actually feel his pain as he considered the thought of her leaving. How was that possible?

"I have looked for you for so long." His thumb brushed her cheek.

He leaned in and kissed her gently. Her heart ached and the bite on her neck began to throb. "Yes."

Abysis grasped her by the waist and pulled her to her feet.

"Yes." Her whole being knew this was right. She needed to be with this man.

"Come, I want to pleasure you." He turned her about and grasped her hand, pulling her toward the door.

"Pardon? I thought we would stay here." Jessica followed without hesitation.

"No, I want to take you to a room where I can heighten your pleasure."

He jerked open the door and glanced down the hall away from where they had come. Nodding his head, he pulled her forward. The cool air, combined with excitement, pricked her skin as they traveled down the hall. She had wanted to see more of the castle and now she would.

They headed up a series of winding stairs; at the top, gay laughter and music filtered through the air. They celebrated the rites. She smiled, wanting to see and experience more of what this place was.

"Abysis, can I see more of your kind?"

He stopped and turned back to face her. *"My queen, you can have anything you wish. I thought for us to have some privacy before showing you to everyone. Is that not what you wish?"*

His brows stooped low over his eyes, and he stared at her determinedly. He was truly concerned about her answer.

"Oh yes! I want to be with you. I . . . I well, I just wanted to know more. See more of this place."

He nodded. *"Then I will show you the hall up ahead. You can watch from above as they prepare for the celebrations that will commence tomorrow."*

A grin curved her lips, and she hopped with excitement. "Thank you."

Abysis laughed and pulled her ahead to where an ornately carved wood railing crossed an arch in the wall. She stopped and gazed down over the edge.

Below was a large dining hall. Maids and gentlemen dressed in servant's clothing hurried about cleaning and decorating for the festivities the next night.

Three large tables were set with vases of flowers. Benches lined each of the tables, and at one end a fiddle player performed on the stage.

The music was gay and happy, and a few younger adolescent cat-men milled or danced about, holding conversations with each other and laughing.

"Abysis, who are the men who are here? Shouldn't everyone be in the rites?"

"No, only adults are allowed to witness and participate. The whelp and adolescents do not. The whelp are mostly abed, but the adolescents are curious, and if we did not give them tasks that need to be done for the celebration, they would surely interrupt the rites. There." He raised his arm and pointed to a young cat-man with ruddy hair and a svelte build similar to his. *"He is my brother, the youngest of my father's line."*

"Your brother? How many siblings do you have?" She never considered that he had a family. A family that she, as his queen, now entered.

His hand lovingly brushed a lock of her hair behind her shoulder. She turned her head toward him.

His eyes sparked with desire. *"I wish to pleasure you now, my queen."*

Her heart raced and a lump formed in her throat. Such passion, such desire. Indeed, she wanted him to touch her. She nodded and his lips pressed with urgent need to hers. Lightly he pinched the flesh of her lower lip between his, then grabbed the top.

His tongue thrust in, and the tip tapped hers repeatedly. She could never get enough of him. Of this intimate touch. Her tongue returned the rhythm, tapping, but she needed more; she wanted to taste every bit of him. She rubbed the surface of his lips and his teeth with her tongue.

Goodness. She never wanted this to stop. Her heart pounded, and her head spun. She leaned into him for support. The instant his hot skin pressed to hers, all his need washed through her. Her knees wobbled and all the passion in her was set free.

His arms wrapped about her waist and she caught his lower lip with her teeth and nipped. He growled.

"More, Jessica, more. I want so much more."

She let her hands slide up his chest and run over his smooth shoulders, digging and kneading everywhere she touched.

He lifted her and sat her on the edge of the railing. Her legs slid about his hips, welcoming him to have her. His hands gripped firmly to her waist, holding her still.

Their lips broke apart and she panted, trying to catch her breath as she admired the look of his wild features. This was the cat, the wild beast in him. Funny how it didn't frighten her; she felt safer than she had in her entire life.

His tongue trailed down her neck, the line of wetness on her skin tingling as it dried. She shivered, knowing that if he let go, she could topple to the floor, but she didn't fear it. He would never let her fall. He possessed her, as she did him. The thought slid straight into her heart.

His mouth reached her breast and circled the plump flesh. His lips settled to the side of the hard nipple and sucked the bloom into his mouth. The pressure prickled like little needles on her skin, and she arched into him, dangling her head back over the railing.

My stars, everything he did to her was fine . . . more than fine. Her eyes fluttered open and below all of the adolescent cats watched them. She stiffened and jerked her hands, dragging her nails across Abysis's skin. He purred, enjoying the harsh caress.

"No, Abysis, look. Look below." She pushed and pulled at him.

He tore his mouth from her breast and gathered her tight against him, nuzzling into her hair.

"Shy, are we now, Jessica? In the ceremony room you wanted to touch me in front of everyone."

She squirmed, remembering her boldness. She did enjoy touching him in the circle, but young cat-beings had not been present. From what he said, she got the impression that they did not know of such things.

"True. But you said they don't participate because they are too young."

He chuckled and his humid breath warmed her skin. He angled his head and growled over her shoulder. The growl she heard as *"Lester"* in her mind.

Jessica turned her head to see his brother step forward and growl back with a crackling voice.

Abysis grunted and meowed.

"Have food and drink in my room when we return from the cell. Brit?"

Another young man with gleaming black hair strode forward and growled as he bowed to them.

Abysis grunted and clicked in this throat. *"You will bring up hot water and a bath."*

It was truly amazing that she could hear him, but strange not to know what the others said. Would she learn over time the difference between one growl and another? At the moment they all sounded the same. She could talk to the servants and to Abysis. For now, that was all she needed.

He cupped her bottom in his hands and carried her from the railing.

As he strode down the hall, she rested her head on his shoulder staring at the castle interior as they passed.

They turned a corner, and a door opened behind them. She glimpsed a small child crying. His head was buried on the woman's shoulder much as she had hers on Abysis's.

The woman ran her hand up the child's back and tried to soothe him. Her heart ached at the intimacy between them. She had never experienced that closeness with another while growing up. Her nurse and governess before her pa died were nice enough, but they never loved her. After he died, no one loved her.

"What is it, my Jessica? I can feel your sorrow."

"It is nothing." She shook her head and pushed the image away. Abysis . . . He had passion for her. That was more than anything she had experienced.

Abysis pushed open a door and then closed it. Flickering candles illuminated the room's circular shape and cast a warm inviting glow. What a strange room. He strode to the side of the room and placed her on her feet.

Tapestries covered the walls depicting cat-beings kissing and hugging, leading each other blindly into rays of light and into darkness. The feeling of trust and a sense of the unknown came from each image. Willingly one followed the other into the unfamiliar, the hidden, the unspoken.

Her eyes settled on the large platform in the middle of the

room. Four poles marked each corner and two more at the center of each side. From each pillar, large gold rings pierced the wood at different heights and angles. The surface of the stage itself was covered with a cushion of puckered silk, like a mattress. What did they use that for? It reminded her a bit of an animal tie.

She glanced around the rest of the room.

"Abysis, what is this room?" *And what do you plan to do to me here?*

He turned toward her and reached for something folded on a stand, then held up a length of dark cloth.

"*This will heighten your pleasure. When you can't see, you can only feel the sensations in their purity.*" He raised the cloth and placed it over her eyes. Wrapping it about her head, he cinched it tight.

His touch ran down her arms, and his hands circled her wrists. "*Come.*" He lifted her and placed her standing on a plush smooth surface.

"*Give me your hands, my goddess Jessica.*" He grasped first her right hand, then her left, and wrapped something soft about her wrists.

A tugging sensation pulled at her wrist and her hand slowly rose until her arm stretched out. Her arm shook, unsure what he was going to do to her.

He gentled the tremor by kissing a trail down her extended arm. Reaching her shoulder, his teeth scraped across her skin and down toward her breasts. Fire slid through that path and her nipples pebbled hard.

She wanted his mouth on her nipples. On any part of her body. She did not fear being unable to see. She trusted him to bring her delight. She thrust her breasts forward, indicating her desire and his mouth left her.

"Wait. No, come back!"

A touch traced the outside of her left breast and slowly spiraled the globe until it neared her nipple. Her chest rose raggedly, waiting for the touch to flick the sensitive peak. The touch disappeared. She reached out for him with her free hand, but he was nowhere.

His fingers sketched a line on the back of her free arm to her wrist. Then, yanking on the soft rope, he pulled and tied the bind tight.

"You are beautiful." His fingers roved over her shoulders, sending twinges of delight through her.

A touch trailed down her spine to the crack of her bum; his finger settled then with tiny touches. As if playing the piano, he circled the curve of her hip and the swell of her bottom. Fever dewed her skin and she trembled. His touch was the most exquisite thing. He made her feel like the most beautiful woman.

Unable to see him, she remembered the preparation chamber and the heat of the skin about his sex. Her skin blazed that hot. His breath labored by her ear. All she wanted was this man to continue touching and possessing her.

"Abysis, I . . . I want to feel your body on mine. Your skin touching every bit of me, your sex joined with me again."

He growled, his tongue tracing the lobe of her ear, then tickling down her neck. His body heat warmed her from behind, and then with a kick of his foot he slid her legs apart. His hands busily tied her feet, spreading her so that she could not move.

Then he was gone.

"Abysis?" Where was he?

"Oh goddess, you are . . . indefinable."

Abysis stood back and stared; it was all he could do. Her beauty entranced him. Stretched wide, every inch of her was exposed for him to touch and see. Her nipples stood at points, the lips of her cunny hung swollen from her exposed extended legs. The muscles of her thighs shook.

He kneeled down before her and placed his lips on her large toe. His tongue slid out and he traced the digit. She jumped and he continued to slide his tongue up the bridge of her foot.

He wanted to lick, suck, and nibble every part of her. His teeth scraped her ankle, and he nibbled his way, kissing and massaging with his tongue, up her leg to her knee. He sampled her skin like a delicacy he never encountered before.

His hands grasped hard onto her thighs, then released to tickle the sensitive inside flesh that led to her sex.

He drew circles in the softness near her curls. Her breath labored in and out, and her muscles shook uncontrollably. Every motion she made caressed him. She was here. She was his.

His breath joined hers in a strain for air. He waited, lightly caressing her skin. Waiting for her to arch with strong need into his caress.

The bliss would come. He felt it build in her with each touch. He had watched this act enough times to know what to do, but now that it was his mate tied to the posts, the torture, as sweet as it was to pleasure her, grated him.

He wanted to enter her, to mate with her a dozen times in a night. He leaned in and kissed her breasts, careful not to touch the sensitive centers.

The sweetest-sounding gasp escaped her shaking lips, and the bliss rose higher. His cock strained, hardening, lengthening at the sensations connecting them.

His touch trailed over the smooth creamy flesh of her thigh to the crease of the buttocks. He never imagined she would be so soft. Lifting her firm swell, dewed flesh scented with hot arousal touched his fingers. He moaned and she arched toward him, pushing her curls directly into his nose.

Sweet goddess. Yes.

He nuzzled the fur, his tongue sliding out along the dripping flesh. She bucked and whimpered, her legs tremoring with need.

His hands separated her cheeks and his fingers delved into the humid flesh, searching for her pucker of sensation. His tongue continued to lap at her sex as his finger circled and tapped at a steady pace, pushing her toward bliss.

She writhed against the restraints as he steadied his massaging and applied steady pressure to the pucker, careful not to enter, just tease.

"Oh . . . Oh . . . !" Jessica's hips arched and pressed into him again, her bliss washing over him. His tongue lapped as his finger pushed into her arse, and she quaked.

She screamed and pulled against the ropes in her release. He smiled. He truly couldn't have wished for a more sensuous mate. Quickly he untied the restraints about her ankles.

He straightened, his ballocks aching with seed for her. He paced around to the back of her and ran his hands about her waist.

"Abysis, you will join with me now?"

His fingers found her nipple and pinched as his other hand angled her hips, pulling her legs closer together. The softness of her bum nestled against his sex, and he eagerly pushed his hardness between. The drenching flesh he had just tasted welcomed him. The head of his phallus pushed into her.

"Oh, Abysis." Her hips pushed back against him, and her flesh slid down the length of his cock.

His legs shook, his hips arched, pulling out of her balmy core. Wrapping his arms about her stomach, he let himself go.

Sweet goddess. His rhythm was rough, harsh as he fucked her. Her cunny caressed each penetration, each thrust of their join. His lips kissed the salty skin of her neck, licking his mark, making her tremble in every pore of her being.

"Oh, Jessica, my queen." His pleasure came on all at once. His body tingled as his seed erupted into her. He jerked and roared, squeezing her as every ounce of him poured into her.

His knees weakened and he leaned into her, panting. He

shook his head, numb from head to toe. No one ever said mating was so involved. He truly felt his entire body flow into her as he spent. He kissed her shoulder. They were truly one.

The first night of their mating would be undisturbed. After that, the celebrations would begin, and he intended to mate with her several times more this night. Abysis pulled himself from her soft petals; swollen with blood, they clung to his cock as he fell from her. Her body shuddered.

"Abysis."

"*Yes, my goddess. Did you enjoy that?*"

"How is it you can give such pleasure to me when I am not of your kind?"

"*It is the way it has always been,*" he said as he licked and scraped her ear with his teeth. "*We cannot breed with our own, only with the human kind. Each generation has a prechosen queen. The heir can only smell her; he is only aroused by her and can only spill his seed into her. I, too, have never experienced this pleasure until tonight.*"

He lowered his head and swirled her nipple into his warm mouth. "*Each year the female Felis who become enheated select their male human to shed their innocence. The male Felis, who participate, are chosen by a lottery and then they choose their mate in order of age.*"

Her body arched and pulled against the ropes that held her. He would bring her release again.

"Oh, so I belong here with you. This was meant to be?"

"*Yes, you more than belong here. You are the highest-ranking female of the Catus.*"

Tears silently ran down her cheeks. "I have never belonged anywhere," she whispered.

He studied her, confused by her tears and the happiness flowing from her. "*Well, you do now and you always have.*" He growled and pressed his fingers to her womb. *"You are the mother to our next generation."*

Jessica sighed. This man, even if not human, desired her more than anyone in her life. For the first time she knew she was where she belonged.

The pleasure is all yours if you're ready to let your fantasies take control and surrender yourself to desire . . .

"The Principles of Lust"
Sleek and sexy erotic art gallery owner Teal Jamison knows what she likes and isn't afraid to let carpenter Zach Dillon know that her current fantasy features him in all his masculine glory. But Zach has a deliciously different game in mind for a woman accustomed to taking charge . . .

"Passion Play"
Quick to follow where passion leads, then back off when things get too close, jewelry designer Mia Jones's sensual odyssey with singles columnist Dominick Jamison is perfect: hot, sweet, and no risk of complications. But how long can her heart stay cold—when she's lost in the heat of a man devoted to every forbidden pleasure her body craves?

"Sexual Healing"
When massage therapist Caitlyn Ellis shows photographer Scott Lowell the joys of sensual self-love for the camera, he can't resist the erotic invitation to take pleasure in her lush curves—or deny himself the hands-on ecstasy of loving a beautiful woman determined to heal his battered soul . . . by setting his body on fire.

Please turn the page for an exciting sneak peek of Sasha White's LUSH, coming next month from Aphrodisia!

Prologue

It was riveting.

At first glance it was rude. But the longer Teal looked at it, the more details she noticed and the faster her pulse raced. The photograph shifted from rude to raw as she looked past the shadowed anus and the pouting pussy lips.

She noticed the strength of the hands caressing those curved hips. The water droplets scattered over taut skin of beautifully molded buttocks and firm thighs, as if recently washed, but not dried. The background was dark, the bodies anonymous. There was nothing else to the photo. Erotic in its simplicity, the only thing that mattered was the touch of those hands and the sensations they created.

The visible wetness that covered the woman's swollen sex made it gleam lasciviously, and Teal almost wished it were her that was bent over, being caressed, being prepared masterfully for a night of erotic attention. She swallowed and squeezed her thighs together as the photograph evolved from raw to luscious.

It was in that moment that the idea came to her. She'd been feeling a little lost and alone, like she didn't have purpose. Her parents were happy in their corner of the world, her brother had found a career he seemed to thrive in. Yet for her, jobs came and went, men came and went. Nothing seemed to challenge her anymore.

She knew there was more to life than partying, and she *wanted* to have goals. She knew she could do anything if she put her mind to it. She'd just never had a clue what she'd wanted to do before. Other than be successful, be independent. But right then, when she looked at that photograph, a lightning bolt struck and she knew.

She knew she could use her ambition and drive, her salacious mind, and her ability to think outside the box to carve her own special niche in the world. A successful and unique one that would be all hers.

And it would be called Lush.

1

It was crunch time. Less than a week until opening day and Teal Jamison didn't have time to fuck around. Especially with something as frustrating as some punk kids spray-painting nasty messages on the front of her building. Pissed off and stressed out about all the piddly little things that kept screwing up her plans, she strode into her soon-to-be art gallery muttering to herself only to stop dead in her tracks.

Anger turned to desire, and excitement of a different sort flowed through her at the sight that greeted her. Soft faded denim stretched lovingly across perfect tight male glutes

All thoughts of temperamental artists, inconsistent suppliers, and juvenile delinquents evaporated as she watched the man straighten from his bent position. She enjoyed the sight of a worn leather tool belt framing his ass perfectly.

Now that's a work of art.

"Looking good, Zach," she purred as she dropped her backpack on the reception desk and continued in his direction. An hour or two of wrestling naked with him would certainly take the edge off her stress.

The carpenter ran a loving hand over the custom-built mahogany shelf he'd just finished installing before turning to her. "Thanks, Teal, but I'm just helping bring your vision of the place together."

"Oh, I've no doubt the gallery will be beautiful, but I was referring to the view when I walked in." She winked at him and gave his impressive form an obvious once-over.

His eyes flared brightly at her brazen comment befor they closed in a slow, lazy blink that made her knees weak. When he looked at her again, the heat was banked and his smile was unhurried. "Well, that's the point of the setup right? That the view be good from every angle?"

Zachary Dillon had come highly recommended as the finish carpenter fot her new art gallery, and she'd made it a point to be completely professional with him. But his work for her was almost done, and she was ready to be more than his boss.

Her eyes followed his movements as he pulled a cloth from his tool belt and wiped his hands. His rough, calloused, manly hands that were large enough to hold her C-cup breasts and make her feel small. Her nipples pebbled in response to her thoughts, and she lifted her gaze to his.

"I was talking about you, darlin'." She couldn't help it. Flirting had always been second nature to her; man or woman, it didn't matter. She flirted and charmed . . . and usually got whatever she wanted.

From the start, just being around Zach had made her blood heat and her pulse race, but she'd remained professional. She didn't want anything getting in the way of Lush's success, not even her own libido. Even now, waiting until his work for her was completely finished would be the smartest thing to do, but she'd had a shit day and her emotions were running high.

She touched his bare arm lightly and gave him the slow sultry smile that usually got her whatever she wanted. "You're looking good."

"Thank you." His voice was a bit deeper as he shifted his weight to his other foot, taking him just out of her reach. He gave her a knowing smile as he reached for the sweatshirt he'd left on a nearby stool and pulled it on over his ragged T-shirt.

"I can't do anything else until I pick up more varnish, so I'm done for the day. I'll see you bright and early Monday, Teal." He picked up an old wooden toolbox and waved to her with his other hand. "Have a good night."

Teal said good night and watched him saunter away.

What the hell had just happened? She'd come on to him; in fact, she couldn't have been more obvious if she'd stripped off her clothes and said, "Let's wrestle naked." And he'd walked away!

Men never walked away from her.

There was a definite attraction between them. She knew the spark of lust when she saw it. By investing all of her savings into opening the very first completely erotic art gallery around, she was betting her future on knowing that look.

So why would a big, healthy, and attractive man walk away from a woman he desired?

A few hours later, she was working in the back room and the question was still on her mind.

"Maybe he's just shy," the perky brunette said from her perch on top of a packing crate.

"No, that's not it." Teal shook her head and pulled the lid off the smaller crate on the table in front of her. She thought about the way Zach moved, the way he ran his hands over whatever he was working on, and a shiver danced down her spine. "He's way too confident to be shy. He's quiet for sure, but he gives off this impression of restrained strength. Very strong and sexy, and completely alpha."

It was just after ten P.M. on Saturday night, and she and Brina Jo were in the spacious back room of the gallery, unpacking the first shipment of items. Teal had spent the last two hours on the phone trying to line up a cleaning crew to come and wash the graffiti off her building, but since the next day was Sunday, nobody wanted the job. She'd lined up a crew for Monday, though.

She'd been enjoying her time alone in the back room. It was the first bit of quiet time she'd had in a while. She knew it was her own fault. When the idea for an art gallery that specialized in erotic art had come to her, she'd run with it. Full speed ahead and complete stop were the only speeds she knew.

Unpacking inventory in the back room was a bit of both for her. She got to work fast and efficiently, but she had also been alone, so she got to turn off her brain for a while and just enjoy herself. Her brain hadn't cooperated, though. Instead, she couldn't stop thinking about a certain well-built carpenter and fantasizing about ways to get him naked. That was until she'd heard someone rattling the locked door of the gallery.

Thinking she might catch the graffiti punks, she'd dashed through the empty gallery only to open the door and find nobody. Well, nobody with a spray can anyway. What she had found was a flyer with the words "House of Sin. You are going to hell" glued to her front door. Slightly creeped out and tired of her own thoughts, she'd called her long-time friend and newly hired assistant, Brina Jo.

By the time Brina arrived at the gallery, Teal had scraped the flyer off the door with warm water and a putty knife, and pushed it to the back of her mind. However, thoughts of Zach would not go away, so she'd blabbed uncontrollably to Brina about the brick wall hitting on him had been.

"If he's not shy, maybe he's not interested."

Teal snorted. "Oh, he's interested."

"How do you know?" Brina asked. "I mean, if he's as distant as you say and he's not gay, then how do you know he's interested?"

Turning away from the crate in front of her, Teal faced her friend. "I can *feel* it. Whenever we're in the same room together, the air fairly vibrates with pheromones, and it's not just me. I've caught him watching me, and I've seen *the look* in his eyes. He wants me too." *Why wouldn't he?*

"What look have you seen in his eyes?" She glanced up from the clipboard she was using to catalogue the items Teal unpacked.

"The look of lust."

Brina Jo's eyebrows jumped. "Lust, huh? Are you sure it's lust and not just tolerance because he thinks you're crazy? He has been in and out of here for the past two weeks; he's seen your moods."

"Crazy is the way your husband looks at you!" Teal threw a handful of Styrofoam peanuts at her friend. "And my moods haven't been that bad. It's just a bit stressful getting this gallery ready to open in less than a month."

Brina cocked her head to the side. "Tell me again why someone with no experience in art whatsoever decided to open an art gallery?"

"I don't need to know art for this particular gallery. I know everything there is to know about desire, hidden and otherwise." Teal arched an eyebrow at her friend. "That includes what lust looks like, even in its subtlest forms."

"If you're so sure of his attraction to you, why don't you just ask him out?"

Teal turned back to the crate in front of her so she didn't have to look at her friend. She hated to admit it, but even though Zach's hard-to-get act just made her want him more, she didn't want to ask him out first. It was silly, but it felt like, if she did that, she'd be giving him the upper hand. And that was something she didn't like.

She tried to think of a way to explain that to her friend as she reached into the crate and dug past the packing. She grasped the bronze sculpture within and lifted it out, scattering the little peanuts everywhere and her jaw dropped. "Wow."

"You're not kidding." Brina Jo hopped off the table she'd been sitting on and stepped forward for a closer look. "That is—"

"Amazing," Teal finished for her.

"That's one way to put it. Are you really going to display it?"

Teal set the sculpture down on the table to her left. She wiped a dust cloth over it lovingly, taking in every detail. It was a couple making love. The female stretched out on her side with the male on his knees, straddling one of her legs while cradling the foot of the other against his shoulder. She was spread completely open. Her head was thrown back, her expression one of pure ecstasy. There was nothing hidden to the viewer as the man plunged his cock into her. His cock was as lovingly crafted as her sex.

Teal turned the sculpture around; it was beautiful from every angle. Every curve and crevice detailed to the point that her own sex clenched in anticipation of being filled.

"Teal?"

Brina's voice broke the spell that had fallen over Teal, and she pulled her hands away from the bronze couple. "Hmm?"

"You're not really going to display that in the main room, are you?"

Teal looked at her friend. "Of course I am. Why wouldn't I?"

"It's very . . . it's so . . ." Brina Jo waved her hand about.

Teal watched her friend's cheeks flush as she searched for the right word. "Erotic?" Teal finally took pity on her.

Brina Jo planted her hands on her ample hips and rolled her eyes. "Yes, *erotic*. But blatantly so."

"Well, that's what Lush is for. I want it to showcase the erotic art that normal galleries think is too 'out there' or 'too edgy.' I can't call it an erotic art gallery and then hide the most erotic pieces in the corner."

"True, but you know you're going to take some flack for it, right?"

Teal shrugged. "I'm prepared. Plus, I know that sex and sexuality is a huge part of human nature, even if some people like to pretend it isn't. I'm banking on a lot of people getting more turned on by these things than they thought possible." Teal smirked at her friend. "Just like you."

"Teal!"

"What?" She laughed. "You going to tell me you're going to go home to Doug after handling all these and *not* want to try out this position?"

Brina Jo's lovely chocolate eyes glittered, and she bit her lip. "That's beside the point."

"No, Brina baby, that is *exactly* the point."

EROTIC PLEASURE
Aspiring actress Gillian Monroe is getting used to rejection. She hasn't been hired for an acting job in months. But that doesn't make it any easier to swallow her boyfriend's over-the-phone break up, claiming they're "not compatible" in bed. Sure the sex wasn't exactly fireworks, but then Steve never wanted to try anything new. Naturally Gillian wonders if there's a man out there who can fulfill her secret longings and take her on a journey of unbridled passion . . .

WET HOT DESIRE
Enter real estate mogul David Wentworth. The man oozes raw sex appeal and his mere touch awakens a wantonness Gillian never knew she possessed. For the first time in her life, she feels free to shed her inhibitions and lose herself in a sensual haze of desire, living out all her erotic fantasies and surrendering to *every* yearning . . .

**Please turn the page for an exciting sneak peek of
Melissa Randall's
SEXUALLY SATISFIED
coming in May 2007 from Aphrodisia!**

1

"Thank you all for coming," said the casting director, clutching his binder to his chest. "You were all terrific and we'll be in touch soon." He gave the six foot blonde with the huge fake boobs a wide grin, which she returned with a flick of her long bleached hair. *If this bimbo can convince the balding old fart that she finds him absolutely devastating, then she's an Oscar-caliber actress who deserves the job,* I thought caustically.

I sighed, picked up my tote bag and trudged to the door with the other rejects. Another bomb of an audition. I couldn't even get hired for a tampon commercial. It had been two . . . no, three months since my last job. If I didn't land a role soon, I'd have to go back to the grind of office temping.

As soon as I opened the door, the heat hit me like a blast furnace. I immediately felt sweat beading on my upper lip and trickling between my breasts. Oh, the joy of New York City in August. The subway was the stickiest, stinkiest sauna in the world.

I staggered up to my third floor apartment, pushed my way in and kicked off my shoes. "Apartment" was a bit of an exaggeration. The ad had described it as a "charming, cozy studio" but "tiny rathole" was really more accurate. I turned on the ancient air conditioner to high; it immediately coughed, sputtered and died. "Goddammit!" I shouted. I hauled out the floor fan, feeling tears of frustration pricking at my eyes.

Five minutes later I was sitting half naked in front of the fan, sipping iced tea. I tried to remind myself of all the good things in my life. My boyfriend of three months, Steve, was the sweetest guy I'd ever met—and extremely cute in the bargain. I was beginning to wonder if he was The One. Anita, my best friend since sixth grade, was supportive and fun and loyal. Even on a sweltering summer day New York was infinitely preferable to boring Hanson, New Hampshire. And I'd had some success with my acting career; if I could just hold on until the big break came . . .

My cell phone rang and before I even flipped it open my telephonic telepathy set in. I just knew it was Steve. We'd talked about getting together tonight, and now I really needed his company.

"Hey Gillian," he said. "Have you melted yet in this heat?"

"No, but I wish I could. I had a thoroughly shitty day." I proceeded to moan and groan and complain, knowing that Steve would be sympathetic. He'd been through enough lousy auditions before landing the plum role of Winston on the long running soap *Nights of Passion.*

I finally ran out of complaints. "So, what would you like to do tonight?"

Steve was strangely silent. Usually he was an expert at pulling me out of a bad mood.

"Is something wrong, Steve?"

He hesitated. "No . . . well, yes. I don't know how to say this, Gillian . . . I planned to get together with you tonight to discuss it. But I think it's better to do it over the phone."

I never understood the phrase "my heart sank" until that moment. "You want to break up with me," I said woodenly.

He heaved a long sigh. "I'm sorry, really I am. I like you so much, Gillian, and we had some great times together. But I don't think we're compatible."

My throat tightened. "I don't understand. We're interested in the same things, we're in the same business, we enjoy doing the same things—"

"It's not that. I just think we're not compatible . . . sexually. In bed. It's never been very good for either of us."

I was stunned. True, Steve and I didn't have the best sex life, but God, I had tried to spice things up. He never seemed interested in trying anything new. It was the same routine every time.

"Look Steve, I understand what you're saying, but we could work on it—"

"No . . . Gillian, I'm really sorry. The truth is that I've met someone else."

My shock deepened. I couldn't speak. I just sat there as Steve rambled on, apologizing, swearing it wasn't my fault . . .

I finally interrupted him. "Okay, Steve, good luck." I hung up abruptly and burst into tears.

Once the worst had subsided, I called Anita's cell. Voice mail, dammit. "Hi Anita, please call me back as soon as you can . . . Steve just broke up with me." I hiccupped. "It came out of the blue. I'm feeling lousy right now . . . thanks."

I washed my face with cold water, praying Anita would call back soon. *I hope she's not having one of her party hearty club nights,* I thought. When Anita was in the mood, she made Samantha from "Sex and the City" look like a shrinking violet. But Anita was so honest and grounded, the only person I could really talk to about deep emotional stuff. We'd met when we were both twelve and dreaming of fame and fortune in New York. A few months after high school graduation, we moved together to the City. My success had been modest, but Anita's modeling career had taken off. She hadn't reached single-moniker supermodel status, but she was well on her way.

My cell rang and I snatched it up. "Anita?"

"Gillian, are you okay? I got your message . . . God, I'm so sorry. What happened?"

"I don't know. He just said we weren't compatible in bed. Then he said he'd met someone else. That was it. The end."

"Well, it's his loss." Anita was indignant. "I'll bet this 'someone else' won't last more than a few weeks."

"Doesn't matter." I sighed. "It's true that our sex life was pretty mediocre. Not horrible, just not all that good. I had to fake it several times."

"Girl, you should never have to fake it! Find some guy who knows what the hell he's doing. Why don't we hit some clubs this weekend?"

"Sorry, I can't. I'm spending this weekend in Easthampton with Aunt Mary. Steve was supposed to come, too. I guess that's why he broke up with me tonight—he couldn't bear the thought of an entire weekend with me."

She snorted. "Screw Steve. There are some great clubs out in the Hamptons . . ."

"Oh Anita, I'm not up for that yet. I'll just spend a quiet weekend with Aunt Mary. I need to get out of this inferno of a city for a few days and relax."

"Okay, but call me anytime if you want to talk."

"Thanks, Anita, you really are the best. I feel a little better already. Let's get together for coffee on Monday."

The train ride to Easthampton seemed endless. I sniveled most of the way. I felt like the World's Ultimate Loser—I'd win a reality show based on that concept with no effort at all. I was a mediocre actress who could barely make a living in T.V. commercials. And apparently I was lousy in bed—couldn't even keep Steve's interest for more than three months.

Aunt Mary met me at the station, and just the sight of her silver hair, bright blue eyes, and broad smile was enough to cheer me up. I had told her on the phone that Steve and I had broken up; she was tactful enough not to press for details. Aunt Mary and I had always enjoyed a close relationship; she was more like a much older sister than an aunt. She had retired from acting a few years earlier, and had always been my mentor and most enthusiastic cheerleader. Mary had never been a hugely successful actress, but she had been well known in New York as a talented and hard working professional.

I was sprawled on a chaise lounge with her cat Jasmine purring on my lap when she came out to the patio with two glasses of iced tea. "Gillian, Jackie and Ken Williams are coming over for cocktails. Ken is bringing his golf partner, some guy named David. Sorry . . . I know you're not in a sociable mood."

Damn! Jackie and Ken Williams were the most boring people on the planet. But they had always been good neighbors to Mary, and she was careful to keep their relationship cordial.

I smiled briefly at Mary. "No problem. Company might be a good distraction for me. I feel pretty skanky; I think I'll have a shower and change." I dumped Jasmine to the ground, ignoring her yowl of annoyance.

I felt almost human again after taking a long, hot shower and changing into a pale blue sundress. I looked at myself critically in a full length mirror. God, I really had to drop ten pounds . . . maybe fifteen. But my skin looked good, tanned to a honey shade, and the strong sun had brought out golden highlights in my wavy brown hair. Perhaps one day, after I got over the humiliation of Steve dumping me, another man might find me attractive and even enjoy me in bed.

The guests had arrived by the time I stepped out to the patio. Mary made the introductions. "Gillian, you remember Jackie and Ken . . . and this is their friend, David Wentworth."

"Hi, Gillian." He smiled and reached out a hand. I gave it a limp shake, trying hard not to gawk. He wasn't conventionally handsome, but he was striking. Somewhere in his early forties. About six feet tall, with the lean, hard physique of a Marine— this man had discipline. Light brown hair just starting to go gray. Full lips, ordinary nose. His eyes were his most stunning feature—glacial blue and penetrating. I felt mesmerized. *Powerful* was the word he brought to mind.

I had a sudden attack of shyness. I dropped my eyes from his face and found myself staring at his crotch. I burned with my easily aroused blush as I looked away, praying he hadn't noticed.

The four of us exchanged the usual pleasantries. I sat on the wicker sofa to alleviate the weak feeling in my knees. David handed me a glass of white wine and sat next to me. Mary, Jackie, and Ken huddled on the other side of the patio, complaining about the hideous new McMansion under construction down the street.

"I understand you're an actress, Gillian." David's voice made me think of brandy—smooth and mellow, but potent.

"Yes." Why did my voice sound so squeaky? I cleared my throat. "Although struggling actress is more accurate. I've performed in a few off-Broadway plays, starred in a couple of commercials . . . nothing really major. And nothing at all recently."

"It's a very tough and frustrating business. But I'm sure you'll make it. You're very pretty, and obviously very bright."

It was a superficial and conventional compliment, but it seemed authentic to me when he unleashed his brilliant smile. Perfect teeth, of course.

"Thanks." My voice had spiraled into Minnie Mouse range again. His thigh seemed much too close to mine; I was sure that I could feel his body heat through the thin cotton of my dress. "So what do you do?"

"Real estate. My parents owned a firm in Denver, so I grew up in the business. I came to New York for college, decided to stay after graduation and work in the industry here. It took a while, but eventually I started my own company."

"Impressive."

"Well, it took a lot of work. I have to admit that I'm a bit of a workaholic . . . but I also take playtime very seriously." His eyes locked onto mine, and my mouth went dry.

At that point Mary, Jackie, and Ken joined the conversation, which promptly turned dull—the weather, golf, politics . . . it was hard not to squirm like a fidgety five-year-old. I was still hugely aware of David sitting so close to me, frequently catching my eyes with his and sending me small, secret smiles. The pheromones were flying.

Finally Jackie and Ken rose to say their goodbyes; David stood as well. I felt a wave of disappointment. How could this devastating man disappear from my life so quickly.

David saved the day. "I'm driving back to New York tonight. I'm parked at the end of Jackie and Ken's driveway." He turned his intense gaze on me. "Gillian, would you walk me to my car?"

"Sure, I'd love to." Dammit—squeaky voice again, plus I sounded way too eager. "I'll be back in a little while, Mary."

Mary raised one eyebrow and gave us a brief, enigmatic smile. "Sure, that's fine. Dinner can wait a little bit longer."

Jackie and Ken decided to walk the beach back to their house, thank God. I couldn't have endured their incessant chatter bursting the bubble of attraction that surrounded me and David. We walked slowly down Mary's driveway and even more slowly down the road to Jackie and Ken's driveway and his car. A midnight blue BMW convertible.

"Nice car." *Great, I sound as inane as Jackie and Ken.*

"Glad you like it. We should go for a drive sometime."

"I'd love to." My confidence was rising; this amazing guy really seemed to like me.

"I enjoyed meeting you, Gillian. I'm just sorry I have to leave so soon."

"Business in the city?"

"Yeah, I have to prepare for an early breakfast meeting on Monday. But I'd love to take you out for dinner sometime. Could I have your number?"

I rattled it off as he wrote it down—gold pen and leather covered notebook. Apparently his real estate business was doing pretty well.

"Great, I'll call you soon." He tucked the pen and notebook into his jacket pocket. Then he reached out and touched my hair . . . skimmed his fingers along the curve of my cheek. I thought I'd swoon.

"You're such a pretty little thing," he whispered. "I wish I could take you home with me." Then he was leaning down, pressing his warm, full lips against mine. The kiss gentle but firm, practiced but somehow surprising. I wrapped my arms around his neck, caressed the taut muscles of his back and his chest. He smelled wonderful—a spicy-sweet scent I couldn't quite identify.

He kissed me harder, more urgently. I felt lost . . .

I'm kissing a stranger in the middle of the street! I dropped my arms and pulled away.

David wasn't fazed; he just gave me a lazy, sexy smile. "I'll call you soon," he said again, and brushed his fingertips lightly against my breasts. My hard nipples were clearly visible through the sheer cotton of my sundress. I felt a slow burn rise in my face.

He quickly got into his car, started it up and put it into gear. "Bye, Gillian."

"Bye, David." I watched his blue convertible turn the corner and out of sight.

* * *

Over dinner, Mary studied me carefully. "David is certainly an attractive man . . . and he was certainly attracted to you. Are you going to go out with him?"

I shrugged, pretending nonchalance. "I gave him my phone number, but I'll doubt he'll call. He's a flirt—probably just likes to collect digits."

"Oh, I think he'll call," replied Mary. "And if you do go out with him, be very careful. You're in a vulnerable position right now, and David has a reputation."

"Reputation? What do you mean?"

Mary took a sip of her wine and fiddled with the glass stem. "I've heard gossip, and I see his name sometimes in the tabloids. After all, Wentworth Properties has made him very, very rich. He must be worth tens of millions."

I nearly dropped my fork. "Oh my God, he's THAT David Wentworth. I never made the connection."

"Yes, he's that Wentworth. People say he's ruthless—used to getting what he wants by any means. And I heard that his divorce—I think it was about three years ago—was pretty messy."

"Well, thanks for the warning, Mary. I will be careful. I doubt anything will happen with this guy anyway. He must be used to having gorgeous women throw themselves at him."

"You're not the type to throw yourself at anyone, Gillian. I'm sure that's very appealing to David."

I thought of our passionate kiss in Ken and Jackie's driveway, and fought hard to keep an embarrassed blush at bay. Thank God Mary hadn't witnessed that little scene.

That night I lay in bed, unable to sleep, my mind whirling. I thought about calling Anita—meeting David definitely fell into the "Major News" category—but it was very late. And for some reason I wanted to keep this stunningly wonderful development to myself for a while.

I tossed and turned in bed for hours. I kept reliving every moment of our meeting—his electric blue eyes and lazy smile, that unbelievable kiss. My heart was pounding. *Please God, let him call me . . . I have to see him again.*

Suddenly Miss Prudence and Miss Hornypants popped into my head. These two voices had first appeared during my adolescence, when my hormones and my good sense were constantly engaged in battle.

"You acted like a complete slut," said Miss Prudence. *"Letting a stranger kiss you and touch your breasts—in public! What were you thinking?"*

"He wasn't a complete stranger," Miss Hornypants pointed out. *"She'd known him a few hours."*

"A few hours!" Miss Prudence was outraged.

"It was just a kiss and a little fondling. It's not like she dropped to her knees and gave him a blow job."

"It was bad enough! He probably thinks she's an easy piece of ass."

"No, he doesn't. He was very attracted to her, and she felt the same way. Why pretend otherwise? They simply acted on their feelings."

"She's going to regret—"

"Oh, both of you leave now!" I demanded.

Once they had disappeared from my mind, I turned my thoughts back to David. What would he be like in bed? I immediately knew the answer—amazing.

I pulled my nightshirt all the way up to my neck. I closed my eyes and massaged my hard nipples, remembering David's fingers brushing gently against them. I imagined his lips and tongue on my breasts, kissing and licking, sucking and teasing . . .

I felt an instant ache growing between my thighs. My breathing quickened. I spread my legs and slowly rubbed my pussy lips together. I was very wet. I slid two fingers inside, imagining David's hard cock, and rubbed my clit with my other hand. Within minutes I came intensely, convulsing and stifling a scream.

I didn't know it then, but it was the first of many incredible orgasms David would give to me.

2

I drifted through Sunday, hoping David would call my cell, knowing he probably wouldn't. He didn't. I fought down disappointment and anxiety. *He will call me, he will call me . . .*

Mary drove me to the station to catch the 4:00 train. I hugged her hard. "Thanks for the great weekend, Mary, it was just what I needed."

"You can visit anytime, Gillian. And please remember what I said about David . . . I don't want to see you get hurt."

"Sure, I'll be careful." I didn't have the heart to tell her that I had already fallen hard for this guy—physically anyway.

The train ride back to the city was blissful, especially compared to the ride out. I thought of David the whole way. I didn't think once about that other guy . . . what was his name . . . oh right, Steve.

The city was still steaming hot. Nothing in my mailbox except a Visa bill with a $240 minimum payment due. Once I'd paid the bill and my rent, I'd have less than $300 in my checking account. I sighed as I realized that I had to go back to temping.

I decided to lift my spirits by calling Anita. I gave her a blow-by-blow account of meeting David, leaving out only Aunt Mary's warning and my orgasmic sexual fantasy about him.

Anita gave a low whistle. "David Wentworth! He's quite a catch. Rich *and* good looking. Elena Hernandez dated him for a few months."

"Oh God, you mean that gorgeous Brazilian model who did the Revlon campaign? I can't compete with someone like her!" I squeaked.

"Elena is gorgeous, but she's also a mean bitch. It's no wonder he dumped her after a few months. And you're gorgeous too, Gillian."

I snorted. "Yeah, right. At best I'm cute. But he probably won't call me anyway."

"Of course he will. And when he does, you have to let me know right away."

I laughed. "Okay . . . you'll be the first to know."

I hung up and started some desultory cleaning. I had the fan on at full blast, but was soaked with sweat within minutes. God only knew when I'd have enough money to buy a new air conditioner.

My cell phone rang. *Anita again,* I thought, *with another tidbit of gossip about David.* "Hello?"

"Gillian? Hi, it's David Wentworth."

My knees turned so weak I had to sit down. I pushed a sweaty strand of hair out of my face. "Oh hi, David, how are you?" I said in my best faux casual voice.

"Fine, and you?"

"Fine." My palms were sweating and I had to work hard to maintain a normal tone.

"I wondered if we could get together tomorrow night. Are you free?"

"Um, yes, I think so. I mean yes, definitely."

"Great. I thought we could have dinner at Francesca's on 52nd Street. Do you know it?"

"Oh, sure." Actually I'd only read about it—Francesca's was the new chic restaurant for celebrities and the super rich. I couldn't afford a cup of coffee at that place.

"I have a six p.m. meeting . . . do you mind meeting me there around eight?"

"Sure, that's fine." I felt relieved. I didn't want David to see my crappy apartment—or my crappy building or my crappy neighborhood, for that matter.

"Perfect. I'm really looking forward to seeing you again, Gillian."

"Me too, David." We made small talk for a few minutes, then hung up. I was so proud that I'd managed to get through the conversation without sounding like Minnie Mouse or making a complete ass of myself.

I immediately dialed Anita's cell. "He called! We're having dinner tomorrow night at Francesca's."

She was almost as excited as I was. "That's fast work. He must be really into you. And dinner at Francesca's . . . he wants to impress you. What are you going to wear?"

"Oh God, I hadn't even thought of that. I don't have anything good . . . what am I going to do?"

"Relax, your best friend is an expert at dealing with fashion emergencies. I have this really cute Versace mini-skirt that would look great on you."

"Anita, I can't fit into your clothes! I'm six inches shorter and twenty pounds heavier."

"Well, okay, we'll bag the mini-skirt idea. But I can bring over accessories and makeup. I'll be there as soon as I can."

Twenty minutes later we were rummaging through my pathetic wardrobe. "What about this long green velvet dress?" Anita suggested. "You always look so pretty in it."

"Too formal and too hot. I usually wear it for family holiday gatherings."

"Okay . . . how about this blue suede suit?"

"Too business like."

Anita refused to be discouraged. "All right. How about the skirt from the blue suede suit with a pretty blouse? This white lace one has a nice low neckline—you definitely won't look too business like."

I tried on the outfit with strappy white high-heeled sandals. I was pleased until I turned around to get a rear view. "Oh my God, my ass looks huge!"

"No, it doesn't," Anita disagreed firmly. "You have a great ass and great tits. I wish I had your assets . . . then I might actually have a shot at the Victoria's Secret catalogue and the Sports Illustrated swimsuit issue."

I turned to look at her. She was dressed in faded jeans and an old T-shirt. No makeup. As usual, she looked spectacular. Anita had incredibly long, lean legs; Audrey Hepburn features; feline green eyes and short jet black hair. It was impossible for her to look bad. I dismissed a twinge of jealousy.

"Okay, I'll trust your opinion. I'll wear this outfit. Now what about accessories?"

We finally agreed on her gold San Marco necklace and matching bracelet, with discreet gold hoop earrings. She also loaned me a white pashmina. She applied makeup and wrote down instructions so I could recreate the look the following night. When I studied myself in the mirror I felt like a princess—a much prettier, more sophisticated Gillian.

"Okay, just one last thing," said Anita. "Underwear."

"Anita, he's not going to see my underwear!"

"You never know." She smirked. "Besides, even if you don't end up in bed with him, pretty underwear will make you feel more confident."

"I guess so . . . I do have a new bra and panty set I bought at Victoria's Secret. Aunt Mary gave me a gift certificate for my birthday." I showed her—a push up bra and modest bikini panties in apricot silk trimmed with ivory lace.

"Perfect. You'll give David Wentworth the biggest hard-on of his life."

"Anita!" We collapsed in laughter.

It was nearly midnight when she left. "Now remember, I want to hear all the details right away. Have a wonderful time." She winked at me as she closed the front door behind her.

The following night I splurged on a taxi even though I couldn't afford it. I didn't want to take the subway or bus to Francesca's and dishevel my appearance. As I stood before the restaurant door, huge moths of nervous tension fluttered in my stomach. I closed my eyes and took three long, deep breaths, trying to center myself the way I did before going on stage or in front of a TV camera.

The hostess was a coolly elegant black woman in a low cut ivory evening dress. "May I help you?" she asked with an imperious glance at me.

"Yes, I'm meeting David Wentworth."

"Of course. This way please." Her voice was a degree or two warmer, but her expression suggested that she still couldn't imagine what I was doing here.

"Gillian. You look wonderful." David rose and leaned over the table to peck my cheek. Even that brief contact was enough to make my heart race.

The hostess dropped a menu in front of me, then leaned far over the table to hand one to David. Her boobs nearly popped out of her gown. I glared at her. She ignored me. David seemed oblivious to the boob maneuver and my outrage.

We quickly ordered wine and entrees. I tried not to feel intimidated by the chandeliers, the priceless Persian rugs, the fine china and crystal.

David smiled and pinned me with his brilliant blue eyes. He was staring at me so intently that I had to drop my gaze and fidget with my napkin to regain my composure.

"When I met you at Mary's I thought you looked familiar . . . I'm wondering if I remember you from a commercial."

"Maybe. My most successful one was for Manhattan Bank. It ran for several months on local stations. I played satisfied customer number one."

"Yes, I remember now. You were excellent as a satisfied customer."

The mild sexual innuendo was enough to make me blush ferociously.

"So how was your meeting?" I asked to change the subject.

"Pretty good. I'm working on a new luxury condo project in Boston. There's been a lot of red tape, a lot of problems with subcontractors, but we're making progress."

Our entrees arrived. My salmon dish was mind-blowing—what Anita and I called "OhmyGod food"—but I was too nervous to enjoy it. David and I chatted casually about our backgrounds. I told him about growing up in rural New Hampshire with Anita; he talked about Denver and his childhood dream of becoming a professional tennis player. A severe knee injury had ended his budding career.

Two hours slipped by; eventually we were the only customers left in the restaurant. David sat back in his chair and again mesmerized me with his gaze. "I just moved into a new apartment on East 75th street. I'd love to show it to you."

I felt a moment of panic. Miss Prudence and Miss Hornypants made a brief appearance in my head.

"He wants to have sex with you! You never sleep with a man on the first date!" cried Miss Prudence.

"Go for it. You might not get a second chance with this guy," urged Miss Hornypants.

Miss H. won. "I'd love to see your apartment."

"Great. My car and driver are just outside." He leaned across the table and softly kissed my lips. My panties were soaked. I knew I was about to experience the most intense sexual pleasure of my life.

No ostentatious stretch limo for David. His car was a sleek black Mercedes with tinted windows. "Gillian, this is Al," he said, introducing me to the driver. Al, a huge, swarthy middle aged guy, opened the back door for me and grinned. I liked him immediately.

In the car David chatted with Al about sports. Taking my fingers in a firm grip, he moved my hand to his thigh. I could feel his potent body heat; I swallowed hard.

The elegant lobby of his apartment building had the hushed atmosphere of a European museum. In the elevator David punched the PH button and then kissed me hard, slowly sliding his tongue between my lips. He ran his hands down my back to my ass. By then my nipples were rising and my pussy was aching. When the elevator doors opened he released me.

"Would you like the grand tour of the apartment?" he asked.

No, I want you to rip my clothes off and take me right here in the foyer. I restrained myself. "Yes, I'd love a tour."

The living/dining area was about the size of a football field. Huge floor to ceiling windows revealed a stunning panorama of the East River. The décor was muted and elegant—steel gray leather sofas and ottomans; large Cubist paintings that appeared to be Picasso originals; a few enormous floral arrangements in crystal vases. I'd seen apartments like this only in *House Beautiful* and *Architectural Digest.* "It's lovely," I murmured, trying not to let my impatience show.

He took my hand and pulled me through the kitchen, the study, the guest room, and finally to the master bedroom. I was disappointed when the tour didn't stop there; I was about to expire from frustrated lust. He showed me the master bathroom and then led me into his dressing room. There he finally kissed me again; I could feel his heart pounding. "Give me your tongue," he demanded. I obeyed.

As he slowly unbuttoned my blouse I reached down to massage the bulge straining at his fly. His cock was extremely hard—and apparently extremely large. I glanced to the right and understood why we were starting here. A full length mirror on his closet door reflected everything we did to each other. It was incredibly exciting to watch.

David pulled my blouse off and expertly unhooked my bra. "God, Gillian, your breasts are beautiful," he breathed. "So round and firm . . . and your nipples . . ." He began to lick and suck; it was even better than my fantasy. My nipples looked like raspberries.

I dropped to my knees and unzipped his fly. I pulled out his straining cock and flicked my tongue over the head, teasing out drops of cum. David groaned. I pulled down his pants and briefs, then attacked his shaft and balls with my lips and tongue. His balls were very tight. David's breathing quickened as he watched me in the mirror. "Gillian, please stop . . . it feels wonderful but I don't want to go off too soon."

"Oh no, we definitely don't want that." I gave him a mischievous smile as I stretched out on the floor. David yanked off his remaining clothes and dropped down next to me. He pulled off my sandals and lifted my skirt. I spread my legs for him, wet and ready, but he made me wait. He gently stroked my pussy through my panties.

"David . . . how did you know how much I love that? My pussy is dripping."

He smiled, slid a finger under the elastic and deep inside me. "My God, you are so wet . . ." He stripped off my panties and spread my lips. "And your clit is so swollen . . ." He started licking and sucking; I felt the deep throb of a building orgasm. I came hard, harder than I ever had before. As I lay there gasping David slowly stroked his cock and stared at my pussy.

When I had recovered enough he knelt between my knees and thrust hard into me. I whimpered. He began to pump slowly, then faster as I gyrated beneath him. I screamed as I came again, digging my nails into his shoulders. He suddenly pulled his cock out, groaned my name and spurted hot cum all over my breasts.

We lay there for a few minutes, trying to slow our ragged breathing and racing hearts. "God, Gillian," he said, "I knew sex would be good with you, but I had no idea . . ."

"That I was such a lusty wench?"

He laughed. "Lusty wenches are my favorite kind of woman. Seriously, you're amazing."

I stretched happily. "You're pretty amazing yourself. Are you going to get hard again?"

"You bet I am."

"Good. I'm going to take a quick shower, and then I'll be ready for another ride."

I emerged from the shower a few minutes later with a soft Egyptian cotton towel wrapped around my body. David was waiting for me in the dressing room, sitting on the leather chair and stroking his hard cock. Without a word I dropped the towel and straddled his leg. I began to rock slowly, rubbing my clit against his thigh as he massaged my breasts. His leg became slippery with my juice. He slid his index finger in and out of my mouth, then parted my cheeks and gently slipped it into my ass. I stiffened for a moment in surprise—I'd never experienced this before—but I soon relaxed and enjoyed the sensation. I rode his thigh harder, excited by the dual pleasure of the friction against my clit and the finger in my ass.

"I was hot for you the moment I saw you . . . even hotter when I caught you staring at my crotch," he murmured.

I stopped riding his thigh, feeling mortified. "That was an accident, I swear it! I felt suddenly shy so I dropped my eyes and ended up looking at . . . that part of you. I was hoping you hadn't noticed."

He laughed. "A likely story."

"But I did want to have sex with right from the start. Somehow I knew you'd be great in bed. When you touched me and kissed me you made me so wet . . ."

"God, you excite me so much." He licked and nibbled my nipples as I rocked faster.

"Oh David," I whispered. "I have so many fantasies . . ."

"I know, darling," he whispered back. "And I want to make them all come true."

We made love two more times that night. Happily aching and sated, I slept deeply in his antique four poster bed. When I woke up late the next morning, I was stunned and disappointed to find myself alone. "David?" I called tentatively.

He entered the bedroom from the dressing room. He was buttoning a crisp white dress shirt. "Good morning, Gillian," he said briskly. "I hope you slept well. Unfortunately I have to run because I'm late for a meeting. There's coffee in the kitchen if you want some . . ." He looked away from me, intent on inserting gold cufflinks in his cuffs.

I wasn't going to allow him to get away so easily. "That's too bad, David," I sighed. "Because I'm feeling incredibly horny this morning."

I flung back the bedspread to reveal my hard nipples. David stopped fidgeting with the cufflinks and stared.

"I guess I'll just have to masturbate. And I'd much rather have your hard cock." I slowly spread my legs and then my pussy lips. I gently rubbed my clit with a finger.

"Gillian, I really have to go—" His voice was hesitant.

I looked at the growing bulge in his pants. "But you don't want to," I whispered as I slid two fingers inside my pussy.

"Oh God." He dropped the cufflinks.

I felt triumphant.